# Slow Dancing

# Elizabeth Benedict

BANTAM BOOKS

NEW YORK · TORONTO · LONDON · SYDNEY · AUCKLAND

This edition contains the complete text
of the original hardcover edition.
NOT ONE WORD HAS BEEN OMITTED.

SLOW DANCING
A Bantam Book / published by arrangement with Alfred A. Knopf Inc.

PRINTING HISTORY
Alfred A. Knopf edition published 1985
Bantam edition / January 1990

Library of Congress Cataloging-in-Publication Data

Benedict, Elizabeth.
Slow dancing / Elizabeth Benedict.
p.    cm.
ISBN 0-553-34811-6
I. Title.
PS3552.E5396S55   1990
813'.54—dc20                                    89–6921
                                                    CIP

Published simutaneously in the United States and Canada

Bantam Books are published by Bantam Books, a division of Bantam
Doubleday Dell Publishing Group, Inc. Its trademark, consisting of the
words "Bantam Books" and the portrayal of a rooster, is Registered in
U.S. Patent and Trademark Office and in other countries. Marca Regis-
trada. Bantam Books, 666 Fifth Avenue, New York, New York 10103.

PRINTED IN THE UNITED STATES OF AMERICA

OPM     0 9 8 7 6 5 4 3 2 1

*This is for Z. and for my family*

Some Girls

*A*s Lexi Steiner walked down the hallway of the federal court building in San Diego, she decided that sleeping with men you didn't care about was an acquired taste and that she had acquired it.

There were four or five of them. David Wiley, whom she was having dinner with that night in Los Angeles, would be the fifth. Or maybe the sixth. She listened to the heels of her high-heeled sandals click against the marble floor. The rubber heels were worn down to the wood. She swung her briefcase into her other hand, took the stairs down to the underground parking lot. The click echoed in the stairwell. She would be okay once she got into her car, once she got on the freeway. She would turn the radio up loud and try to forget what had happened in the courtroom upstairs. The sting would be gone by the time she got to L.A. By Monday, when she had to report to Mark, she would be better. With any luck, between now and then, closer to now, she was going to get laid.

She opened the door of her old Toyota and threw her brief-case across to the other seat, ignoring the papers that fell out of it and landed on the floor between the Styrofoam cups and empty beer cans.

"Miss Steiner. Is that you?"

She looked around. A woman with glasses was scuttling across the lot, holding out a small piece of paper. "I work in the Judge's office. I have a message for you."

Lexi reached her hand out of the car window and took the piece of paper. "Thank you. Sorry for the trouble."

"Glad I found you before it was too late." The woman walked away. The message read: *Call Mark—Important.* She crumpled it into a ball and flicked it over her shoulder into the back seat. She rarely made him wait, but this time he would have to. She would stop on the freeway and call him. Maybe. No. She would, but not now. She drove up the ramp into the sunlight and lowered the visor to keep it out of her eyes. When she stopped to call Mark, she would try Nell again in New York. They had been missing each other's calls for days.

She drove north on I-5 and wondered about David Wiley's sudden interest in her. In the year she had known him, all his solicitations had been strictly professional, all could be answered on the telephone. He had called her a few days before, just as she was leaving for the trial in San Diego. He was in L.A. for the week and wanted to talk to her about Esterbrook's charges that illegal aliens had been registered to vote. They hadn't been, she had told him. There wasn't much to say. Reporters had been calling about this for two weeks and she was getting tired of denying it. Wiley was the last person she had expected to hear from on it. He didn't usually write about immigration.

"It's not an immigration story," he had said, "it's an election story. Esterbrook's running for Congress."

"But there's no story."

"Then why's Esterbrook spending so much time telling me they're being registered?"

"It's the only thing he says that anyone pays attention to."

"But how can you be sure he's wrong? Where's the evidence?"

"Ask him. He's the one trying to make the case."

"Sounds like you've been through this a few times today."

"Let's put it this way. The Center has better things to do than answer for Esterbrook."

"Things like what?"

"It would take a while."

"I've got time."

"I'm sorry. I don't right now. I'm leaving for San Diego in a few minutes and won't be back until late Friday. I'll have plenty of time to talk on Monday."

"I'm going back to New York early Saturday."

"Let's talk on the phone sometime."

"I'd rather not." The negotiations continued. Could she be back in L.A. for a late dinner on Friday? She wasn't sure what time she'd be through in San Diego. He was loose on time, he said. "I don't mind eating late—and I really want to see you." The timbre of his voice had shifted suddenly; a quiet, unexpected leap from the professional to the personal. She froze, the receiver wedged between her ear and her shoulder. After a long pause, she said. "It can be arranged." Good line. Two can play this game. Avoid personal pronouns when the stakes change. I'd love to. Don't give him that, especially when you don't know what he wants. "I'll call you when I get back to L.A. Where can I reach you?" A bit sultry, easing into the part. If he wanted information about immigration, she could give him that on the phone. But if he wanted something else—

"The Bonaventure. By the way, what are you doing in San Diego?"

"Suing the cops. They arrested some Mexican-Americans because they couldn't prove they were U.S. citizens. But you're slipping, Wiley—that should have been your first question."

He laughed. This was getting serious, Wiley laughing. In a year of talking to him, she had never heard him laugh. "Tell me more," he said.

"You blew it. I'll let you know Friday."

"And bring whatever you can—transcripts, briefs."

"You never stop being a reporter, do you?" She liked playing with him, once she could feel him bend.

"Rarely."

"Did you ever think about getting an honest job?"

"What's wrong with reporting?"

"It's kind of sleazy. You know, knocking on people's doors, asking nosey questions."

"I think there's more to it than that." But he didn't sound sure.

"Let's talk about it Friday."

Today was Friday and she fiddled now with the knobs on the radio. Nothing was coming in clearly, except the sound of David Wiley's disembodied voice, which was the only thing about him she could recall. They had met briefly, only once. Their calls until the other day had been short, unchatty, to the point. She had decided a long time ago that he was either bored or boring, but sometimes useful, with a name, a phone number, a piece of information.

She had come to like reporters and the shorthand of their trade: I think I've got a story for you. I can't go on the record with this, but I can tell you who might be able to. Are you on deadline? Another fraternity, another set of passwords, but swifter and simpler than her own. She said something on Wednesday and it was in the paper on Thursday. A touchdown. Her own work was more like a primitive military campaign. Minus the heroism anyway. Except the night Mark got very drunk at a bar in South Texas, in the next town over from where they had just argued a case, and banged his fists on the table and ranted, "Let's go kick some redneck ass," and the bartender said did he want to go out back and see whose ass would be kicked or did he just want to leave real quiet and not come back.

But as for Wiley—he would probably be easy and take her someplace nice for dinner. Reporters always had big expense accounts. So did some of the others, the ones who lived in different places around the country and came to L.A. on business, or arranged to meet her in the cities where she went on business. She saw them at conferences, courthouses, cocktail parties. And hotels. She almost forgot hotels. Assignations in expensive rooms with color televisions, brand-new faucets and deluxe shower nozzles, matching furniture and wake-up calls. So perfect it was camp, kitsch, a model room in a department store not meant for living. But there you were anyway, and quite often with a man.

It occurred to her that the best part was telling the stories to Nell. Which reminded her to stop at the next exit to call her. She negotiated her way across the five lanes of traffic just in time to take the truckstop turn.

"Jesus, Lexi, where have you been?"

"San Diego. I've tried you seventeen times. I keep getting that fucking machine. That was me, hanging up all those times."

"You should see some of the other crap my brother's got around this place. Gadgets out the wazoo. He and Marie have this thing hooked up to the tv so they can play space games. He's thirty-two years old and he's playing games with little dots called Space Invaders, for hours at a time—*what* is that noise?"

"A truck."

"Where are you?"

"A truck stop on I-5."

"Are you serious?"

"Of course. Listen." She opened the phone-booth door and held the receiver up in the air for about ten seconds. "Did you hear that?" she shouted. They laughed wildly.

"Lexi, what are you on?"

"Nothing, except diesel fumes. Which reminds me. Boz came by the other night on his way to Mexico, and he left some dope that even he wouldn't bring into Mexico."

"Guess who I'm having dinner with in an hour," Nell said.

"Who?"

"You've got one guess."

"Oh no. Eric Lord."

"Uh-huh."

"Was he surprised to hear from you?"

"I'd say so. It sounded like he dropped the phone. And you'll be pleased to know that he asked about you. I told him we were still as hot an item as ever, even though you made me move to California and I hate it."

"I didn't make you move. You followed me to San Francisco."

What was I supposed to do—stay in New York by myself?"

"You're the one who moved to L.A.," Lexi said. "I followed you there."

"Yeah, but I think you still owe me one. Anyway, Eric was delighted to hear you've made something of yourself—I gave him a few highlights."

"I would have thought you'd have other things to talk about after all these years."

"You and he *do* have something of a past."

"I've done worse things than dance with a married man. Even if it was your man."

"Not exactly mine. And for the record, he's not married anymore."

"Really?"

"Don't you remember, he called me when he got divorced?"

"I thought that was what's-his-name."

"He did too. Listen, do you think I should get married?"

"To Eric?"

"No, in general."

"You've been telling me for years that getting married is a lot of hokey crap."

"Are you blaming me for the fact that the institution of marriage stifles and oppresses over one half of the race in every possible way?"

"A minute ago you wanted to get married."

"What?"

Lexi shouted, "Wait a second!" and waited for a truck to pass. "A minute ago you wanted to get married."

"I changed my mind. Maybe I just want to get laid."

"I thought you're going to write the definitive book in praise of single womanhood. Aren't you going to talk to that editor on Monday?"

"Yeah, but I'm getting cold feet. I've been thinking that maybe it'll have a surprise ending—just kidding, folks, they're all miserable."

"Do you think they are?"

"Aren't you?"

"Of course, but if I were married I'd be really miserable."

"But don't you think it would be nice to have someone to hang out with?"

"You can hang out with me."

"Lexi, you work all the time. I haven't seen you in two weeks."

"That's because you've been in New York all week. When are you coming back?"

"Thursday. Jesus—what time is it?"

Lexi looked at her watch. "Four-thirty."

"That means it's seven-thirty. I'm about to be late for Mr. Lord. I've got to run. I may have to call you later, if this dinner is a disaster."

"I won't be home. I'm having dinner with this guy tonight."

"Which one?"

"A new one."

"Who?"

"A guy named Wilcy."

"Talk louder. I can't hear you."

"A guy named Wiley."

"I still can't hear you."

"There isn't a truck anywhere. Have you gone deaf?"

"The connection just got awful. Call me tomorrow. Lexi, can you hear me?"

She dropped another dime into the phone and called her office in L.A. collect. Mark wasn't in. Did she want to speak to Emma? Yes. Emma was the secretary they shared.

"Two things," Emma said. "One. Call Nell. She's called three times. Do you have the number?"

"Yes."

"Two. Someone from Channel Seven invited Mark to do a news show on Sunday afternoon, but he's got to go to New York. He wanted me to find out if you were going to be in town."

That was Mark's shorthand: if you were in town, you were automatically available. And if you weren't, you made yourself.

"Yes," Lexi said, "I'll be in town. What's the show about?"

"The election—what else? It'll be a ten-minute debate between you and Esterbrook."

"Not again."

"I'm afraid so."

"I think I'm going to move to Orange County just so I can vote for whoever's running against him." She twirled the phone cord around her forefinger. "If you leave the information on my desk, I'll pick it up Sunday morning."

"Good. How'd the trial go?"

"I think the bad guys won. Again." She noticed she was tapping her foot against the floor of the phone booth, in time to the clattering of her nerves. She stopped. "One of our clients had a little too much to drink at lunch. The U.S. Attorney made him look like a fool. But do me a favor. Let me tell Mark about it."

"Sure. I haven't heard a thing. Did I tell you Nell called?"

"Yes. Anything else?"

"Take the rest of the day off."

"I plan to. See you Monday."

Back in the car, she tossed her shoes into the back seat, rolled a joint of Boz's dope and headed out the serpentine road to the freeway. She slipped into the second lane from the shoulder. She thought about having dinner with David Wiley. She wondered if she would have anything to tell Nell when it was over. She wondered if men confided in each other the way they did. Or did men only confide in each other about the liaisons that pulled at their heartstrings? If Lexi and Nell waited for those, they would have nothing to talk about.

Lexi had taken only a few of them, the four or five in this series of men she didn't care about, to her house in Venice Beach, at the edge of Santa Monica. It was rundown, cluttered with books, Mexican rugs, photographs of friends, a freeway sign that said, TURN AROUND YOU ARE GOING THE WRONG WAY. Leaky faucets. No television. A collection of small cacti Nell had given her because she could never remember to water anything. And let's face it, Nell had said, you're never fucking home. Sometimes when she returned from a trip, Nell had flowers sent to the house, "You are my everything" scribbled in the florist's hand on the small card stuck in between the chrysanthemums.

The men Lexi slept with these days were older, distinguished, smooth. They fit better in hotels than in her house. Serious practitioners of law. Dedicated purveyors of seduction. The first one so taken with himself that he had barely noticed how green she had been on their first date, just out of law school and starting her job at the L.A. Immigrant Service Center. She had been hungry then for grownup sanction—though what she usually ended up getting was a pat on the ass. Now, three years later, there was really no excuse for being such a groupie. Fucking for the disadvantaged and the undocumented: her clients, the clients of the men she slept with, sometimes their mutual clients.

What bothered her now wasn't that she had slept with them but that it had mattered so much at the time, until she learned to be cool about it, like they were. Water off a duck's back. Call it Sex and Adventure, not Love and Ambition.

Love and Ambition was what she and Nell had agreed in college kept them going. It was Nell who introduced the phrase into their vocabulary, Nell who assigned small worries grand titles: Love and Ambition, The Conservation of Misery in the Universe, an Extreme Case of the Human Condition. Or a flight of metaphysics: "What, say, is the point of a green light that's not green long enough for you to cross the street?"

It was Nell's theatrics that had first impressed Lexi when they met at the beginning of their senior year in college, in the campus apartment overlooking Broadway that they were assigned to share. Lexi was suspicious at first, thought Nell was just playful and cute, not seriously interested in either Lexi or herself. Nell wasn't going to be boring, or dull, but she might be terminally flip. Lexi wasn't sure and she couldn't tell from looking. Nell was tall and blonde and full, blue-eyed, dimpled, more in the mode of the Vermont Maid than Marilyn Monroe. All sturdy, country innocence, always in overalls and hiking boots. She talked about climbing mountains in the Northwest. She talked about getting laid.

"Let's see if I've got this straight," Nell said a few days into the semester, standing at the kitchen counter in their apartment. "You left this guy after living with him for a year because you were bored." Nell broke three eggs into a clear glass bowl. Lexi watched her. Maybe Nell wanted that—not to be sized up, but to be the center of things. "But now he's getting it on with someone else and you're miserable." She nodded. "I've got one of those too." Nell poured the eggs into an oiled pan. "But the person he's getting it on with is his wife." The eggs sizzled. "You want some of this omelet?"

"What's that smell?"

"Feta cheese. Or maybe it's the dead mouse under the refrigerator. God, this place is a dump. Did I tell you I might have VD?" Lexi started. "I'm not kidding. I met this guy when I was taking the train across Canada on my way here, a few weeks before school started. He called me yesterday and said I should go to a doctor."

"You made it with him on the train?"

"Yeah, under my sleeping bag going through Winnipeg. It was fun except my ass got a little cold sticking down between the seats. This omelet is awful. Do you want some?"

Lexi almost said, "Sure" before they got the joke and laughed.

"But the thing I'm really worried about," Nell said, looking in the refrigerator, "is that I gave the married guy VD, which means he gave it to his wife, which means—shit, I don't know what it means. Is this your orange juice?"

"Yeah, take some. What about the married guy?"

"It's on and off. This week it's off. But I had to call him today about the penicillin, so it might be on again any minute. You lived with this guy you just walked out on for a whole year?"

"Yeah."

"I lived with someone once. The summer before last, for three weeks. That's all I could take. He wanted to get married and I wanted to get laid. It was a disaster. How could you live with anyone for a year?" She guzzled orange juice from the container.

"Sometimes it was nice—the idea of it was nice. Being attached to someone. But I was bored out of my mind."

"How could you not be?"

"I wanted to be in love. I wanted to be in love the way Madame Bovary wanted to be in love. Thunder, lightning, lots of velvet."

"You know how long that lasts? About as long as one side of a forty-five—and even if you want more, you're usually too wiped out to get up and flip the record over."

"But don't you think the point is to end up with someone?"

"Maybe after you've done everything else you want to do."

"What else do you want to do?"

"Go to Nepal."

"For a career?"

"For an adventure."

In her college bedroom Nell kept a carton of old plates she had bought at an auction near her parents' house in upstate New York. When she was upset she would take a few plates up to the roof of their building and hurl them against the brick heating unit that extended the length of the building. "Here, try." She handed a plate to Lexi.

"What do I do with it?"

"Smash it to smithereens. You'll feel terrific, for about fifteen minutes. Did you ever try shrieking?"

"No."

"If you're in the woods, you get yourself to the top of the biggest hill you can find. But here you have to go to the subway. You stand on the platform between the cars and shriek your guts out."

"Like Primal Therapy?"

"More like confession. It just keeps you going till the next time."

"Did you ever go to a shrink?"

"No, I just went to confession. Did you?"

"Yeah. My parents thought it would encourage my artistic sensibilities if I thought I was neurotic from an early age—you know, the same way hardship is supposed to build character."

"So what happened?"

"I think it backfired. I'm going to law school."

"To show them it didn't work?"

"No, I think they knew it hadn't worked a long time ago. Sending me to a shrink was their last-ditch effort to see if I had the makings of an artist. When I was five they sent me to a summer camp for artistically gifted children."

"My parents' idea of culture was the Reader's Digest collection of Christmas music. Eight records' worth."

"Did they make you go to summer camp?"

"We couldn't afford it. But how did your parents know when you were five that you were artistically gifted?"

"They didn't. They own an art gallery and they go abroad for the summer to look for new artists. When I was a kid they didn't want to take me, so they found this camp and told the owners who they were and about all the artists they knew. It's how all those exclusive places work. If the parents are smart, they think the kids'll be smart. If the parents are arty, they think the kids'll be arty. My parents thought the same thing. They made me go to art lessons at the Museum of Modern Art, dance lessons at Juilliard, piano lessons with someone famous. I hated them."

"Your parents?"

"The lessons. I hated having to go someplace and have a good time. I mean, I hated the assumption that I was going to like whatever they told me to like. I hated everything when I was a kid, except for being with my parents and their friends. Mostly I liked their friends. I liked being an adult more than I liked being a kid, and when I was with them they treated me like an adult. Or I acted like one, so they treated me like one. And the fact that I was a kid who acted like an adult was adorable to them."

"Did they make you go to camp every summer?"

"No, that was the lesson I learned. That if I acted like a kid they would send me away to some bullshit place for artistically gifted children, but if I acted like an adult they'd take me with them."

"You figured that out when you were five?"

"No, that's what the shrink told me. The only useful thing she said."

"But I still don't understand why you want to go to law school."

"I took Towers' Feminism and the Law course last year. Towers is brilliant and all the women she invited to be guest speakers were—they weren't all brilliant, but they were all really smart, and they were doing things I admired. Or that I came to admire. After two classes I was hooked on Constitutional law. It was like discovering Cézanne."

"What do your parents think about it?"

"They don't understand what could have made me stray."

That semester Lexi and Nell often sat in the kitchen of their apartment and talked until two in the morning, about their families, their lovers, their ambitions. And sex. Endless detailed conversations, uproarious laughter, confessions. There was something majestic to their intimacy, even though its revelations were crude and prosaic. Nell at age three in the bathtub, a strange, exciting sensation as the water drained, tickling what she did not know then was her cunt. Lexi had not expected to hear that word. She always groped awkwardly for another, something medical or neutral, understood only because of an antecedent or a gesture. When, Nell asked, had Lexi first felt a sensation there? Twelve, thirteen. God, what she had missed! It wasn't that she hadn't tried, it was that she didn't know where to touch.

"It takes men forever to figure it out too," Nell said. "A woman I know said the best she ever had was with someone she slept with once and never saw again. Can you imagine?"

"What's the best you ever had?"

"Let me think."

"You have to think about it?"

"I have to think about how to describe it."

"Well?"

"I think I need something to eat."

"There's some stale bagels on the bottom shelf. You can have one."

"Thanks."

"There might be some rotten cream cheese in the butter cooler. You know how it gets yellow around the edges when you haven't wrapped it right?"

"I see. You could kill someone with this bagel."

"So who was the best?"

"I thought I asked you first."

"I thought I asked *you* first."

"This fucking toaster doesn't work."

"You want to go get some donuts? The place on 114th Street is open all night."

"Yeah."

They walked through the college campus holding hands and laughing at everyone who stared at them. "You'd think they'd be used to it by now," Lexi said. "Half the women in our class are gay."

"And the rest of them are living with their triple-bypass-heartbeat boyfriends and applying to business school."

"What about us? What are we doing?"

"We're fugitives," Nell said. "We'll never do anything the way they do it."

Lexi had never thought of herself as a fugitive before. Before, she was sometimes a recluse, sometimes someone's girlfriend, almost always lonely. Fugitive took in all of that and added a dimension of urgent, continuous movement. Gone before anyone noticed you were there. A life of mystique and notoriety. Fugitives were lonely, but they had fabulous adventures.

Sitting at the kitchen table, Nell drew a graph for her. "This is most people's lives." She drew a straight horizontal line across the page. "And this is our life." She turned the page over and drew a line that peaked and plunged like an outline of the tips of the Himalayas. "Amazing highs and terrible lows."

Nell made Lexi feel less lonely and also more like a fugitive, which she liked better than any of the things she had been before.

The only thing Lexi and Nell didn't talk about was the electric air between them. When Lexi was talking on the phone one night, Nell sidled up and pestered her. Lexi yelled, "Leave me alone," and Nell slithered away. Following her as far as the phone cord would reach, Lexi held out her hand for Nell to take. Wordless reconciliations, guilty looks, uncontrollable smiles. Lexi dreamed one night about kissing her passionately. She dreamed another night of Nell carrying her like a child in a long nightgown down the hallway to her bedroom, to her spartan single bed, whose churning springs she had occasionally heard, and there— She woke up and tried to stamp out the dream's conclusion from her thoughts. For weeks, asleep and awake, she dreamed, and tried not to dream, of the explicit physical completion of her attraction to this woman. She knew it was only partly that she hadn't gotten laid in months.

The point in those days had been to keep from being bored. But now, on her way to dinner with David Wiley, Lexi wasn't sure what the point was anymore. Sex and Adventure— maybe not the point but among the effects. Love and Ambition. Maybe that was closer. She knew she had more than a few gold stars in the Ambition column. Girl Most Likely to Succeed. The problem was that she had had no idea back then how much the gold stars would cost. What she had become was not at all what she had had in mind. Other people's children were not as cute as

they used to be. Her bookcase full of English novels and modern poetry belonged to someone else. A month ago she had
given away her cat because she was on the road too much to
take care of him. But after he was gone a few weeks she realized
it was because she didn't like having him around anymore, un-
derfoot, wanting something from her, Cat Chow or to have his
head scratched.

She did not know when she had begun to crave loud music, bad movies, cruel men.

David Wiley sat in his hotel room in downtown Los
Angeles and waited for the phone to ring. At his feet were a pile
of news clippings he had torn out of the morning's L.A. *Times,* a
thriller about the CIA he had picked up at O'Hare a few weeks
ago, *The Collected Poems of Wallace Stevens, The Bald Soprano,* a
manila legal file labeled MEXICAN-AMERICANS, and a paperback
copy of *Passages.*

In his lap was a recent issue of *Conservative Digest.* He was
going through it with a red pen, drawing little stars in the mar-
gins, underlining a word here, a paragraph there, and turning
down the top corner of the pages on which he had made notations. On the last page was a headline: YOUR CHRISTMAS GIFTS
CAN HELP STOP THE LIBERALS. He grunted and closed the magazine and tossed it across the room. It hit the wall and landed flat
on the floor next to the television, the glossy cover photograph
of Ronald Reagan face up.

David's eyes wandered to the view out of the twenty-
third-story window of his hotel room. A cluster of tall, shiny
office buildings, several with mirrored surfaces, glistened in the
fading sunlight. An unusually clear day, the first blue sky he had
seen in almost a week in L.A. He stood up and walked to the
window. His eyes dropped fifteens stories, to the side of an old
brick building on which was printed in black letters, each as tall
as a door, BELIEVE IN JESUS. In smaller but still discernible letters,
*For More Information Call . . .* He had been in the hotel for a week,
often perched at this window, waiting for the phone to ring, or
for room service to arrive with a meal or a pot of coffee. His

gaze always fell to the puny building, tucked in between the skyscrapers, with its bold, pathetic message. He wondered who still believed in Jesus, whether anyone called the number it advertised, and what the two people said to each other when the phone was picked up. Five years ago he might have called the number to find out. Ten years ago he would have.

He was waiting for three phone calls. One from a press secretary in Washington, D.C., who would let him know when and where David could interview his boss, a rising young conservative congressman who was running for a Senate seat he would probably win when the election was held, eleven days from now. David had told the flack the interview would be fairly short and *pro forma*. A lot of flacks grilled the hell out of the reporters before they let them at their bosses. It was best to catch these guys off guard, go in for what was billed as a perfunctory interview. Let the guy think all he'd have to do is answer a few questions about his voting record—and when things got rolling and the guy got comfortable, hit him with whatever you had. Evidence of a dubious business venture, a suspicious tax return, an incriminating memo. David loved to watch them squirm, though it was not often he had information that good. But he was pretty sure he was onto something with the congressman whose flack had promised to call him within the hour. David needed to talk to the guy before the election—though the congressman certainly did not need to talk to him. He looked at his watch. It was after eight on the East Coast.

He was also waiting for a call from his fourteen-year-old daughter, Louise, and/or his ex-wife, Gretchen, who would be calling to remind him of the opening of Louise's school play in New York the following night. Not that either had said she would be calling, but he had come to expect a second or third reminder when he promised he would attend anything. Even with the extra reminders he was often absent, called away at the last minute, or stuck in someplace like Tuscaloosa for a day longer than he expected. But this performance was one he could not miss. Louise had been chosen for her role over a girl two grades ahead of her. There was that, and there was the fact that he had spent most of the last three months on the road, writing election stories. The one weekend he had been free, Louise had told him she was going to the Berkshires with her mother. He had not seen her since August.

The first reminder had come two nights before when Gretchen called at two minutes after eleven. He could picture her waiting until then, maybe calling the time to double-check, to make sure the cheapest rates were in effect. Not that she had to count pennies, between the child support and her own practice. Clinical psychologists in New York charged at least sixty dollars a session. The discount phone call two nights ago just another reminder that their relationship had been reduced to two things. Money. And Louise.

"Louise said you were coming to the opening night," Gretchen had said. David carried the phone to the television and lowered the sound. When he was in hotels he liked to watch reruns of *The Rockford Files,* or whatever adventure shows were on.

"I told her I would come to the opening night the first night she told me about it," he said and fine-tuned the hue knob, sharpening the shades of green.

"So you'll be there."

"Yes, Gretchen, I'll be there." He walked back to the bed and kept his eyes on James Garner.

"She's counting on you."

"I know."

"We both are."

"My plane gets into Kennedy at five-fifty. What time is the play, eight?"

"Eight-fifteen."

"So I'll see you there?"

"That's one of the reasons I'm calling. I'm going to be away for the weekend, until Sunday. I'm going to the Sunday performance. I thought I'd give you the opening night and I'll pick up when some of the wrinkles get ironed out. Unless it closes in Philadelphia." She laughed nervously. David laughed too, in spite of himself. The low-keyed importuning, the bit of cleverness, the little joke: it was part of Gretchen's latest role, the cheerful, nonthreatening ex-wife. Or maybe she was just in a good mood. Whatever it was, it was infinitely more tolerable, even with the disingenuous jokes, the forced laughter, than the way she used to be. Classically bitter, for most of the five years since the divorce. Though, Lord knows, he had probably deserved her wrath, had missed God knows how many school plays and parent-teacher conferences, had often canceled the weekend visits and once a trip to the Bahamas the day he and Louise were to leave. The news, he explained to her. Her silence on the other end of the line had been incriminating. Gretchen must have picked up the pieces while he was in Biloxi writing about a plane crash, or in Oklahoma covering a tornado, whatever disaster it had been that time. The larger the disaster, as always, the better. Before long—his eyes wandered again to BE-LIEVE IN JESUS—Louise would be canceling weekends on him instead of the other way around, and it would not be because she was going to the Berkshires with her mother.

"*The Bald Soprano*'s a wonderful play," Gretchen had said two nights ago. "You might want to read it before you come."

"I read it last week."

"Louise plays the maid."

"She told me. I thought about her doing the part as I read it."

"She's nervous out of her mind, poor thing. Lots of dreams about falling off stages and forgetting lines. Like dreaming you'll flunk the exam the night before you take it." Gretchen's homespun wisdom, never profound but always on the mark. Perhaps her gift as a therapist. Certainly one of the things that had drawn him to her during their last year of college. He remembered the night in his student apartment in Ann Arbor when Gretchen sang "My Guy" *a cappella* into his mouth. "You best be believing I won't be deceiving my guy," she crooned and moved closer to him. "He may not be a movie star, but when it comes to being happy, baby, we *are*."

"Nervousness is only natural," David had said to her two nights ago. "Tell Louise I'll be sitting in the front row. And tell her not to break a leg—from me." He laughed. Gretchen said they might run into each other if he was in New York Sunday night. He said he was not planning to be.

"But you never know," Gretchen said. "I mean *you* never know."

"You're right, I never do."

"So maybe . . ."
"Yes, maybe."
"Take care, David."
"You too, Gretchen."

The third call David was waiting for at five that afternoon was from his editor. Ingstrom made it a point to call at least once a day, even though David would not be writing anything for several days. Ingstrom was a nervous type, new to the job, and eager to keep up with his reporters, probably afraid that they would tip out, trip off to the beach, or drink all afternoon at the Polo Lounge. He didn't believe—or pretended not to believe—David's faithful descriptions of smoggy afternoons waiting for the phone to ring in the hotel room. Ingstrom was like a kid who thinks L.A. is all beaches and bus rides past the homes of the stars.

When he called, David would tell him that his research on the electoral strength of Mexican-Americans was completed. He had spent the better part of the week talking to Chicano politicians and community activists. Beneath their enthusiasm, their graphs and independent studies, he sensed despair. All you had to do was look at the numbers. Chicanos made up twenty percent of the state, but only about fifty percent of them were registered to vote, and nowhere near that number would turn out. But a few days from now, when he actually sat down to write, he would highlight the enthusiasm and the potential, and soft-pedal the facts. He would quote Cesar Chavez at a get-out-the-vote rally. He would describe the poster in the family clinic in East L.A.: the little Chicano boy looking plaintively at the camera, beneath the words: SU VOTO ES SU VOZ. Your vote is your voice. Maybe not in this election, but it would not be long before . . . End it on a positive note. And leave out the subterranean story, not because it wasn't interesting but because it had nothing to do with the assignment: the electoral strength of Mexican-Americans.

The subterranean story was that there were something like

a million illegal aliens in L.A. alone, and Esterbrook had gotten a lot of ink in the L.A. *Times* last week when he charged that some Chicano community leaders had registered illegal aliens to vote. Esterbrook had heard, he said, that this was going on. Some of his Chicano friends, he said, had told him. In the papers and on television the Chicano community leaders disavowed the charges. Off the record, one of them said to David, "We don't have any Republican *friends*."

As far as the election went, David knew he had lucked out. All he had been doing for the last three months was writing about what he called The Alternative Electorate, the unorganized voices, or the newly organized voices, the people you haven't had to answer to yet, the people you still may be able to ignore. Farm workers, gays, Mexican-Americans, women, the New Right, the Old Left. In Pensacola, Florida, and Cairo, Illinois, he had found a few other desperate voices in the night, working up hopeless petitions, running candidates on losing tickets, trying to matter, as earnest and dreamy as kids who ran for class president.

It was a good assignment, especially considering the alternative: the campaign press corps. He had told Ingstrom last summer that he would rather write about the electoral potential of sheepherders than rot away on an airplane full of drunken reporters who had to transcribe what a bunch of drunken politicians had to say to a bunch of Iowa farmers about grain subsidies and school prayer. He had covered the last two presidential elections. He had been a good soldier, had waited until the day after the last election to tell his editor that he would quit the paper before he would cover another. Ingstrom called David's current assignment "Back Roads of the Campaign Trail." He couldn't stand the idea that David had gotten his way with the paper. He needed to remind his reporter that he was not all that far from the beat he had wanted to avoid.

At the moment, what he really wanted was the story on illegal aliens being registered to vote. The idea intrigued him. Their status intrigued him. They were at the very bottom of the list of people who were getting fucked over, a list that he kept in his head and that grew in a downward direction just when he thought he had reached the bottom. Something he had learned from Orwell: however far down the bottom is, there's always someone beneath it.

When the election was over, he might propose a few stories on illegal aliens to Ingstrom. Earlier in the week he had called some contacts to get an idea of where to begin. He had called an old friend, Roger Gaston, who wrote about immigration now for the L.A. *Times,* and they had had dinner together. They had worked together in Washington years ago. They kept track of each other's bylines. In the two years since David had seen him, Roger had stopped smoking, gained weight, and now drank light beer instead of martinis. It looked like three light beers for every martini he used to down. Two distracted glances to every woman who entered the dining room. And a saucy comment when he saw anything out of the ordinary.

"Where should I start with this immigration story?" David had said.

"Which story? There are three dozen you could start with."

"What about the allegations that illegal aliens are being registered to vote?"

"Makes good copy, doesn't it?"

"But wouldn't it be easy to register them?"

"Sure, Wiley. Send the ladies from the League of Women Voters into the sweatshops with a stack of voter-registration cards and a copy of the Constitution in Spanish. The place would empty out in twelve seconds."

"All right. But you haven't convinced me it's impossible across the board."

"If you find out it's going on, give me a call."

"Who'd know?"

"A guy at the L.A. Immigrant Service Center. Mark Peyser. If you can't get hold of him, Lexi Steiner."

David nodded and said, "I know her."

"You know her well?"

"Not very. I met her once or twice. Talked to her a bunch of times on the phone since then. Do you?"

"She lives next door to me." Roger smiled.

"Don't tell me, you think she's gorgeous, right?" Roger

thought three quarters of the women he met were gorgeous. He thought the rest of them were dogs.

"She's not bad. Kind of exotic-looking. Little birthmark right here." He pointed to the top of his nose. "But of course you've met her."

Roger turned to look at a woman dressed in a suit that made her look like a career girl in a 1940s movie. The backs of her calves caught his eye and, seconds later, David's eye as he followed Roger's glance. The woman walked briskly past the pastry cart. In the place where her stocking seams should have been were painted two thin lines of bright purple glitter. "What if those aren't stockings?" Roger said. "What if she just glued the goddam glitter right onto her skin?"

David laughed, turning away from the twenty-third-story window. He pulled *Passages* from its usual place on the bottom of the pile of books and magazines. He had started to read it three times and after twenty pages—any twenty pages he opened to—he became so incensed by its pop psychology that he tossed it aside, across whatever hotel room he was in. But he carried it with him wherever he traveled, because Louise had given it to him a few months ago for his thirty-sixth birthday. He was sure there was something in it she wanted him to know. Maybe something like: Grow up, Daddy. He slumped into the armchair by the window with the shiny paperback, its edges scuffed and worn from the abuse it had taken at the bottom of his suitcase for two months.

Actually, he was waiting for four phone calls, but the fourth would not come until about eight-thirty. Lexi Steiner was going to call about dinner when she got back from San Diego.

"She knows immigration law inside out," Roger had told him later during their dinner. With a few more light beers under his belt, Roger also passed on to David some of his notions about Lexi Steiner's other interests. Nothing conclusive, mind you, Roger had said, but a tempting theory. David listened to

Roger's theory and shrugged his shoulders, secretly interested, but unwilling to share Roger's voyeuristic pleasure in the details of her personal life. Or Roger's version of the details. When they had worked together in Washington, Roger had constructed elaborate tales of the sexual habits of all the White House aides and their spouses that he knew. This one liked it that way, couldn't you just tell by the way she answered the phone. Or that one, always on top, especially when her old man had just returned from a late-night meeting with the President. That was when you needed a feisty woman the most, wasn't it, Wiley? Imagine the poor schmuck, his manhood torn to shreds in the Oval Office at two in the morning. The therapy itself was worth the price of the job. David would laugh, imagine fleetingly Roger's rendition of the hot scene in the semi-official bedroom and return to what he had been writing when Roger interrupted him, gesticulating over his typewriter.

David opened *Passages* to the chapter called "Why Do Men Marry?" and began to read.

Ahead of her was a swarm of signs hanging over the freeway: LOS ANGELES, SAN BERNARDINO, RIVERSIDE. For several distinct seconds, the length of time you lose the sound on the radio driving under an overpass, Lexi forgot where she was going. Then she said aloud, as if the sound of her voice would confer sanity: David Wiley, dinner, call him when I get to town. She paused for a moment, then continued speaking to herself in a prosaic monotone, like a spy reciting back complicated instructions he has just been given. David Wiley wants to talk about Esterbrook's charges. And he wants to talk about immigration. And he really wants to see me. Or maybe he really wants to see me because he really wants to talk about immigration. She followed the signs for Los Angeles, took the freeway around a sharp bend, hedged where the traffic merged into five lanes of speeding cars. She inhaled, accelerated, sped into the middle lane.

She considered a proposition: there were things besides immigration that she really wanted to tell him about. Or tell someone. Someone who was a man. A man who really wanted to see you. She wanted to tell a man this story. Two weeks ago in the Delta terminal of the Dallas–Fort Worth airport, when she had been changing planes at three o'clock in the morning and hadn't slept in twenty-eight hours, she had wanted to sit down on the floor under the video terminals announcing arrivals and departures and bury her face in her hands and cry, like a child lost in a department store. The next night when she got home from work, she drank half a bottle of red wine. Sometime after midnight she walked the three blocks from her house to the beach. She left her sneakers in a spot where the wet sand met the dry sand and danced in the foamy water of the low tide to music without words going through her head. Da da da dump da da da, da da da dump, da dump, da dump, da da, da dump. She invented melodies and splashed through water up to the middle of her calves as if she were doing a square dance, even though she had no idea how to do one. Who needed to know how to do-si-do as long as there was wet water and warm sand and stars in the sky, as long as— She kicked her foot through the water as hard as she could and watched her glistening wet toes shoot up into the air. She held her foot above the foamy water, extending her arms to keep her balance, then lowered it and threw her weight on it, leaping through the air and the receding waves, water splashing all over her shorts. She kept running in huge leaps until the shorts were drenched and she was out of breath. Then she turned and walked slowly back down the beach, squeezing wet sand between her toes: postcard of a girl ruminating at the water's edge. Wish you were here. Wish someone was here. She stopped and lifted her head slowly toward the sky, careful to focus her eyes on the first star that came into view, and said softly: I wish I may I wish I might have this wish I wish tonight. I wish. I wish. She stopped cold. Her eyes still pinned to the star, she wished she could think of what to wish for. She kicked the water and walked back to the place where she was sure she had left her sneakers. They were not there. Carving an X in the sand with her foot where she stood, she walked thirty paces to the left, thirty paces back to the X and then thirty paces to the right. The sneakers were nowhere. She gave up and headed over the cool, dry night sand toward the parking lot, her feet caked with fine black sand, thinking over and over again: I should have wished I'd be able to find my fucking sneakers.

A little way south of San Onofre, Mick Jagger came in clearly on the radio: "I got nasty habits, I take tea at three." Lexi turned it up loud and rolled down the car window, letting her arm hang out of it, suspended in the wind. "The meat I eat for dinner must be hung up for a week. My best friend he shoots water rats and feeds 'em to his geese. C'mon now honey, doan cha wanna . . ." She drew in her arm and lighted one of the joints Boz had left with her as he passed through L.A. on his way to Mexico. Still driving the beat-up '67 VW Bug he had had when they were in law school together in San Francisco. Now his Bug had 180,000 miles on it, he boasted, and a cracked windshield that he had taped with invisible acrylic tape. Drunk awhile back, he had driven off the side of a road down a steep, wooded hill. He'd smashed his forehead and the windshield and dented the passenger door so badly that it no longer opened.

He had arrived four days ago unannounced at midnight, on his way from San Francisco. He had tried calling from a truck stop in Bakersfield, but there was no answer. "C'mon in. I just got home." With her back to him, she took a deep breath and closed the front door. He sauntered through the living room and into the kitchen. "There's some beer in the refrigerator."

"You want one?"

"I've got one." She sat down on the couch, the only real piece of furniture she had. A navy-blue modern thing she had bought for three hundred dollars last year. Boz would probably say something about it, probably ask how much it cost, and she would stammer, thinking of the fifteen-dollar couches they had bought at the Good Will when they lived together in San Francisco. It was on sale, she'd say. Have a seat.

He stood in the doorway between the kitchen and the living room holding up a can of beer as if he were in a commercial, so she could see the name of it. "Lite." He smiled and said, "What are you drinking this shit for?" meaning it but aware of his nerve. She couldn't stay mad at him long. He was all-California: white-blond hair almost down to his shoulders, sparkling blue eyes, scraggly beard. A long face, always sunburned, with full, baby-faced cheeks. He wore a skin-tight tank top that was bleached colorless from years of washings. His shoulders stood out muscular and freckled from the sun, from weekend river-rafting trips and afternoons at the nude beach north of San Francisco. From his shoulders down he was lithe and narrow. Unless you got up close and could see the wrinkles beneath his eyes, he could have been nineteen.

When they had met years ago at a club in San Francisco and he told her he was a student, she was sure he meant an undergraduate. It turned out he was a year ahead of her in law school and he was thirty-one. Before he went to law school he had been a nuclear physicist. When she asked him why he'd stopped doing that, he said, "I was doing angular-momentum calculations and I might as well have been driving a cab."

Now she smiled back at him as he opened the can of beer. His thumb pried loose the flip top and he held out his palm to catch the bit of foam that sprouted out of the hole. He licked his fingers.

"If I'd known you were coming, I'd have bought a six-pack of Schlitz Malt Liquor. The Bull."

"I knew I should have called again from the road." He smiled and sat down on the director's chair next to the couch. His eye caught the large freeway sign leaning against the wall. TURN AROUND YOU ARE GOING THE WRONG WAY. "You still have that sign."

"Remember when we found it? Coming back from—where was it?—Yosemite? Shasta?"

"Yeah, I remember. I think it was Shasta. That's how I feel

about my life these days: turn around, you are going the wrong way. So I'm going to Mexico. I think I need to take it easy for a while."

"Boz, you've been taking it easy since I've known you." She got up and went to the kitchen for another beer. She called out, "You should visit my parents when you're there."

"Where do they live again?"

"Cuernavaca." They had moved there from New York three years ago, to retire. Had moved to Mexico at the same time Lexi started her job defending people who moved in the other direction across the same border.

"I'll be lucky if I make it to Tijuana at the rate I'm going."

She returned to the living room. "How long are you going to be away for?"

"No more than two weeks. I've got to come back to vote."

"You vote?"

"Of course. Always. I write letters to congressmen. I do all that shit." He shrugged his shoulders. "I believe in the system, for what it's worth."

"Your belief or the system?"

"Both." He smiled. "Did I tell you I just won a case?" She shook her head. "Do you have any rolling papers? I ran out on my way here." He uncrossed his legs and stretched them out to reach into his pocket. He took out a small plastic bag of marijuana and said, "This is part of my fee. Some guys in Sonoma County got busted for three hundred marijuana plants and I got them off. Illegal search."

"And all you got was dope for it?"

"It's good dope. They're the only clients I've had in the last two months except for Goldstein." Goldstein. Another friend from law school. Back then the joke was that Goldstein was going to be a lawyer because he got arrested so often it would save time if he could defend himself. Never anything serious, but he had landed in jail a handful of times. For things like not having the thirty-cent duty charge at the border crossing in El Paso in 1973, and when they searched him they discovered he didn't have a draft card either and threw him in the El Paso jail for a week. Or a cop stopped him for throwing a cigarette butt out the window of his car in downtown L.A., then did a computer check on him and found there was a warrant out for his arrest because of two hundred dollars in unpaid parking tickets.

"What did he do now?" Lexi said and handed Boz a packet of E-Z Wider and a magazine to roll a joint on.

"Passed a cop on the right one night. We were both pretty drunk."

Lexi laughed.

"But I've got big plans. I'm going to sue all the banks in California for improper disclosure of interest rates. When I get back from Mexico."

"Let me know when you do. I want to be an injured party. I had to take out a personal loan to buy this couch."

"I was wondering what you bought it with." He balanced the magazine on his knees and spilled out a small mound of marijuana from the plastic bag.

"How's your love life?"

"I'm still on the ropes from the last one. Did I ever tell you about Jane?"

"One night on the phone, Boz. I think you were drunk."

"I probably was." He licked the edge of the rolling paper. They often spoke each other's names at the end of a sentence, even the simplest, most neutral declarative statement. A substitute for the more intimate names exchanged between lovers or between people who had once been lovers. Early on, when it was all new to Lexi, in her first year of law school, she and Boz would stay out late, drinking, playing pool, driving to clubs in Palo Alto or Cotati, and return to Boz's flat in the Mission to sleep for what was left of the morning. When the sun was up and they had to be in law school in an hour and a half, Boz would put a record on the stereo and turn it up loud. Lynard Skynard sang, "I fought the law and the law won," and Boz would sing along, the sun blaring into the room as loudly as the music inside it. I fought the law and the law won. They would stop for coffee and *pan dulce* on their way to school.

She had never been as wild as she had been that year, her first year out of New York. She took the LSD he offered her and they drove, tripping, to a hot springs in Sonoma County. Or they took off early in the morning with three of Boz's room-mates to the mountains, five people and gear piled high in Boz's old Bug. One of them had probably thought to empty the beer cans out of the back seat. The gesture of Boz's she liked best: taking the last swallow of a sixteen-ounce can of Schlitz Malt Liquor and theatrically tossing the empty can into the back seat. The back seat of the car for which he had no insurance and no intention of ever getting any. When he first told her, she had said, "Isn't that illegal?" "So's smoking dope." He craved caf-feine, kept a bottle of No-Doz in the glove compartment. She declined. She imitated him tossing the beer can over his shoul-der. Often back then in the mornings she woke with black rings under her eyes, evidence of the beer, the dope, the lack of sleep. The dark marks pleased her peculiarly, like the swollen jaw of the man who had been in a barroom brawl the night before: no regrets, even though it hurt like hell in the morning. Sometimes she and Boz had slept together and sometimes, occasionally, they slept with each other's friends. Boz with Nell, Lexi with Goldstein, Boz with another friend of Lexi's from law school, Lexi with several more of his friends. She told him what she had done one weekend. Grinning, he said, "You sure are having fun with all my friends."

"I sure am."

The wildness that year was a rite of passage, something other than a response to the constraints of law school. Maybe a response to the constraints of everything in her life up to and including law school. Nell had given her the idea to get with it, and then Boz showed her how. Showed her how to toss beer cans into the back seat, how to fuck with impunity, how to take off in the middle of the night without a destination. A one-liner from back then: Reality is for people who can't face drugs. Very funny the first time you heard it, especially if you were stoned.

Four nights ago in her living room, Boz had said, "Don't you have any friends for me, Lexi?" and passed her the lighted joint.

"I thought you already slept with all my friends." They laughed.

"That was years ago. Don't you have any new friends?"

"Do I go around asking you for lists of your friends every six months?" She inhaled deeply.

"It's a good thing you don't because I'd just have to shine you on. What do you think of the dope?"

"Give it a minute to get into my bloodstream, would you?"

"Sure, Lexi. Where's Nell at?"

"In New York, trying to get a publisher to give her a book contract."

"You women from New York are such hustlers." He smacked his lips loudly.

"And you guys from California are so mellow." She smacked her lips in imitation. "How's Goldstein doing? Is he going out with anyone?"

"No. He's pretty miserable—you know, just going through the motions."

"How come?"

"I don't know. He's lonely. He wants someone to come home to and to sleep with. He wants to be in love like everyone else does."

"Why is it so hard to do that?"

"Fuck if I know, Lexi." He shook his head and got up and looked through the long row of records in Lexi's bookshelf. "Do you have *Some Girls*?"

"The Stones?"

"Yeah."

"No."

" 'Rich girls they want Cartiers, Italian girls want cars, American girls want everything in the world you could possibly imagine,' " he sang and took a record from the shelf. He put the record on the stereo and took off his shoes. When the music started he began to dance around the floor with his eyes closed, holding his arms. Otis Redding sang: "I been loving you too long, I don't want to stop now." He drew out each word, breathless and torn, drowning in violins. Boz rolled his shoulders, opened his eyes suddenly and said, "I don't think I ever loved anyone that long."

"You know he was twenty-six when he died?"

"Shit. When I was twenty-six I was writing a dissertation at Berkeley and taking LSD every weekend just to get *by*. We fucking made our own acid in the chemistry lab." He closed his eyes again and swayed his hips to the music. "Poor fucking Otis," he said. "Poor fucking me."

"Hey."

"Yeah." He kept moving.

"You're not taking the dope to Mexico , are you?"

"No, I thought I'd leave it here and pick it up on my way back."

"I've got to get up early. I'll get you some sheets for the couch."

"Don't need no sheets, Lexi, got my sleeping bag."

"Don't forget to turn off the power on the amplifier."

He opened his eyes and smiled, "I won't, Lexi."

He would probably be returning to her house in a few days to pick up the dope. She thought of him coming home to vote, believing in the system, and took another long drag of the joint she held between her fingers. She wanted to forget herself on this stretch of the freeway.

She moved into the far right-hand lane to pick up 405, which would take her to the Harbor Freeway and then into downtown Los Angeles. David Wiley was waiting for her call.

David was in the middle of the chapter called "Men's Life Patterns" when the phone rang. When he picked it up he heard a scratchy, cavernous sound. Long distance. "Daddy. It's me."

"Hello, you. How are you?"

"Okay." She sounded tentative.

"I thought you'd be at dress rehearsal tonight."

"It was this afternoon."

"Are you studying your lines?"

"Not right now."

"Is something wrong?"

"Do you know about Tarot cards?"

"Sort of."

"I bought some today and I've just been reading them. You know, they tell you everything about the past, the present and the future." She paused. "They said something horrible is going to happen tomorrow."

"Did they say what?"

"Something to do with travel and death."

"How can you tell?"

"First, you spread the cards out in a cross and then you read them. I've got this book. And the book said—I mean, when you match up the cards to what the book says they mean—well, whatever the book says."

"What did it say?"

"It said—wait a second, let me read it to you. In the card that's supposed to tell you about the future, I got the Ace of Swords. In the book it says that the key phrases are—are you listening?—news of sickness or death; difficulty in adjustment; talk of a melancholy nature; division of ideas; inability to talk fluently."

"It sounds like it's about your play—inability to talk fluently. Maybe you're afraid you'll forget your lines."

"But what about the sickness and death?"

"I don't think everything on every card is supposed to come true. Maybe it'll turn out differently if you read them again."

"I read them twice. That's when I got scared. The second time, in the future card I got the Lightning Card. The book says that's part of the Major Arcanum. What does that mean?"

"I'm not sure."

"What's arcanum?"

"It's from arcane. It means obscure. But I don't know what it means in terms of the cards."

"The book says the Lightning Card's key phrases are accident or catastrophe and applied creative energy. *Both* future cards said something about death."

"But both of them didn't. An accident could be anything. You could cut your finger on a piece of paper or drop a carton of eggs."

"What about catastrophe?"

He strained to follow the details of her talk, the dramatic words imbued with vivid lives of their own in which, somehow, she believed their own lives would become entangled. Louise latched onto another bizarre philosophy every few months and believed in it utterly, like some girls believed in every new boyfriend, until a new one came along. For Christmas last year she had had his astrological chart read and sent him a tape about his personality prepared by the astrologer. He had been surprised at the time by how accurate it was. But all he could think, then and now, was that all of this hocus-pocus was her way of rebelling against him and Gretchen. He with his facts always in print, Gretchen with her psychology, willing to listen to the smallest thing and spend an hour with you to figure out why it bothered you. There was nothing mystical about it except her incredible patience, unless you were her ex-husband.

"There might be a hurricane in Manila," he said. "It would be a castastrophe for everyone in Manila."

"You don't understand, do you?"

"I guess not."

"Something *awful* is going to happen tomorrow, Daddy. I think it might happen on your flight to New York."

"Louise, it's just a bunch of cards. Calm down."

"I don't think you should come to the play. I think you should stay in California."

"Where's your mother?"

"In the Berkshires."

"What the hell is she doing in the—"

"Daddy, you know she goes there every weekend."

He had forgotten. "What's the name of those people next door?" he said.

"You mean the Fergusons?"

"Yes. Maybe you should spend the night there."

"Why?"

"So you won't be afraid."

"I'm not afraid *now*. I'm afraid for what's going to happen tomorrow."

"Louise. Louise."

"What?"

He didn't know what to say next. He sat down on the bed and felt something underneath him. He stood up and saw *Passages* where he had sat down. "You'll never guess what I was reading when you called." Thank God it hadn't been *The Economist*. Maybe he could get her to stop talking about the cards. "*Passages*. I'm on page 192."

"Do you understand yourself better now?"

"What do you mean?" So there was something she wanted to tell him.

"Mom said it was for grownups who wanted to understand themselves."

"Did she say I needed help along those lines?"

"She doesn't say mean things about you anymore."

"Since when?"

"Since Curtis."

"Who's that?"

"This guy she goes out with. He's the one with the house in the Berkshires. He's also *heavily* into Tarot cards."

"Is he a psychologist?"

"Everyone she knows is one."

"And he's into Tarot cards too? I didn't think they went for that kind of thing."

"Mom didn't think so either. But he reads her cards all the time. I think she likes it."

"So you think he's a nice guy?"

"He's all right." She sounded unimpressed. Over the years she must have seen a lot of Gretchen's men come and go. "But he keeps asking me if I want to be a psy*cho*logist when I grow up. That's how he says it."

"You don't, do you?"

"You *know* I haven't wanted to be one since seventh grade."

"I knew, I just thought that maybe . . ." His voice trailed off. Actually, he had forgotten that it had been two years since she called him up and announced that she was going to be an actress instead of a psychologist and wanted to take acting lessons at the Neighborhood Playhouse. She had called to ask him for money. "Mom said you should pay for the lessons," Louise had told him.

"Is she there? Put her on the phone."

"She's out."

"She's always out."

"She says you're always out too and that's why you got divorced."

"If she comes back before seven, tell her to call me at work. I'm going to Detroit tonight. If I don't hear from her today, tell her I'll call her from there."

"Are you going to pay for my lessons?"

"One of us will."

"When are you coming back?"

"I'm not sure. I might go to New Orleans after."

"For work?"

"Yes, for work."

"She says all you ever do is work."

"She's told me that many times."

"She says it's neurotic too."

"Louise, you don't even know what that means."

"I do too. She told me."

"Jesus Christ."

"Are you mad at me?"

"No, I'm mad at her."

"You're always mad at her."

"I'm not always mad at her."

"I don't know why not. She's always mad at you."

"You know, for someone who's a shrink, she really—" He stopped. For a second he had forgotten he was talking to his daughter. He knew what his failures were—Gretchen had catalogued them—but bitching to Louise about Gretchen, the way Gretchen bitched to Louise about him, was not one of them. He figured that one of them, one of the adults, had to exercise some modicum of restraint, some vestige of civility, in the rearing of this child. Though she, the child, challenged his definition of childhood every time she opened her mouth. She might as well have been twenty-six instead of twelve the day she called to ask for money for acting lessons. As if she needed acting lessons.

Now she was fourteen and some boyfriend of her mother's had filled her head with nonsense about Tarot cards. But if it was true, as Louise had said, that Curtis' arrival had brought a halt to Gretchen's sniping about him, maybe there was something to be said for the guy. Even with his pack of cards, scaring the hell out of Louise the night before her play.

"So you'll stay at the Fergusons' tonight?" he said.

"No. They're weird."

"I know they're weird, but at least you won't be alone."

"I like being alone."

"I know you like being alone, Louise, but you don't like being scared, do you?"

"I told you, I'm not scared now. Nothing bad's going to happen until tomorrow."

"All that's going to happen tomorrow is that you're going to have stage fright. Everyone has it. Even Laurence Olivier has stage fright."

"You're still going to come to the play, I can tell."

"Of course I'm coming. I'm even going to take you to Sardi's after."

"What's Sardi's?"

"It's a restaurant where theatre people go after an opening. It's a tradition."

"I don't think I can go. The teacher who's directing the play is having a party at his loft in SoHo. He says it's really huge. I guess you can come if you want to."

"Do you want me to?"

"It might be boring for a grownup."

"I'm never bored."

"My ass you're not."

"I've never heard you say that before." He was trying not to laugh.

"Curtis says it all the time. We're walking down Broadway by Zabar's and Curtis says, Do you want to get something to nosh on and Mom says, No, I'm not hungry and Curtis says, My ass you're not, and then we go in and he buys thirty dollars' worth of cheese and fish and cookies and Mom stuffs her face when we get home."

"He sounds like a pretty colorful guy."

"Actually, I think he's a jerk. Except for the Tarot cards."

Lexi drove fast, too fast, eager to get there but also eager to keep going, to keep moving. Something Nell had said once: It's easier to keep your balance when you're in motion. She thought of how much she and Nell enjoyed taking risks, seeing how much they could get away with. Driving too fast, dealing drugs, sleeping with other women's husbands. Nell had outdone them both a few months ago. The phone call had come late at night. "Listen, I need your advice," Nell said, breathless already. "Remember that guy I told you I ran into at the supermarket who said he'd seen me at that party in Malibu and said he might have a job for me writing tv treatments and then never called? I'm with him at some Italian restaurant and he thinks I'm in the bathroom, so I can't stay on too long." They giggled furiously. "I ran into him—I think he said his name was John, or maybe it was Ron—anyway, I ran into him at the parking lot around the corner from *New West*—they want me to write that piece about punk clubs—and we had a few lines of, uh, in the car, and then he took me here. But I'm not sure where we are. Jesus, I don't know what I would have done if you hadn't been home. Anyway, he's gorgeous. But that's not why I called." Peals of laughter on both ends of the phone. "He's driving to Las Vegas tonight and he wants me to go with him. What should I do?"

"Don't do *anything* until you find out what kind of car he has."

The guy, whatever his name was, was what Nell called off the record. Which meant that you could tell him your name was Penelope and your husband was on a business trip in Abu Dhabi and it was the maid's night off. You could be whoever you wanted to be, because you would never see him again. Even if you did, you wouldn't owe him anything. You could make up your identity as you went along. Along for the sex, the adventure, the thrill of trespassing. A joy ride. A phony passport. The edge of suspense, as narrow as the ledge of a cliff that has been traversed enough times to make it into the guidebook, but not without a warning: sharp curves, falling rocks, experience only.

Lexi had acquired a collection of gold stars in experience from Stephen Shipler, the first in this series of smooth lawyers, Minor Mentors. Experts in hotel relations. Just recently out of law school and two weeks into her job, she was sent to represent the Center at a conference in New York. Stephen Shipler conducted a seminar on *pro bono* legal services at the Roosevelt Hotel. Lexi asked a lot of questions. He held court, knew a hell of a lot about getting fancy law firms to do legal work for Your Cause. He cornered Lexi later at a cocktail party. He had noticed her that afternoon. She had asked *good* questions, he said. How long had she been with the Center? Only two weeks. He was handsome and rugged, had bloodshot eyes—golden boy who's been working too hard in his three-piece suit. He admired the Center's work and invited her to dinner at a Japanese restaurant across town. She was not sure it was she who inspired the distinct sparkle in his eyes.

Only later, in her room an hour before they were to meet, did it occur to her that all she had to wear were the clothes she had on: a faded denim skirt and gauzy Indian blouse she had bought in college, intending, four years before, to wear it for "special occasions." In the full-length mirror of her room in the Roosevelt Hotel, her dinner clothes looked as smart as pedal-pushers. Nothing to do with smarts, which she knew she had plenty of. But maybe not as many as she had always thought. They should have told her there was more to being an attorney than passing the California Bar. They should have told her to get some new clothes for her trip to New York.

She stood in front of the mirror and undressed herself. She decided to take a bath. Crouching in the tub, she shaved her legs carefully, moving the Schick single-edge razor up the side of her calf, gently over her knee, in a straight line to the top of her thigh and down again, brushing the blade against the stubble around her ankles. The Bible she and Nell pored over in college, when one of them felt a lump in her breast or a pain in her side, *Our Bodies, Ourselves*. It did not have a chapter on how to shave your legs. Someone probably had told her that there was more to being an attorney than passing the Bar. She ran her wet palm over her suede-smooth kneecap, which bled slightly through a childhood scar. Someone had told her all of it, but she had not been listening.

On their way to the restaurant, Stephen Shipler walked with an expansive strut and held doors open for her. When she got the rhythm—linger a few seconds at the door, hands at your sides, and *wait* for him—it annoyed her less than she had expected it would. Either he was old-fashioned or a revisionist. His hair was a few inches longer than his law firm probably wanted it, a vestige of graduating from Yale in '68 and Harvard Law in '71. He wore the three-piece suit he had worn for his lecture and carried an expensive briefcase. The right costume. The right instincts. He had exploited Lexi's handicap, she thought now. The fact that she had not yet learned how easy it is to swagger.

If he could see her now. The khaki suits in warm climates, the herringbone suits and snazzy blouses for court appearances and trips back East, drawers overflowing with pantyhose, and two dresses from I. Magnin, the only two she owned. And she didn't want to do what you had to do to be able to afford more of them, even on sale. Like work for a Washington law firm, the way Stephen Shipler did.

That first night, he bounced around names of senators and their aides and told Lexi whom to call for what kinds of information. When you get your feet wet, he said over sushi, you should get into the testimony circuit. Some committee or other would pay her way to Washington. He would show her around. There were some terrific restaurants and Washington wasn't as dull as it was cracked up to be. Did she like to dance? He took off his jacket and his shoulders looked firm under his pure cotton Oxford shirt. He wore a staid striped tie. Was she up for some jazz or was she as tired as she looked? Jet lag, she said, and she was a little drunk. Or maybe it was something in the food. She'd thought it was only the Chinese who doused their food with MSG. They ordered more to drink. They laughed. A trip to Washington might be fun. And she loved to dance, but hardly ever went. Though tonight she was probably not up for it. Had he ever been to the Crazy Horse, up Pacific Coast Highway south of Malibu? Maybe next time he was in L.A.

Later in his hotel room he used his hands to hold her head, moved her head with deliberate but tempered force—far more than a suggestion—from a spot on his neck to his chest to himself. He kept his hands pressed firmly around her head and played with strands of her hair. He moved her head then away from himself so that he could feel her breasts there, between her breasts, and he pressed them close around it, which no one had ever . . . It was weird having it pushed into her face, pushed against her, as casually as if it were a finger. He was so sure of himself. So cock-centered. The phrase had never occurred to her before that moment, when it was locked between her breasts.

When he was inside of her later, she felt the same taut, sure strength in his hips as they pressed into her, forcing her to press back. He must dance really well. He shoved a pillow under her buttocks. With his hips he pulled her along to the edge of sensation and then let her pull back ever so gently, and back and forth and back and forth. She felt as if she were getting ready for a dive, jumping up and down on the end of the diving board to get a feel for the springs. Tighter than she had expected. Though she offered no resistance and came right before he did.

When they caught their breath and pulled the covers back up, Stephen kissed her on the cheek, a quick goodnight kiss, and rolled over and slept by himself.

In the morning she pretended to sleep while he dressed and packed. He strutted around the room as if he were about to whistle, looking over the front page of *The New York Times* as he buttoned the buttons on his shirt sleeves. Lexi thought about telling him she was awake, but she didn't know what to say after that. Sleep well? Anything new in the news? It was better under the covers, and he wasn't looking for conversation anyway.

He parked his bags at the door, and as he turned toward the bed, she closed her eyes. He leaned down and blew lightly in her ear, kissed her hair. "Don't sleep too late," he whispered. "I won't," she whispered back and opened her eyes. He stood up and smiled as he turned to the door. "I'll talk to you soon," he said and left. The door clicked shut.

Lexi turned over, drew the covers up around her and thought: How many women has he left like this in hotel rooms? A bit surprised by the cheap drama of the thought, and how it had come to her full-blown, like a jingle from a commercial or the refrain of a song, mass-produced and ready for consumption by the broken-hearted. She was a little broken-hearted, but she was also intrigued by the constellation of circumstances: his law-firm smooth, his odious charm, his cock. The wallflower gets laid by the captain of the football team and even though she knows it's not love—and it may not even be romance—it's its own sort of triumph. Even if you have to keep it a secret. Stephen Shipler would open doors for her, he would know when to call a cab, when to call person-to-person. With the hotel covers pulled up around her shoulders, she could practically hear Boz clucking his tongue, making his pronouncement: "If you ask me, Lexi, he's just one more tight-ass East Coast lawyer who wanted to get laid."

She knew Boz was right, but she also knew there were some things she wanted to learn from Stephen Shipler. One of them was that captain-of-the-football-team confidence. Whatever she did, she liked to look like she had been doing it for a long time, like she knew what she was doing. So she had tried to be cool about taking drugs with Boz, and sleeping with his friends, and him sleeping with her friends, though at first she had felt a lot less cool than she had acted. But putting it on that way had had a palliative effect she hadn't expected. Eventually she became the act.

But the etiquette for lawyering was different and Stephen Shipler knew what it was, even though he was not the kind of lawyer she wanted to be. He wasn't even the kind of man she would want to have around on a regular basis. One of the ones you see three times a week, introduce to your friends and spend a lot of time talking to about where your relationship is going. She knew where her relationship with Stephen Shipler was going. Though she would not consult him on any of this, he would teach her to be comfortable in fancy restaurants, he would teach her to dress like a woman instead of a college student, and he would teach her something about fucking. Something about taking what you want when you want it, which seemed to be one of the things he did best.

Still, she was pleased that Stephen Shipler had taught her his coldness, and taught her some of the other things she had had in mind. It made it easier the next time.

The next time was Lexi's local counsel in a case against the Pima, Arizona, police department. Then a lawyer in New York who was writing a book about preparing expert witnesses and who talked freely about his wife and children. Then a tv producer in Dallas whom she remembered chiefly because he took her to a party at a mansion where there was an enormous cage of doves at the edge of the swimming pool, and in the middle of the pool a multi-colored sculptured fountain. A Texan's idea of Bernini.

Between trysts Lexi and these men talked on the phone about filing motions for extensions of time, about taking depositions, about who was going to write the post-trial brief, and who was going to get the guy they knew in the Attorney General's office to get the government moving on its *amicus* brief in the case that was in the Supreme Court. And when that was done, they sometimes talked about the possibility of future trips to Los Angeles. Maybe they would find time to fly to New Orleans for a weekend. Would she be in Washington to testify on a bill that would increase the quota of immigrants from Mexico?

She came to be fascinated by the choreography of seduction. The moment, the gap, the glance, when the game took a spin and switched from Old Maid to Black Jack. She liked it even at its most banal. There's a terrific view of the city from my room. Even if it was Cleveland. She would notice his wedding band. She would have to ask about his wife. She always asked about their wives. She thought that if you married someone, you would think about things like the *quality* of your marriage and the *quality* of your feeling for your wife, the way a connoisseur would consider a fine meal: an implied level of excellence beyond which judgments were based on nuance. She always listened for shades of feeling, ready for Stravinsky—something complicated and unordinarily lovely. Instead it was like the morning traffic report on the radio: Sure I like my wife.

She got very good at it. Learned to avoid hanging around for breakfast. Learned to avoid thinking about the pieces of her behavior that five years ago would have been unthinkable. In college she had known a man who moved furniture in New York during the summers. He had said that one of the things you had to be able to do to haul a couch up five flights of stairs is to turn off your brain. You had to be able to do other things too, but if you couldn't turn off your brain, none of the other things mattered. Sometimes now, Lexi tried to turn off her brain.

Sometimes in bed she could do it. Sleeping with men she didn't care about, she came nine times out of ten, but quieter now, and deeper. More moans these days than grunts. Three out of the five men she counted had said she was terrific in bed. In so many words. The only joke she ever remembered: Two friends who see the same psychiatrist decide to trick him, tell him, in separate visits, the same dream. After the second friend has finished, the psychiatrist says, "I can't believe it, you're the third person today who's told me that dream." Terrific, I mean really terrific, in bed.

She thought now that it might be nice to have someone around, someone who would take note, have expectations, think she was complicated. Not contrived, but rich. The difference between Agatha Christie and George Eliot. It didn't matter that you knew what happened in the end. The journey, not the arrival. Or someone who just appreciated the edges of things.

She had thought briefly about taking Richard Healy to

bed. He was a first-year law student at UCLA who worked part-time in her office and was assigned to her Monday and Wednesday afternoons. He was tall, lumbering and smart. He went hiking on weekends and came in Mondays tanned and brimming. He was not a wimp, but he was a kid. He would be too grateful. Nell agreed.

David Wiley had fallen asleep with his head propped against the wall at the head of the bed. Turning in a dream, he pulled a muscle in his neck. He opened his eyes and saw the President's face on the tv screen. "We've got problems now," the President said. "I don't want to underestimate them. There are no simple solutions. But our country, when we were united and when we understood the problem or the challenge or the obstacle, has never failed, and I don't have any doubt in my mind as President of this country that the United States of America, a united people, as we face the future . . ." Now David couldn't remember turning on the television or lying down to take a nap. Ingstrom hadn't called, the flack in Washington hadn't called, Louise had called and told him his plane tomorrow was going to crash. Lying on his back, he rubbed his eyes with his hands, trying to remember whether he had dreamed that or whether she had actually said that to him. The rest started to come back. The Tarot cards, travel and death, catastrophe, Gretchen in the Berkshires with Curtis. He had not dreamed any of that.

He had been dreaming of swimming across Lake Tahoe with Melissa deKalb. They were doing the crawl in perfect, identical strokes, but she was coming up for breath on her left side and he on his right, and they opened their eyes and looked at each other with each even stroke. Her eyes were as blue and clear as the lake itself, and her blond hair was, somehow, after swimming almost two miles, completely dry. They were headed for the beach at Stateline, the little Las Vegas just over the California border in Nevada. They were going to play the slot machines, and, turning her head to him to take a breath,

Melissa said, "I know you want to, darling." Then she dropped her head back in the water and moved her arms over her head, keeping the rhythm of their strokes. With her next breath she said, "But you can't fuck me here."

It hadn't happened that way in real life. In real life they had driven from San Francisco to Stateline in Melissa's white Corvette because David had to be there to talk to someone who was attending a convention of police chiefs. They swam late that first night in the hotel's kidney-shaped swimming pool, with oversized tumblers of margaritas waiting for them at the edge of the pool. Melissa had taken off the top of her bikini and had floated on her back. Her breasts rose out of the water, illuminated in flashes by the hotel searchlight beaming down from the roof in elliptical patterns. David's head felt cavernous and clumsy. They had smoked pot before in their room. She had taken a joint out of her pack of Marlboros and held it between her lips, waiting for a light. When he saw it was not a cigarette, he said, "Are you sure—" "Darling," she'd answered in her soft, honey-coated voice, "we're in Nevada." He was not used to smoking pot, not comfortable with either the activity or the sensation it produced. Later he swam to the edge of the pool and the back of his head felt like it was sinking. He remembered that in their room she had said it was Jamaican and would do strange things to his head. He had thought that was just hippie drug talk, phrases borrowed from teenagers they interviewed on *60 Minutes*. What year had it been? '73. '74. Not exactly the dawning of the counter culture, but a baptism of sorts for him. He was new to smoking pot, to margaritas in oversized tumblers, to cheating on his wife. "I know you want to, darling, but you can't fuck me here." She had said it that night in the swimming pool, not a warning but a tease. She would have fucked him there—if he had not been afraid someone would catch them. Oh, you and your middle-class morality. She paddled away, topless. Right about what the marijuana would do to his head, and right about his morality. Except for what happened later that night, and the night after, in their room. He smiled, turned on his side, felt a tightening in his thighs, his buttocks.

He remembered his flight a few days later back to New

York. All the way across the country he had felt contrite and incredibly juicy. A sense of floating in liquid, in something thicker than water but not as thick as her own fluids. He would have liked to fuck her in the swimming pool. Anywhere. For long stretches of the flight his desire for her had overshadowed his anxiety about returning home. He was sure Melissa would show, and even if she didn't, that she had become the new standard. Gretchen would never meet it.

But he did not develop much of a taste for smoking pot or for cheating on his wife. Melissa saw to the second and, because of its association with her, also the first. She called his house twice in the middle of the night. The first time, several weeks after their two-day trip to Stateline, David was home and answered the phone. They had a bad connection. It took him a good two minutes, between the echo on the phone and being awakened from his sleep, to figure out who it was. "Are you sleeping?" she had said. "It's only eleven-fifteen here." He was suddenly alert but speechless. He said, "I . . ." And then, "Could you . . ." I can't talk to you now. Could I call you tomorrow? But instead he was silent, then trapped in his silence, Gretchen awake too now and asking, "Who is it?" twice. "You must have the wrong number," he said finally and hung up the phone. To Gretchen he said, "It sounded long-distance. He asked for Alice." Surprised by how easily the lie had come to him.

"Calls in the middle of the night," Gretchen said drowsily. "I always think they're bad news."

He could not fall back to sleep that night. Ashamed of the phone call. Ashamed of Gretchen's trust, of himself, of the worm of desire he felt at four in the morning for Melissa deKalb. He wanted to tell her that on his flight back from California he had thought of fucking her: he in his seat and she, sitting up too, straddling him, at thirty-five thousand feet. Floating above the clouds in her liquids. Something surreal, phantasmagorical but at the same time bluntly pornographic about the image. Something his wife would never . . . Maybe it was just a seven-year itch. Someone had introduced them in San Francisco and she had flirted furiously. So impressed with who he was, what he wrote about—though when they were alone together, she didn't mention his work. His apartment at five the morning of her call was eerie. The couch, the collection of plants along the window sill, the toys in the corner. A darkened museum. Someplace not his own.

Six months before, Gretchen had said she wanted to leave because he worked all the time, because she was tired of waiting for him, because the time she called him at work to tell him that Louise had been thrown against a car when her skateboard collided with a ten-speed bicycle and they were in the emergency room of Mount Sinai, he had said, "I'm on deadline, I'll be there in an hour and a half," and was an hour late. She reminded him that that was only the most recent incident she could point to. For his part, he made the usual promises of the excessively ambitious. A long vacation, just the two of them; only one day of the weekend at work; a sense of perspective.

In the dark of his apartment the night Melissa had called, he walked to the kitchen, listening to the sound of his bare feet against the hardwood floor. He poured a cup of milk into a saucepan and added a spoonful of vanilla extract to it, turning on the flame under the pan. The vanilla spread in a paisley pattern through the milk. He watched it dissolve until the milk began to bubble gently along the side of the pan. He poured the drink into a coffee mug and sat on the step-stool by the kitchen window. The night was ending. Streetlights were dimming, several people were walking dogs ten stories below, the doormen were coming out. Steam rose from the hot milk and condensed on the window, blocking David's view of a schnauzer lifting his leg on the corner of the building across the street. He sipped the warm milk obediently, even though he did not like the taste. The way Louise gave in to Gretchen when Gretchen fixed her warm milk with vanilla, Louise too tired to protest but anxious enough to need the anodyne.

The second time Melissa deKalb called, David had been out of town. She and Gretchen spoke. "At length," Gretchen said to him, relating the event a day later in their bedroom while Louise, aged nine, ate lamb chops and French fries in the breakfast nook. "Or, I should say, long enough," Gretchen said. She sat in the armchair and drank red wine, looking out the window as she spoke. "I didn't think you had time for Melissas too." She seemed remarkably composed. She continued to look out the window. "I was wondering this morning whether you had set yourself up. Screwing around with some darling Lolita—she never said, but she sounded awfully young, David. So young she doesn't know you're not supposed to call married men at home. In the middle of the night, no less. Or maybe that's how they do things in California." She gulped the wine as if she were gulping whiskey on a bet. "She'd call, I'd find out and you could finally leave. I mean, you wouldn't have to keep telling me it was the paper." In the same calm voice, eyes focused steadily on the north face of the apartment building across the street, she said, "I talked to a lawyer this afternoon." At that moment Louise burst into the room and said, "I'm allergic to lamb chops. I wasn't sure I was, but now I am." When they stared at her in silence, because their own thoughts were light-years away from allergies and lamb chops, and because in the last six months Louise had proclaimed her allergies to corn flakes, lima beans, vitamins, classical music, math homework, and Justin Bradley, who had called her once and said, "Listen" and then farted into the receiver, she said the one thing she knew would break their silence, because it had worked so many times before: "Don't you care what happens to me?"

David was shocked now, five years later, by how little care he had shown his wife and daughter. Shocked as you are when you recall a childhood antic, pointedly mean. A smart-ass phone call to a girl whose mother had just died. Tossing raw eggs from a warehouse roof into a playground at noontime, aiming for the head of the infant in the white bonnet. Cringing thirty years later at your cruelty, grateful for your lousy shot.

He got up from his king-size bed at the Bonaventure, put on his glasses, turned on the light next to the bed and the light in the foyer. He reached his arm into the bathroom and flipped the light switch. He saw himself in the mirror that stretched across the wall. He needed a haircut, a shave, a clean shirt. Ingstrom said he should get rid of his hippie glasses, round, wire-rimmed. Ingstrom's idea of how a reporter should not look. Ingstrom himself, he told David, wore contacts. Soft contacts. David asked if he had had a vasectomy too. Ingstrom said he didn't need one, because his wife's tubes were tied and he didn't make a habit of sticking his thing in places where it didn't belong. No need to say: Like you do, Wiley. Ingstrom was wrong about that too, carried away by the popular mythology—and his capacious resentment of David. A different Melissa deKalb every night. She had been instead like a bad LSD trip. It had made him never want to do it again. He unbuttoned his shirt and turned on the shower, rubbing his cheek to double-check the stubble. He would shave for his dinner with Lexi Steiner.

Under the hot spray of the shower he did not know if what he was feeling was lethargy from spending all day in his hotel room, waiting for calls that hadn't come, or a deeper dullness because of something he had done or hadn't done a long time ago, something he had never thought he would have to pay for. There was some reason he had dreamed about Melissa, recreated that awful, endless event, because he did not usually dwell on the past; another one of Gretchen's complaints about him. What else would you expect from a shrink? Maybe it was that book that had made him dream about her. *Passages*. Louise making her mark again, even three thousand miles away. Hundreds of pages of personal anecdotes about people you were supposed to "identify" with: Marsha, 31, has been seeing Todd for three months. . . . Like reading a collection of letters to Dear Abby, or the police blotter. David Wiley, 36, bright, young reporter. Though they were all bright, young reporters. At one time Ingstrom had been one too. Trying to recapture his youth now with soft contact lenses and loose talk about sticking his thing in the wrong places.

And what if he, David, had not become a reporter? In college he and taken a career-choice test which said he was suited to be either a mathematician or a spy. Something from a spy novel: "We prefer to call them agents." All right, then, call them agents. International overtones. CIA, not FBI. He was something of a spy, an agent. Last week a friend had called to ask if he would be a guest speaker for a class in Investigative Reporting at the New School next semester. One class, one hundred and fifty dollars, name in the full-page ad the New School runs in the *Times* and the *Voice*. Talk about whatever the hell you want, Wiley. Tell them about the time you cracked the story about the D.A. in Memphis covering up information about a local drug manufacturer using prisoners as guinea pigs without their consent. Or how you got the real story on Roman Polanski and the thirteen-year-old girl. Everyone loves that story, Wiley, even if you'd rather forget it ever happened. Everyone has at least three of those. When you were just starting out you thought you would sleep with your grandmother if it would get you on the front page. Years later, when you took inventory of the things you had actually done to get a story, incest sounded as tame as tiddlywinks. In the course of things, he had made more than one woman cry. He had dated and slept with the high-strung daughter of a high-level government official in order to pump her for information about her father. The girl had an enormous crush on him and called him hysterically when she saw what he had written in the morning paper about her father. She returned that afternoon, as scheduled, to Bennington, to complete the spring semester, and he never knew whether she had been upset because he had been using her or because she had read that morning in the paper, right beneath David Wiley's byline, that her father was a crook.

He thought he heard the phone ring over the roar of the shower. Though it might be the phone in the room next door. The sound was too muffled to tell. Several more faint rings. His body was covered with lather from a full soaping, the hair on his legs, chest and arms so dense that ordinary soap clung to it and thickened mysteriously in the air between the follicles. It would have taken a good five minutes to wash it off. Whoever it was would call back. It gave him a lift, the call itself, his certainty that it would be returned. Thick mounds of white lather, as thick as shaving cream, collected at his feet.

The phone rang again as he was dressing. It was Ingstrom. It was after eleven o'clock on the East Coast on a Friday night and it was Ingstrom. He wanted to say hello. He sounded loaded. He wanted to know if David had been sleeping alone. David said no one in Southern California ever slept alone. "Except you, Wiley." "Right, Ingstrom, no one but me." Then Ingstrom asked him why he hadn't been writing anything about all the illegal aliens who'd been registered to vote in California. He had just seen something on the wire.

David couldn't wait until the election was over, even if Reagan won. At least he wouldn't have to talk to Ingstrom every day.

It had been dark for some time when Lexi pulled up to the gleaming mirrored towers of the Bonaventure and drove her Toyota into the parking entrance of the building, down a slick-surfaced ramp and around a pristine circular indoor driveway. She gave her keys to the valet and went inside, up two sets of escalators, to call David Wiley on the house phone in the lobby.

He said he would be down in a few minutes and thought a moment as he picked out a place where they should meet. "The lobby's a zoo," he said. "I can't remember the name of the coffee shop there—it's supposed to look like an outdoor café. I think the word patio is in the name."

"I'll find it," Lexi said.

She hung up the phone and turned to her left. David Wiley was wrong. It was not a zoo, it was a giant, deluxe, space-age shopping mall in every direction. Ahead of her were clusters of tables surrounded by rattan chairs. Beyond them, an illuminated fountain, bright yellow lights shining from within its thread-thin jets of water shooting three feet up into the air. To her left, an irregular-shaped pool of calm water, the edge of the pool about hip level, hundreds of new pennies sparkling on its floor.

At the farthest end of the pool, an elevator descended in an illuminated glass shaft and seemed to land, from Lexi's vantage point at the registration desk, in the water. The elevator door opened and people poured out. Bustling, well dressed, Oriental. High-priced tour groups. People everywhere, as crowded as Santa Monica beach on a hot afternoon. She kept walking. A long, straight second-story balcony abutted a circular ramp that rose in a spiral for several stories above the lobby, like a cross-section of the Guggenheim Museum. On the upper levels were stores, their windows lighted up, filled with things for sale at eight-thirty on a Friday night. "Is there a coffee shop around here?" she asked a man in a uniform. He pointed. Ordinary directions were useless here. Take your first left. That didn't mean anything in the jungle. The air itself was different: purified, filtered, controlled. Like in an airplane or a mortuary. "Lexi." The sound seemed to come from one of the balconies. She looked up. "Lexi." It was closer now. "Over here." She turned around and looked across the sprawling pool in front of her. She had not remembered his glasses.

"What do I do now?" she called to him across the pool.

"There are some elevators right there." He pointed to his left. "I'll meet you there."

At the bank of elevators they shook hands. Lexi said, "Do you stay here often?"

"This is the first time."

"Doesn't it make you dizzy?"

"You've never been here?"

She shook her head. One of the elevator doors opened and two people walked between them, and a horde of people walked around them.

"C'mon," he said and held out his arm, guiding her through the crowd. "We're going to get stampeded."

"Where are we going?"

"The car. I assume you don't want to eat here."

"Not unless—"

"I can tell you don't. We'll figure something out on the way." He took long steps, must have long legs underneath his trenchcoat. She had thought they only wore them in the movies. She took two steps for each of his and was still a bit behind, asked a question into the back of his shoulder: "What about Mexican?"

He stepped on the moving steps of the escalator and turned around to look up at her from two steps below. "You must eat that all the time."

"It's the only thing I can afford."

"What about Drake's?"

"I've never been there."

"It won't make you dizzy, I guarantee." He smiled, turned and stepped off the escalator, marching straight through the glass doors leading to the garage, holding the door open for her with his foot. A bit of comedy, maybe just unevenness, about his movement. A famous person walking through a crowd, shoulders hunched slightly, his conspicuousness a fact of continuing liability, like not having any money. Or a teenage boy, the sleeves on his shirt too short and his pant legs too long, afraid of being carded when he buys a six-pack.

A big new car with four doors drove up to the sleek indoor driveway where they stood. David walked toward the driver's side, reaching into the pocket of his khakis beneath his trenchcoat. Lexi opened the passenger door and slid onto the seat, pushing aside the collection of newspapers and magazines. Through the window on David's side she saw him press his white hand into the black hand of the man who had delivered the car.

They drove up the ramp and onto Fifth Street. David said, "What are you smiling about?"

"Your car."

"What about it?"

"It's so big."

"I thought everyone in California likes big cars."

"And all the women are tall and blonde."

"Speaking of women—" he smiled—"I talked to someone a few days ago who knows you," David said. "Roger Gaston."

"My next-door neighbor."

"That's what he said."

"How do you know him?"

"He used to work in Washington when I was there. You must know he writes about immigration now."

"Of course. He even misquoted me once and had a federal judge on my case until they printed a retraction. But what does he have to do with women?"

"What?"

"You said, 'Speaking of women,' and then talked about Roger."

"Oh that. I guess I shouldn't have said anything. How did the trial go?"

They went to Drake's and drank margaritas. David said it was his favorite restaurant in L.A. He didn't look like someone who would make a big deal about liking such a fancy restaurant. In his khakis and wire-rimmed glasses. He didn't look like he belonged in a Cordoba, even if it was rented.

Lexi looked at the menu. "Melon and prosciutto for seven-fifty? You can buy a crate of melons for that much."

"Don't worry about it. The paper's paying for this. By the way, do you still think reporting is sleazy?" He put down his menu; a serious question.

"Did you take me here to prove it isn't?"

"Not at all. I thought you'd like it."

"Oh, I do." She was starting to. She was on her second margarita.

"But you didn't answer my question."

"Do I think reporting is sleazy?" She licked some salt from the rim of the glass. "Sure it's sleazy. As sleazy as most things that look glamorous. Politics, Hollywood, being a rock star. When I was a kid I had a friend whose parents were divorced and her father came to visit her a few times a year and took her out to dinner and to the movies every night for a week. I thought having divorced parents was glamorous." She was enjoying herself.

He smiled. "Are you hungry?"

"Not very."

"The salads are good."

She picked one out to have.

"What year were you born?"

"Fifty-one," she said. "Why?"

"We'll order a bottle of wine from fifty-one." He motioned to the waiter, who was there in seconds, a compact, tidy Frenchman with a thick accent; he said his name was André. David ordered the wine and their dinner, and when the waiter left he said, "What's wonderful about this place is that it's got real class, not fake class. Fake class is when the waiters hover around your table and ask whether everything is okay every five minutes. Real class is when the service is so good you don't even notice it."

"Sounds like an advertisement in *The New Yorker*."

"Do you read it often?"

"Just the ads. And the cartoons."

"What else do you read?"

"Cases. Statutes. Regulations." She reached for her glass. "Proposed regulations." She smiled. "What do you read?"

"I've been reading in the L.A. papers that illegal aliens have been registered to vote."

"I've been reading that too."

"Is it true?"

She took the last sip of her margarita, felt the crushed ice melt against her tongue. All she had to say was that Esterbrook was wrong, repeat what she had told him the other day. But she just sat there for a while, like she didn't know the answer. She was tired of questions about Esterbrook, tired suddenly of being called on to represent The Truth about everyone but herself.

"Off the record," David said.

"What?"

"Off the record." He held up his hands, an innocent man about to be frisked: no weapons, no notebook, no pen. I give you my word, no record of this conversation. She closed her lips, understanding in a split second that he had mistaken her bemused silence for concealment.

"Esterbrook is desperate for publicity," she said. "I told you that the other day."

"If the charges were true, would you tell me?"

She was silent for a moment. She had not expected this to become a test of her integrity. "You're turning this into something it isn't. There's nothing to expose. Except that Esterbrook enjoys taking advantage of people who aren't likely to talk back."

"But if there were something going on, would you tell me?" The repetition sounded studied, prosecutorial.

She chose her answer carefully, took the widest possible berth. "Maybe," she said. "Is that good enough?"

"I guess it'll have to do. For now."

"You'd love it if there were something going on, wouldn't you?"

"If there's something to write, I'd want to write it. I suppose you think that's sleazy."

"As sleazy as most things that look glamorous."

He smiled.

André returned and presented the bottle of wine, swaddled in a light pink napkin, like a jeweler with his wares. David nodded. André filled his glass, waited for a second nod, filled hers and left.

"How much do they pay you?" David said.

"Sixteen-five."

"How do you live on that?"

"I don't hang out in places like this." She raised her glass.

"Where do you hang out?"

"Do you always ask so many questions?"

"Just when I'm interested in the answers. Does it bother you?"

"Not at all. But I'm suspicious of people who make a profession of it." -

"Who besides reporters?"

"Shrinks. Stanford-Binet. The IRS." She stopped a moment—this was new material. "At best it's a sign of unquenchable curiosity. At worst—" another pause, this one for effect—"it can indicate a certain unhealthy selflessness. Voyeurism perhaps." She was so clever when she was drunk, she was so pleased with herself.

"Which am I?"

"I'm not sure yet."

Their salads arrived. André refilled their glasses. They kept talking. Immigration, the Center, some of her cases, the mood of the country, California versus New York, Venice Beach versus the Upper West Side. He poured more wine into her glass.

"I expected you to be more self-righteous about your work," he said. "So many people in causes are."

"Which rap do you want to hear?"

"What do you do besides work?"

"Not much."

"Are you alone?"

"Not when I'm working." She looked at him and smiled, so he wouldn't think she minded. "But there is this friend," she said.

"Oh."

"A woman."

"And?"

"We're very close."

"What does she do?"

"She's a journalist. Freelance. You may have seen—she did a piece for the *Times* about the gay scene in San Francisco, and she's working on a book about single women."

"Is she gay?"

"Why don't you ask if she's single?"

"Everyone's single."

"And if she's gay, then I am too?"

"Not necessarily—but that's what Roger thinks."

"Roger from next door?"

David nodded.

"Is that what he told you that you wouldn't tell me before?"

"Yes."

"What did he say?"

"He said there's a woman who hangs around your house a lot and he thought you might be gay."

"Do you want to know if I am?"

"Yes." His interest was acute.

"Of course with some people you can tell by just looking. The butch dyke, the men on Castro Street with their tight jeans and stuffed pants."

"Neither of which you are."

"Do you thing André is?" She cocked her head in the direction of the kitchen.

"I hadn't given it any thought."

"I'm not, and neither is my friend."

"Roger's been wrong about a lot of things."

"Though I can see where he might have gotten that impression. We do cultivate it. Lots of holding hands and hugging in public."

"It's too bad that always has to mean so much. Why you can't put your arms around someone you care about without— Have you ever been married?"

"No, have you?"

"A long time ago. Before I knew I'd end up being married to a newspaper."

"Will you be a reporter forever?"

"No. God, no."

"Too sleazy for you?"

He let out a short, full laugh. It was so nice to make him laugh; noisy, explicit approval. His attention otherwise, she decided, was quiet and smooth, but not slimy. He asked nosey questions without apologizing. She also recognized the gruffness she had always felt from him on the phone, but saw now it was just his bluntness and his tempered, patient silence. She tried to figure out how that would translate in bed. cool, careful appreciation, but a bit clumsy with the particulars. Or maybe he would ask a lot of questions.

"It's not sleazy," he said, "but it *is* undignified for a grown man to go tearing around the country making people talk to him. Someone in a Kingsley Amis book said that we all specialize in what we hate most."

"But you don't hate it."

"I don't hate it, but it's something to do when you're a kid, not when you're forty five. If I last that long, I might not make it through the election."

"You have doubts?"

"My daughter has doubts I'll make it to New York tomorrow. She's in a school play tomorrow night. I got a very strange phone call from her this afternoon. She was reading Tarot cards and her cards said my plane tomorrow was going to crash."

"The cards said that?"

"Not in so many words. They said something about— what was it?—catastrophe and travel. Travel and death. Something like that. The plane crashing was her interpretation." He lifted the glass and looked into its cradle of deep red wine. Perhaps admiring the color, or hoping to read something in it, something other than what the Tarot cards had said. "She said I shouldn't go to New York tomorrow."

"How old is she?"

"Fourteen. Going on twenty-six." He drew a knife through the salad on his plate. "Last year for my birthday she had my astrological chart read." He stuck his fork into the leafy greens. "At first I thought the whole idea was ridiculous. But I was surprised by how accurate it was."

"What did it say?"

"I forget most of it now."

"What didn't you forget?"

He paused, either surprised by the question or delving into his memory through the night's liquor. "It said I was single-minded about whatever I did. Sometimes verging on the mani-acal. I think my ex-wife helped write it." He lifted the fork to his lips. "She didn't like being a reporter's widow. Not many of the wives do." He washed down the salad with wine.

"What will you do if you stop being a reporter?"

"That's the question. What will I do? What does anyone do? Do you settle down or do you keep running?" He shook his head, more to register confusion than to answer a question. "And if you stop, how do you live? I can't go back to writing about two-alarm fires and car accidents. I don't even live any-where now."

"What do you mean?"

"The place where I was living went co-op about six months ago and it was twice as much money as I wanted to spend, even for an insider's price. I moved my things into stor-age, and before I could look for a place to live, I went on the road for a few months. I haven't gotten around to finding an apartment since then. Christ."

"Where do you stay?"

"When I'm there, which isn't very often, I stay with friends or in a hotel. I've even stopped thinking it's strange not to live anywhere. . . . Jesus, I'm very drunk. I shouldn't be tell-ing you all of this. I should be asking you about illegal aliens."

"But I've told you everything." She smiled.

"You know, there's a rule about this," he said. "The rule is that you should never get drunk with your sources." He sounded serious, sober.

"Is the corollary that you should get your sources drunk?"

He looked surprised. "Look," he said quietly, "I didn't invite you to dinner with the intention of getting you drunk and plying secrets from you."

"Why did you invite me to dinner?"

"I told you."

"I thought for sure—" She was drunk, had trouble hearing herself, as if her ears were stuffed with cotton. If it came out wrong, she wouldn't be able to hear it. "When you called me three days ago you said something—I can't remember what it was—something about wanting to see me—I thought for sure . . . It sounded urgent. Like it didn't have to do with work."

He took a swallow of wine and placed the glass on the table carefully, as if there were a circle drawn on the table and the base of the glass had to fit into it. The navigations of the inebriated. "I wanted to talk about your work and I wanted to talk to you. I met you once for five minutes and I've been talking to you on the phone for a year. I wanted to know who I've been talking to."

"Are you satisfied?"

"I've enjoyed this immensely, Lexi. You're quite—" He stopped.

"Bold?"

"That too. But the word I was thinking of was—" He stopped again. André appeared at the table and picked up their plates. He asked if they would like coffee or dessert. They shook their heads in unison. When he left, David said, "There's another rule you should know about. Reporters don't sleep with sources."

She finished the wine in her glass. "Have you broken that one too?"

He looked at her and then at the table, sadly, or maybe stumped. He reached for his wineglass, slid his fingers around the stem, but did not lift it.

"Excuse me." She got up, walked across the dining room and asked a waiter where the bathroom was. Downstairs to your left. She held the railing going down the stairs and staggered into the ladies' room. What was all that hurrah on the phone about wanting to see me? Rushing back to L.A. It couldn't wait. He *had* to see me. So that was his style. Wine and dine your sources. They'll spill the beans when they're drunk. Jesus, that *was* sleazy. She looked at herself in the mirror and held her hands up to her face, as if the gesture, hands against her cheeks, holding her face, spreading her fingers over her skin— she recited each step—could sober her up. Her cheeks were burning. She could not possibly drive home like this.

When she returned, there were two glasses of cognac on the table. Small, rounded glasses half filled with bronze liquid. The candlelight gave them golden highlights. David noticed her looking. "Courtesy of André."

She sat down and said, "Really?"

"No, I ordered them." He smiled. "Are you all right?"

"I'm fine." She lifted her glass and waited for David to raise his. "To André," she said and they touched glasses. "Do you know what I think about André? I think his real name is Ralph and he's from Pasadena."

David laughed.

"Do they have a special course in charm for reporters?"

"What did I do that was so charming?"

"Saying you were going to order wine from the year I was born. Or was that just a line?"

"I don't have any lines."

"That's a line too."

"Why are you so cynical?"

"You ask wonderful questions. You know, hardly any men do." She brought the glass to her lips and drank. The liquor felt hot in her throat. "This is grand, and André is grand, even if he is a fraud." She looked at David and thought he looked stern, impatient. "Jesus, Wiley, I don't know."

"I'm sorry you're unhappy, Lexi."

"I'm not asking for your pity."

"I didn't think you were."

"Or your judgment."

"I wasn't judging you."

They were silent. David motioned to André for the check. David watched him filling out the piece of paper and Lexi watched David. She thought he looked sad. She thought it was all her fault. Sometimes she did not know when to shut up.

André brought the check and David looked at it. He held it up for Lexi to see. Eighty-six dollars. "How did that happen? All we had was salad."

"And a twenty-five-dollar bottle of wine and fourteen drinks." He took a credit card out of his wallet.

"Do you do this a lot?"

"No, do you?" He smiled a little as he said it.

On their way back to the Bonaventure, where Lexi had left her car, she pulled out the armrest on the seat between them and lay her head down on it. When she tried to stretch her legs out, they hit the car door. Lying on her back, she kicked off the shoes, lifted her legs and stuck them out the open car window. The air felt good on her ankles. Her skirt rode up her thighs. She pulled it back down. She heard a hum and felt her calves rise several inches as the window rose. The window went down an inch and then up a few inches. David could make it open and close with a button on his side. "You want me to pull my feet in, don't you?" "Not at all." He sounded playful. He raised the window a few more inches and left her legs dangling against the edge. On her back she could see the streetlights, huge globes of light that disappeared over the car every few seconds, and the leaves of palm trees in between the flashes of light.

"Where are we?" she said.

"On our way to the Bonaventure."

"No, I mean what street?"

"Wilshire."

"Wilshire and what?"

"We just passed La Brea."

David tuned in a station. Chamber music. "Hey," she said, "do you like disco?"

"God, no. Do you?"

"I love it. I love to put it on in the morning when I get up." She tried to think of a Donna Summer song and a wave of nausea crashed in her throat. "Oh God," she whispered and brought her legs in, turned over on her side and curled up on the seat.

"Do you want to lie down in the back seat?"

"No."

"Do you want me to turn off the radio?"

"No."

"We're almost there."

She closed her eyes and the universe spun. The violins on the radio screeched. She felt his hand on her shoulder, stroking the cotton of her blouse until his warm palm touched her bare arm, just above the elbow. He stroked her skin down to her fingers and ran a finger over each of hers. "Touch my head," she said. "It feels like it's floating."

He wrapped his hand around her head, pressed his fingers through her hair, massaged the back of her neck. "I don't do this very often."

"You do it fine."

"No, I mean—"

"I know what you mean. I'll drive home when we get back to the hotel."

He held her neck, extended his hand to reach her ears, wrapped strands of hair around her upturned ear. She shivered. He said, "I'd like it if you could stay."

They were silent taking the escalator up to the lobby of the hotel. Lexi carried her shoulder bag in one hand and the canvas overnight bag she had taken to San Diego in the other. David wore his trenchcoat and walked with his hands stuffed in his pockets and his shoulders hunched over. "Where are we going?" Lexi said. She had to walk quickly and concentrate so that she wouldn't lose him. At one-thirty in the morning, the place was mobbed.

"The Yellow Tower."

"The what?"

He held up his room key. The end with the room number engraved on it was covered with a bright yellow strip. "There are four towers in this hotel," he said. "They're color-coded. I guess it's easier than giving them letters or numbers."

Lexi thought the lobby looked like an amusement park, the ascending circular levels lighted up like Ferris wheels, the flashing fountains, the artificial ponds. The shops along the balconies that hung over the lobby. David shuffled ahead, impatiently cutting through the crowd. Lexi put her arm through his. "Let's go shopping," she said. "I need a new outfit." He didn't laugh. "You could buy something too. A genuine Western belt buckle. You might like something for the home." He kept walking. "Though you may be right. The stores may not be open all night." She let go of his arm.

"Here we are." He stopped and pointed to a bright yellow banner suspended just ahead of them, hanging from high unseen beams and fluttering against the cement surface of the elevator shaft. "The Yellow Tower."

"Home," she said. "Remind me again why you stay here." The doors of the glass-walled elevator opened and they stepped inside. It rose quickly through the glass shaft in the lobby. By the sixth or seventh floor they were above the lobby and traveling up on the outside of the building, the elevator doors seemingly the only things attached to the structure. Lexi turned to look at the city as it spread out below them, through the thick gray-tinted glass elevator walls. The hotel swimming pool was the first thing she saw, illuminated from within and from above by stationary spotlights around the edge of the pool, a prize sapphire built on an overpass above a city street. To the left of the overpass, several streets away, was an old building with some words painted on the side in big letters: BELIEVE IN JESUS. Lights from the hotel swimming pool shone on the sign. "Funny sign," she said quietly, almost to herself, "for this neighborhood." She turned back to David. "You never did tell me why you stay here." The door opened on the twenty-third floor.

"It's not boring."

The television was on when they walked into his room. "Do you think the maid left it on?" Lexi said.

"I did." He walked across the room and turned it off. "I hate coming back to a quiet room." The room was dark now, except for a dim light in the foyer.

He went to the bathroom and closed the door. Lexi took off her skirt and draped it over a chair. She heard the water running for a long time. He came out still dressed and walked past her to the windows as if she weren't there. She went into the bathroom. She should not have come here with him. He looked glum, put upon, like some awful relative had shown up unexpectedly. He should not have asked her to stay. She took three aspirin from a bottle next to the sink and swallowed them with a large glass of water.

She left the bathroom and took off the rest of her clothes. She walked in darkness until she hit the bed with her knees. "Where are you?"

"On the other side," David said.

"How come you have such a big bed?"

"It came with the room."

"Can you see me?"

"Sort of."

The bed was huge. She stretched her legs under the covers. She touched his leg through the bedclothes. He was lying on top of them. She curled up on her side and thought about going to sleep. The sheets were cold. The elevator went up and down just outside the window. Strings of light that decorated it flashed by, the harshness muted by the drapery David must have pulled closed while she was in the bathroom. She lay with her back to him and closed her eyes. She felt him pull back the covers. Then there was a hand on her hip. About time. She remained still as a statue. Let him feel his way on his own. Let him feel his way.

"I don't think we should do this," he said. He rubbed the small of her back with his palm.

"That's what I thought you thought."

"But you feel so good."

"You thought you'd come back here alone. Is that why you left the tv on?"

"Yes." He pressed his thumb against her spine and moved his hand slowly up her back.

"Until when?"

"After the cognac."

She turned and reached for him. He was dressed. He brought his hands to her face, his lips to her mouth, and kissed her carefully, exploring her mouth.

"I liked your arms when we were having dinner," he said.

"What about them?"

"I don't know. I just liked them." He reached again with his hands for her face. She was surprised by the weight of his tenderness, by the tenderness itself. She undid one of the buttons on his shirt and he said, "Wait," and kept kissing her. He kissed the skin between her breasts. She rested her chin on the top of his head and wrapped her arms around his back, stroking his shirt. "Tell me about your friend," he said. "The woman."

"What about her?"

"Why she writes about gays."

"It's a story."

"Nothing else?"

"I thought that's what reporters did."

"Not all of us write about gays."

"You think she's a closet dyke who sublimates by writing about it?"

"She might be."

"That's awfully simple."

"But that doesn't mean it's not true. Did you two ever . . . ?"

"I told you we didn't."

"But you want to."

"Are you asking me?"

"I'm telling you. Or maybe you're telling me."

"What did I say?"

"It's not what you said. It's that you brought her up at dinner. It's that you like talking about her so much."

"We used to want to sleep together."

"When?"

"The first few years we knew each other. The intensity diminished after the first few months, but it didn't go away completely for a long time. I don't know. Maybe there's still a little left. Or maybe it's curiosity. I think we decided it would be more fun to talk about than to do."

"Would you do it if the constraints were removed?"

"Civilization imposes great sacrifices." She began again to unbutton his shirt. He did not object. He helped her with the bottom button. Their fingers fumbled together and locked. He licked her lips. His mouth engulfed hers, slowly discovered its curves. He sucked on her tongue.

"But you didn't answer my question," he said, the words garbled, his mouth full of her.

"I'm not sure what it is anymore." She slid her foot over the sheet and rested her leg on his thigh. "If it's any comfort to you, I'm quite fond of men." He rubbed her knee. She saw him now in the dark, the gray silhouette of his profile. She could even see his eyelashes. Sensory adaptation, the only thing she had remembered from the biology class she had flunked in college. Your senses adapt to the atmosphere, you get used to the dark, the noise of the refrigerator humming, high altitudes, hotels. He kissed her knee.

"You remind me a little of a woman I used to know in New York." He got up, took off his pants and tossed them onto a chair. "She was an upper-class girl from South America who liked to hold up banks. Wanted to do her part to redistribute the wealth."

Lexi laughed. "I remind you of a terrorist?"

He got back into bed with his shirt still on and lay on his side, head propped up with his hand, a girl at a slumber party telling secrets. "She was very adventurous," he said. "Unfortunately, she's dead now."

"One adventure too many."

"What's the most exotic sexual experience you've ever had?"

Unlikely places came to her. The dunes at Jones Beach. The floor of a VW van. The floor of a cement shower stall at a campground in Mexico while American hippies sang "Love Me Do" around a campfire and assaulted an out-of-tune guitar. But nothing as large as an experience. Then she remembered Leon.

"I've got one," she said and rolled over on her back. "I was in San Francisco for a conference last summer, this yearly meeting of women lawyers. I was on a panel about the problems of women aliens. After the first day it was hideously boring, and that afternoon I left the hotel and started walking toward North Beach. I was wearing a herringbone blazer, wool skirt—my lawyer uniform—and carrying my briefcase. It was cold and foggy the way it is in San Francisco in the summer. I turned up the collar of my blazer and heard someone say, 'Hey, baby, why you walkin' so fast?'

"It was a black guy, about thirty-five, kind of attractive, wearing high pirate boots with his pants tucked into them and a long scarf around his neck. Very San Francisco. I started talking back to him—'It's not me, man, you're the one walkin' so fast.' We kept talking like that, jive talk. Hey this, hey that. Not really saying anything. When I asked him what he did, he'd say, 'Little a this, little a that. Collect antique cars, play some music. What about you? What do you have in that briefcase?'

"I said I worked in an office and sort of set the tone: that we wouldn't tell each other anything about ourselves. I think I even told him my name was something else. We went to a café in North Beach and drank wine. I could smell the liquor on his breath. Old liquor, like he'd been drinking all day for days. It was only about two then. He asked me if I had an old man. 'Sure,' I said, 'you got an old lady?'

"'Course.'

"'Then where will we go?'

"He said he knew a hotel up the street that cost ten dollars. 'Is it nice?' I said. 'Course it's nice. You think I'd take you someplace that wasn't nice?'"

David laughed loudly. He was lying on his side watching her, her voice clear and steady in the dark. "I felt safer after he said that," she said. "But a conditional kind of safety, like you must feel walking through a war zone if you have a gun of your own. And I couldn't believe there was a ten-dollar hotel anywhere.

"It was up Columbus by the Transamerica Building. We walked up a flight of stairs to a window, like a ticket window in a train station, and Leon—that was his name—gave this old Chinese guy ten dollars and asked for room number eight. He whispered to me that it was the best room in the place.

"The bathroom was down the hall, and they opened the door to our room, but didn't give us a key. I still don't understand why. The bed took up most of the room except for a chair and a sink in the corner. It looked like a Hopper painting. Naked light bulb, distorted mirror above the dresser. I went to the window and opened it a few inches, trying to be nonchalant. I thought I could shriek out the window if he did anything horrible.

"He didn't. He was sweet. And slow. He said I felt like I hadn't slept with anyone in a long time, by the way I held him. . . . I didn't think it would show. . . . Technically he was—"

Lexi stopped and turned to David. They lay facing each other in the gray light, several feet apart. She liked the way he listened.

"Technically he was—" she lay back down on her back and spoke slowly into the air—"very proficient. Extraordinarily so, like an old lover but without the predictability. Old lovers who've just had a fight and still sort of hate each other, and the anger makes the sex pure and completely selfish. He kept panting, 'Do you want it, do you want all of it?' and the bedsprings were churning like a cement mixer, and the fuck-talk and the noise and, I guess, the anonymity made me come in whirlpools. . . . I don't remember his coming, I just remember that he fell asleep on top of me and snored. I wanted to get out of there.

"When he woke up I said I had to go and got up to dress. 'That's all right, baby, just like a woman, you get what you want and then split. I understand.'

"He was still in bed, and I stood there dressed in my tweeds, holding my briefcase—of all things—and he said, 'I wouldn'ta thought someone who wears those kinda clothes would like to fuck as much as you do.'

"Then I left. I remember walking back down Columbus to my hotel, to a conference full of feminist lawyers." She laughed. "Feminists. I used to think that meant something." She crossed her hands, laid them on her stomach and tilted her head back into the pillow, thinking. "I don't think they would have approved of what I had just done."

"Why not?" David said. "You were a free agent. Like Leon said, you took what you wanted and then split. That's more than most of them could have done."

"Tell me a story now," she said.

"You want a story." He lay on his back. "There are a few." Lights from the elevator rising outside made a brief stippled pattern against the drapes. Lexi thought of the swimming pool downstairs, the bizarre lobby, probably still full of people, like the subway in New York hours after midnight. Downstairs, the vacationing couples in the lobby on their way to the Yellow Tower, the Green Tower, to the revolving rooftop bar. Sweet drinks in odd-shaped glasses, the finely crushed ice and the food coloring that you sipped through a straw. Tropical delights, obsequious waiters. David would have called it fake class, not real class.

"I knew a woman a few years ago, maybe five years ago— it was when I was still married. She was very adventurous."

"The one from South America?"

"No. Melissa didn't have any political convictions that I knew of. I never really figured out what she did, or how she lived. Except that she seemed to have a lot of money, a lot of spending money. A sports car. We went to Stateline together in her car. Got very drunk, very stoned. She wanted me to tie her up." He stopped talking.

"Did you?"

He nodded. "To the bedposts, with pantyhose. I'd never done that before."

"Then what?"

"I teased her. It drove her mad. It was very exciting to me, the way she was thrashing around. I don't remember a lot of what happened, but I remember her moving wildly."

"Then what?"

He laughed quietly. "The usual." Maybe laughing at himself, at having only been up to doing the ordinary. "Which wasn't bad," he said and laughed again. "The next night—when we were quite a bit more sober—she set out to, I guess you'd say, break down my defenses, which at the time were pretty substantial. She tried awfully hard. Put on something of a command performance. She made me sit on a chair and she lay on the bed and constructed this elaborate fantasy of two or three women with her on the bed, and maybe a man somewhere around—I can't remember. She described everything everyone was doing to everyone else in the most explicit detail. It was weird."

"Exciting?"

"Unbelievably."

"Then what?"

"She made them all go away."

"Then what?"

He laughed. "The usual."

"It hadn't worked."

"What?"

"Breaking down your defenses."

"No, it did. It worked very well that night."

"What about the next night?"

"There wasn't one. I went home."

"To your wife?"

He nodded.

"Did you ever see her again?"

"No. I talked to her a few times on the phone. For about a year after that, I thought of calling her every time I was in San Francisco, which is where she lived. But I couldn't. She was bad luck."

"Why?"

He shrugged. "She just was."

"I don't understand."

"I'll tell you about it sometime."

"Did you ever do what she did in her fantasy? A group?"

"No, but I've thought about it. For about twenty seconds at a time."

"Why so short?"

"I don't know. The phone would ring. The plane would land." He laughed. "Life's little interruptions."

"I think it's in the category of things that are more fun to talk about than to do. Less complicated too."

"Let's talk about it."

"Not now."

"What should we talk about?" They held hands, moved their legs under the covers until they touched each other's feet.

"Tell me about your daughter. Are you going to her play tomorrow?"

"If my plane doesn't crash." He laughed.

"You think the cards are right?"

"Of course not."

"Aren't you afraid even a little?"

"She's not psychic. She's an impressionable kid who happens to be a good actress. On stage and off."

"What plays have you seen her in?"

"She's doing *The Bald Soprano* tomorrow night. That's tonight, isn't it?"

"Yeah. What time is it?"

"Three. Three-ten."

"What plays have you seen her in?"

"The Christmas play when she was in first grade. Nothing since then. Last year she was in *The Prime of Miss Jean Brodie* and the year before she was in *Bye Bye Birdie*. I was out of town both times."

"Where were you when she did *Jean Brodie*?"

He turned over to face Lexi, propped his head up on his hand, dug his elbow into the bed, shifting positions to fill up the silence. "San Francisco. Writing about the trial of revolutionary killer and heiress Patricia Hearst."

"What about *Bye Bye Birdie*?"

"Memphis. On a wild-goose chase. It turned out to be a complete waste of time."

"Why are you going this time?"

"I always intended to go before, but at the last minute something came up. When a dam breaks and twenty thousand people have to be evacuated, you can't say to your editor, 'Look, Tom, I've got to go watch my kid in a production of *Bye Bye Birdie*.'"

"What if your editor called right now and said the Bonneville Dam had just broken and you had to go to Oregon on the next plane?"

"No comment."

"What would you do, Wiley?"

"I'd want to tell him I couldn't go."

"Tell me something that's not obvious."

"Your collarbone is magnificent. I've been looking at it for an hour."

"What if the Bonneville Dam broke?"

"It would be a terrible mess and some poor reporter would have to go write about it."

"And it might be you."

"It might be, but I don't think so. That's part of going to the play this time. It's a test."

"It won't be much of a test if the Bonneville Dam doesn't break."

He rested his open palm on her collarbone; the V his thumb and forefinger made circled the base of her neck like a necklace. "It will be if I can't take my hands off of you."

"Did you think—"

"Be quiet for a minute."

"Why?"

"I hear something."

"What?"

"Shhhh."

A clatter of voices outside the door, moving quickly.

"Them?"

"Fire engines." She didn't hear them. "I guess they're gone now. I always wonder what would happen if there were a fire in a place like this."

"You love disasters."

"I don't. They scare the hell out of me."

"I've got one for you."

"What's that."

"One night two weeks ago I went to Venice Beach and lost my sneakers. I put them someplace and went wading and when I got back they were gone."

"Do you think someone took them?"

"No, there was no one around. It was dark. I just couldn't find them."

"What time was it?"

"About twelve-thirty."

"You went to Venice Beach alone at twelve-thirty? Weren't you afraid?"

"If I'd thought about it I would have been. I was drunk."

"Are you a lot?"

"Lately."

"What are you going to do?"

"I don't know." She took his hand and returned it to her collarbone, the patient guiding the doctor's hand: this is where it hurts. "I'll have to buy another pair of sneakers. Maybe I'll be at K Mart when they're having a Blue Light Special. Do you know about those?" He shook his head. "Someone explained it to me once. They make a blue light go on on top of some product for about five minutes and knock the price way down and sell out the stock." She laughed and then got serious. "What are you going to do, Wiley?"

"Go to Louise's play tomorrow. Hope the Bonneville Dam doesn't break between now and six o'clock."

"Six?"

"I've got to get up then to catch my plane."

"Should we go to sleep?"

"Do you want to?"

"No, do you?" she said.

"No."

"What should we do?"

"Talk. Fool around."

"I think we should have a very weighty conversation about—what about the philosophy of justice?"

"Too late for that. We have to talk about the decline of morality in America. That's what they want us to talk about."

"Who?"

"Falwell. Those people. I spent two days with him last month for this series I'm writing about the election. You know what he does? He has his church give money to poor people in Haiti and to Vietnamese boat people. You know why? To cover his fucking ass. So no one can say he's a racist." He paused. "I'd rather spend a week with the head of the Klan. At least he's not going to try to convince me he's anything other than what he is."

"What did you write about him?"

"Not what I wanted to, but I couldn't figure out how his empire works. Where the money comes from and where it goes. It's like trying to get a budget for the CIA."

"Do you think he's right?"

"Falwell? About what?"

"The decline of morality."

"He's wrong about everything."

"I don't think he's wrong about what the problems are. Teenage pregnancy, crime, the deterioration of the family. Things like that."

"He doesn't get any points just for understanding the problem. It's like mathematics—it doesn't count unless you get the answer right too."

She shook her head and raised herself up on her elbow. "It's not like mathematics. It's like suing the government. They win even when they're wrong."

He looked at her hard, as if she were still speaking. As if she had more to say.

She slid her leg across the bed and pressed her bent knee against his thigh. He drew her to him, straightened out her leg and lifted it, slowly, to press his thigh between her legs, the mood of his motion cautious, exploratory, his interest sustained not by the promise of what was at the end of the expedition but by the artifacts he discovered along the way. She massaged his chest. Their legs tangled, untangled, fell slowly into place, limbs from head to foot entwined as tightly as braided bread. But when they began to move, they were awkward, out of synch, heart set on the perfect wave, the one that will carry you to the shore whole, exhilarated by the rush of the tumble, by the body's willingness to be carried. Instead their bodies heaved and flopped. He lifted his torso above her with his arms, perhaps a countervailing gesture of his good intentions. He opened his eyes and looked at her. The tails of his shirt brushed rhythmically against her stomach, like strands of seaweed in a gentle undertow. He lowered himself gently down onto her and suddenly clasped her shoulders, tensed himself and relaxed, a silent, an utterly silent, orgasm. His heart thumped against her breast. She hoped he would not apologize.

He rolled over and sighed, a long, pleasurable sigh. The sudden shaft of air between them chilled her and she went back to him, warmed herself against the wet heat of his chest.

"What am I going to do with you?" he said.

"What do you want to do?"

"Take you home, stay here with you. Go roller-skating on the boardwalk in Venice. Eat tacos for breakfast."

"Have you ever eaten tacos for breakfast?"

"Never. Have you?"

"Once in Texas."

"So you'd know what kind to order?"

"Absolutely."

"Then that's what we'll have."

"When?"

"Next time I see you."

"Will you be a creep in the morning?"

"Of course not. Are they sometimes?"

"Yes. But so am I."

"I have to go away in a few hours."

"I know."

"But I'll come back."

"When?"

"After the election. Maybe before. Maybe both." He curled up next to her and kissed her cheek. "I think I should try to sleep for a few hours," he said. He held her cheek with his palm. Fading fast, already on his way.

"Good night, sweet." She swallowed the sweet. Endearments of one syllable; another acquired taste. If you said them quickly enough or quietly enough, you could pretend you didn't mean it.

Maybe he hadn't heard her. He buried his head in the curve of her neck. He kissed her collarbone, ran his hand over her hip. He kissed her nose, her cheek, her chin in his half-sleep. Then he was gone. Outside against the window, the elevator lights flickered in a downward progression. She was wide awake. She listened to him sleeping and considered the odds, the pluses, the minuses. Her thoughts came to her in disparate fragments, what you expect to hear when you spin the dial on the AM radio driving the interstate through Iowa in the middle of the night: the wind-chill factor in Cleveland, in the name of the Lord, in the name of Jesus Christ, I found my thrill on Blueberry Hill, at the center of your dial, all-news radio, all day and all night, rescue me, take me in your arms, now here's a message from the Dairy Farmers of Wisconsin, it's late out there brothers and sisters wherever you are, gone away and left me all alone, put your hands together and sing so that the brothers and sisters all over the great state of Missouri can hear you, rescue me—

# Sweeping the Country

The windows of the loft on Spring Street went from the floor to the ceiling and the ceiling was two stories high. The exposure was southern. The light poured in and warmed the place where Nell stood in her brother Sean's kitchen at nine o'clock Saturday morning, cutting navel oranges in half for the orange juice she was about to make. The sunlight coming in through the wall of windows felt to her like summer heat. Like Los Angeles heat. The volume on the stereo was turned down low and Sarah Vaughan was singing Gershwin: "'S wonderful! 'S marvelous! That you should care for me!"

She counted the orange halves and downed a tall glass of ice water in one gulp. Her third or fourth glass since she had returned from Eric Lord's apartment an hour ago. The headache from her hangover was gone, but she was still thirsty.

She called across the counter top into the living room, where Sean was leafing through a stack of records. "Want a glass of juice?"

"Sure."

"Piece of toast?" She was on her third.

"Sure." She popped four more slices into the toaster. She inserted an orange half into the machine and pulled down the long arm on its side that would squeeze the juice from the fruit, like the arm of a slot machine. But with a juicer, she thought and pressed down hard, you win every time. With Eric Lord she had barely broken even. She tossed the spent orange across the counter top and looked at the clock next to the refrigerator. It was the middle of the night in California. Hours before she could call Lexi. She burped. The sound reverberated in the open space of the loft, like an explosion with a slow fuse.

"Jesus, Nell," Sean called across the room.

"Am I going to ruin the tape?" He was making a tape for the party he and his wife, Marie, were having that night.

"No, but you might ruin my eardrums."

"Your toast is ready." She opened the refrigerator and scanned the shelves on the door. "You want some of this fancy-ass marmalade?" Everything in the place was top-of-the-line. That's what happens when you marry an heiress. You could teach at a private school like Sean did, and still have a thousand dollars' worth of stereo equipment, while your wife spent her time taking aerobics classes and painting the weird pictures that were hanging all over the loft. If Nell thought too much about Marie, the marmalade and everything else about her brother's life, she wouldn't have any anger left over for Eric Lord.

Sean came up from behind. "Just butter," he said and took the glass of juice on the counter. "You're awful quiet this morning—except for your stomach."

She unscrewed the lid of the marmalade jar and kicked the refrigerator door shut. "I had a little too much to drink last night." She didn't think Sean would want to hear about what else happened. Sarah Vaughan continued to sing, "'S awful nice! 'S paradise! 'S what I love to see!" Nell spread a thin coat of marmalade over a slice of toast.

"'S awful dumb song," she said.

"'Scuse me."

"What time is the party tonight?"

"Nine-thirty. Ten. Whenever people can get down here. I'm taking off as soon as the record's over. There are some last-minute costume things to take care of. Want to come uptown with me?"

"I don't think so."

"Sure?"

"Yes, I'm sure."

"What's wrong?"

"Nothing's wrong."

"You sound terrible. You're walking around like somebody died."

She turned her back to Sean and ate her toast in three bites.
She wiped off the counter with a paper towel and left the
kitchen, saying, as clearly as she could with her mouth full,
"I've got to get out of here. I'll see you later."

"Nell, wait."

She turned around.

"Did I say something I shouldn't have?"

She chewed hard and swallowed. "I just need some air."
Nothing's wrong. Nobody died. No one she could talk to Sean
about anyway.

As she left the apartment a few minutes later, swinging her
canvas bag over her shoulder, Sarah Vaughan was singing,
"They may take you from me, I'll miss your fond caress. But
though they take you from me, I'll still possess—" At the front
door, Nell stopped and dug into her bag to feel around for her
wallet, remembering a minute later to tune back into the song,
to see how it turned out. "The way your smile just beams, The
way you sing off key, The way you haunt my dreams . . ."

Eric Lord still had a nice ass, no doubt about that. She
walked west on Spring Street toward Sixth Avenue, dodging a
line of teenage punks walking four abreast on the narrow sidewalk, strutting between the garbage cans along the curb and the
stacks of empty liquor cartons piled high in front of the burned-
out storefront SoHo Community Center. She stopped to read a
notice that had been slapped on the window: The building had
been designated for restoration and might be designated a His-
torical Landmark. You were invited to inquire, to sign a peti-
tion, and to attend a meeting next Wednesday sponsored by the
Spring Street Block Association. Three of the four punks had
Sony Walkmans in their ears. The fourth punk, a girl, had a
butch haircut streaked bright purple and wore a leopard-skin
mini-skirt that shone like vinyl.

Next to the burned-out community center was the SoHo Patisserie, its window filled with Napoleons, miniature kiwi tarts, chocolate-covered cream puffs, macaroons and swirls of meringue, large light bits of candy, the whole thing just a swirl, like the swirl at the top of a dish of frozen custard. Nell knew the sugar would go straight to her head, like a stiff drink. It wouldn't do much for her ravenous appetite, but it might take the edge off her depression. She went inside and took a number. The clock on the back wall caught her eye. It was nine-forty-five. Still too early to call Lexi.

When the time came, she picked out three pastries, slipped the paper bag into her shoulder bag and headed out to look for a park where she could sit down and eat them. On the way, she would buy a quart of milk. Low-fat. You had to cut corners somewhere. Even when you were so depressed you couldn't see straight. Which she realized she was as she crossed Sullivan Street. Suddenly so down she didn't even know why. She'd lost track. And didn't know if she wanted to get back on track, sort things out, categorize her angst.

She stood on the corner of Sullivan and Sixth and couldn't decide which way to go. She looked uptown. The Empire State Building was forty blocks away. She turned around, looked down Sullivan and saw the two towers of the World Trade Center. She was surrounded by some of the tallest buildings in the world. She decided she wanted to feel wretched and miserable for a while, just give in completely. And she also wanted to eat. She was going to start with the pastries. She headed downtown.

She had come to New York to go to college ten years ago for the reason that everyone comes to New York. Because it was the big time, the big city, and also because to her parents New York represented everything that was evil and fast and loose. Her desire to go there as well as her actual journey had pissed the hell out of them for years. It had been precisely the reaction she had wanted to provoke. If New York did not exist, she would have had to invent it. Who'd said that about God? Pascal. Diderot. One of those guys. Lexi would know. It was still too early to call her. She eyed the street for pay phones anyway.

Now, ten years later, she was back, but not because it was

the big time anymore. These days it was more like her home-town, and she had come this time in part to show everyone—her brother, her brother's rich wife, Eric Lord—that she had made something of herself. Though what that was, at the moment, she did not know. She crossed Grand Street against the light and remembered her book. Her fucking book. Single fucking women. The surveys said that of all groups—married men, single men, married women, single women—the happiest were married men and the second happiest were single women. Fat chance. Though that was supposed to be what her book was about: an ode to single-womanhood. That was what she was supposed to go in and tell this editor at Doubleday on Monday morning.

It would take everything she had to go in there and do a hard sell, partly because she wasn't sure she believed any longer in the idea, and partly because she wasn't sure she believed any longer in herself. In her capacity to persevere, in her attention span. It was easy to see the end of a news story or a magazine piece. But seeing the end of a book was like standing on Venice Beach and looking west, looking for China. It was there all right, but you had to travel a good long way before you were close enough to see it, even from a distance. She dreaded the journey. She dreaded finding out that she wasn't up to it. She was sure that's what she would find out. Had a momentary image of herself in the crow's nest of a ship, looking into the horizon, looking for land—when a storm hit suddenly, sinking the works with a single wave.

She shoved her hand into her purse and felt around for the bag of pastries. As she concentrated on crossing Canal Street, her fingers hit a mound of thick cream. When she took her hand out, stepping up to the curb, it was covered with chocolate-, mocha-, and lemon-flavored cream fillings. The three pastries had been smashed together in her purse, the flavors combined, indistinguishable. She licked her fingers. They were delicious.

Too bad she didn't have a spoon. She'd be able to eat the cream filling faster. Maybe it was just as well. That much sugar at once would make her reel. She was probably hypoglycemic. She had read somewhere that there were probably more people in the United States who were hypoglycemic than who weren't, though no one knew for sure because so few people who were were aware that they were. So it was probably just as well she didn't have a spoon. Though it would have kept the sugar and saliva from making her fingers stick together. She shoved her hand back into the bag to feel around for a piece of pastry, not the cream this time but the dough. Something she could get a grip on.

She stopped at a pay phone at the corner of West Broadway and Worth. She didn't have a watch, but figured it must have been half an hour since she'd seen the clock in the bakery. She would call collect and person-to-person, and they had done this enough times for enough years so that Lexi would know to say that she wasn't in and to ask for a number where she could return the call. The operator let Lexi's line ring six times, told her to try again later and to have a nice day. She slammed down the receiver. She didn't want to have a nice day. And even if she'd wanted to—

All right. Pull yourself together. Time to settle a few scores. Time to get out of the wretched-and-miserable mode. And the only way out is through. Take it from the top. Keep walking. It'll hurt less if you're moving. Eric Lord will hurt less if—if what? He used to be a hero and now he isn't. There's nothing more decrepit than a fallen hero. Maybe he feels like one too. Or maybe he's got a new crop of starry-eyed violin students bending over backward to get his attention, to win his approval. The associate professor of music who moonlighted with some big-name quartet, had played Carnegie Hall, Alice Tully, Tanglewood. It doesn't sound like much now, but back then it put him in a class apart. And you wouldn't know to look at him that he was a world-class lover. Absolutely top rank. You don't come across too many of those in a lifetime. The first one is always a surprise, because until you have one, you have no idea what all the fuss is about.

Lord knows, she had made a fuss over Eric Lord. Looked up to him the way girls who are six look up to their fathers. Now he was just this guy whose wife had left him, and had taken most of the furniture from the apartment that Nell had seen for the first time last night. The dreary, dusty Riverside Drive apartment that didn't even have a view of the river. That had cockroaches in the bathroom and a refrigerator that was empty except for a bottle of gin and a jar of peanut butter. Pathetic. Absolutely pathetic. Fallen heroes don't fall from heroism to the median, where they can just hang out with everyone else. Fallen heroes fall far below the median, because they start from so much higher up and the extra height increases the speed with which they fall and hence the impact of the fall. Fallen heroes are lucky if they land in one piece.

Nell stopped at the next pay phone and called Lexi again. There was no answer. She hung up before the operator said have a nice day. She kept walking down West Broadway, huffily, stalking the sidewalk. The World Trade Center towers rose out of the ground and into the sky like mutations, like they'd been given hormones to make them extra big, but someone had screwed up the doses and things had gotten out of hand. Or maybe they were supposed to be that way. If one of the buildings fell on its side, it would hit New Jersey. She stopped at a deli called Eat and Run and bought some milk.

West Broadway was chilly and gray, the sun obliterated by the Trade Center. She wanted to talk to Lexi and Lexi wasn't home. Maybe she was out of town. Maybe she was still in San Diego. It came back to her as she crossed Reade Street, sipping the milk out of a quart container through a straw, that Lexi had had dinner the night before with a guy, a new guy. She hadn't heard anything else during the end of that phone call except the word new. A new one. Even if Lexi had gotten around to telling her his name, it wouldn't have done her any good. Bad form, really bad form, to call Lexi at his house on their first date, even if it was an emergency. An emergency was when Nell really had to talk to her. This, getting high on cream-filled pastries and low-fat milk, this was an emergency. Just as well Nell didn't have the guy's name or number. It would have been too tempting to call. And maybe he was one of the ones who didn't live in L.A. He probably was. Lexi had explained to her once what the rules were: no one in her office, no one in L.A., and it was all off the record. Like Eric Lord. Someone you couldn't talk to your brother about. Someone you couldn't bring home for Thanksgiving.

A record store called Shake Your Groove Thing was across the street. Nell stopped a minute and considered going in. She wanted to buy an album of the loudest, crudest punk rock she could find and sneak it onto the tape her brother was making for his party that night. Sarah Vaughan could sing, " 'S wonderful, 'S marvelous," and before anyone realized there had been a mutiny, the Dead Kennedys would be singing, "Nazi punks, Nazi punks, Nazi punks, FUCK OFF." But she had spent her last three dollars on pastries and milk. She didn't have the guts to do it anyway.

Standing as close to the building as she could, she craned her neck and looked straight up the side of Tower Number Two, all hundred and ten stories. From her angle, the supports of the building were flat, solid white lines that drew her eyes heavenward. With her body pressed against the base of the building and her face toward the sky, she was thinking that it was time to find someone who wasn't a hero. Or someone who wasn't going to pick her up in a parking lot in downtown Beverly Hills and ask her to drive to Las Vegas that night to make a connection with a drug dealer. Or someone who wasn't like the rest of them: boring, perpetually stoned, perpetually married, or all three. It was time to take this one step further. Give them all up. Not that it would make a big difference. As it was, she spent twenty-eight out of thirty nights alone. But celibacy wasn't enough if what she was after was a thorough overhaul. Her neck began to ache from looking up the side of the building that was half a mile high. She realized she would have to do more than give up sex. She continued walking downtown on West Street. It ran along the Hudson, and once past the World Trade Center, the sky returned.

She held up her thumb, counting. One: she could give up sex. Her forefinger. Two: she could give up writing her book. Her middle finger. Three: she could give up—well, there wasn't much else, unless she counted giving up on the entire country, which she had been thinking about for years. She could just leave. It was one of her old formulas, and well worn. When she hadn't known what else to do, she had left New York, When she hadn't known what else to do, she had left San Francisco. She didn't know what to do now, where to go next. Europe, India, Africa. She almost didn't care as long as it was extremely different from where she was. She imagined a map of the world and herself charting a course around it. And she would have to go by herself, because Lexi was busy. Lexi was always busy with some case or conference. Lexi had the most incredible attention span. She could actually stand on Venice Beach and see China. Or if she couldn't, it didn't bother her. She trusted that it was there and that she would eventually reach it. She just kept paddling.

The sidewalks in Battery Park were thick with leaves. She drew her feet through them slowly, as if she were walking in sand. At the end of the walkway was a concession stand. Forty feet beyond that was the tip of Manhattan. Nell bought a postcard with her last quarter, a picture of a shiny red apple with I ♡ NEW YORK printed across the bottom. Wooden signs pointing to the Statue of Liberty ferry hung on the railing that circled the river walkway. Nell walked in the other direction.

She sat down on a bench and took a pen out of her purse. Laying the postcard on one of the flat slats of the bench, she wrote:

Dear Lexi,

Why aren't you home when I need to talk to you? Remember the line from Rosencrantz & Guild. Are Dead? "What a fine persecution—to be kept intrigued without ever quite being enlightened." The news here is that enlightenment might be just around the corner. For one thing, Eric Lord isn't The Whole Truth anymore.

Most Love, N.

The Statue of Liberty was out to sea and on her right, holding up her salt-eaten torch to the poor, the tired, the huddled masses yearning to breathe free. Jesus. Had they really meant all that? They certainly didn't mean it now. They ought to tear the thing down or put it in a museum, like an arrowhead or a steam engine, to teach people about the way things used to be. Lexi would never go for trashing the Statue of Liberty. Lexi took all this stuff very seriously, even the symbols. Could go on forever about the history of U.S. immigration policy, the operations of the Immigration Service, ideals of international justice, all the persecuted people who want to come here but aren't allowed in.

Nell wasn't thinking about any of that. All she was thinking about was how long it would take her to save up enough money to get the fuck out.

"May I take your tray?"

David Wiley shook his head. He couldn't believe how tired he was. How hungover he was. He was still working on the flattened, chilled croissant that had come with the flattened, chilled scrambled eggs and the canned fruit salad. Half a maraschino cherry topped the slice of grapefruit, slightly off center in the square plastic dish next to the wilted croissant. "More coffee?" He shook his head. She moved on down the aisle. Half a cup of that coffee couldn't keep a laboratory rat awake, but still he didn't want anything more to interrupt the sleep he had been thinking of since the wake-up call at five-forty-five that morning. He washed down what was left of the croissant with what was left of the pre-packaged container of orange juice. Sawdust and sugar. He wanted more.

He remembered what had happened after the shock of the wake-up call. He would never get used to its sudden blare in what seemed like the middle of the night, jolting him out of a deep sleep, wherever he was. He slept deeply, soundly, wherever he was. He remembered getting dressed in the darkness of the hotel room, putting on glasses, pants, shirt, belt. Lexi asked him what time it was. He could not find his socks. Almost six, he said and stooped down to look for them. Then, curled up in the corner of the king-size bed, she had said, "Are you all right?" The question had seemed oddly accusatory. He was on his hands and knees, still looking. He poked his head up and said, "It's not that I'm being a creep. I'm just tired. And hungover."

"What are you talking about?" Her mouth was half in the pillow. He found one of his socks at the foot of the bed, under the ruffle of the bedspread, and then crawled to the side of the bed where she lay. Her eyes were half shut: everything in halves at this hour. Half a pair of socks, half a statement, half of his brain at work. The thick black ends of her hair made an eerie pattern on the edge of the sheet that was pulled up over her shoulders, up to her lips. Half a mouth. He was inches from her now, kneeling on the floor, a sort of modern supplicant.

"You asked me last night if I would be a creep in the morning." He had remembered that much.

"I forgot. What else did I say?"

"That I ask a lot of questions."

"Wiley," she said softly, "that was the best part."

He leaned forward to kiss her, tasted the starched hotel sheet on his lips, her lips. Half a kiss.

He rang for the stewardess. He wanted to ask her whether there was an extra croissant and an extra orange juice. "Sir?" He heard her voice before he saw her coming up to him from behind. "I was just wondering." He tipped the empty plastic cup in his hand. "Are there any extras? And maybe a croissant too?" The hangover had made him fiercely hungry. He could have eaten three of them.

"I'll check," she said. Cheerful as a buttercup. She probably hadn't spent most of the night drinking, talking, asking all of those questions.

Waiting for the stewardess to return, he thought of all the questions he hadn't thought to ask Lexi last night. Like, why do you care so much about illegal aliens? Like, what's the second most exotic sexual experience you've ever had? Like, why didn't you sleep with your friend? What held you back for all those years? And finally: Were you mad at me for making you leave the hotel when I left, because it was six o'clock and you wanted to sleep?

Ten minutes later in the lobby of the hotel, he had led her to a couch and said, "Would you wait here while I pay my bill?" "Why here?" He was embarrassed to tell her, embarrassed by his peremptory request, but still committed to it. "I'm funny about hotels. Anyone could see us." The more he said, the more ridiculous he sounded.

"Not if I were sleeping upstairs." Lexi smiled, sat down—with maybe mock obedience. But obedience nonetheless.

He walked across the lobby. Hotels were such public places, and there were rules and conventions to observe. They were not places to be seen at six o'clock in the morning with one of your sources. He did not like the idea that, with Lexi at his side, the hotel cashier might find some way to ask whether Mr. Wiley had in fact had a single room. He reached into his pocket for his wallet, his MasterCard.

When he returned to the couch, Lexi was standing, holding out a stack of newspapers. "I bought them for you while you were paying your bill. And also—" something appeared in her palm—"a souvenir of Los Angeles. A paperweight that snows. Never mind that it never snows here. If you get mad, you can throw it through a window, like a brick." She moved as if to hurl it, then passed it gently, as if it were an egg, into his hand. "The letters look fluorescent, don't they?" she said. "Maybe it's a nightlight." He stood stiff as she tipped her face up to kiss his cheek. "For heaven's sakes, it's just a kiss. Rona Barrett's sound asleep. Like everyone else in L.A." Blinking lights of the lobby, blinking everywhere but within the circumference of her face. They made his head throb. She touched his cheek. "Don't be sad," she said, "it's Saturday."

It hadn't occurred to him until that moment—maybe the way she had just said, "It's Saturday"—hadn't occurred to him that the moment didn't have to end, that it was in his power to prolong it, or at least to make the offer, which, the second it came to him, he knew was as outrageous as the snowing paperweight of Los Angeles in his hand. "Do something crazy," he said.

"Anything for you." She was looking up at him shyly, hesi-
tantly. Eyes as brown as chocolate, her hair not a darker shade of
brown but the absence of color entirely: black. They had been
in the dark so much that he had not noticed her coloring until
now. If he thought too hard about the crazy thing he wanted her
to do, he would change his mind.

"Come to New York with me," he said.

"When?"

"Now."

"That's crazy."

"I told you it would be."

"Are you joking?"

He shook his head.

"What about your daughter?"

"Come to the play with me."

"You've flipped, Wiley."

"Well, if you don't—"

"It's not that. It's really not that. It's— For how long were
you thinking of?"

"I guess a few days."

"A few days?"

"Is that too much or too little?"

She smiled, looked straight at him, and then her compo-
sure collapsed. She laughed quietly, shaking her head. She was
making fun of him.

"Look, forget it," he said. "It was a stupid idea."

"It wasn't," she stammered. "It isn't."

"But you won't come."

"What about work?"

"Tell them you're sick."

"What about your work?"

"I'll be sick too."

"And we'd stay at your place?"

"I don't have a place—remember?"

"Then—"

"Fuck, I don't know. Maybe the St. Moritz. On me. The
whole thing."

"You don't have to."

"I know I don't have to."

"I'll pay for some."

"You don't have to."

"I know."

"It would be fun," he said.

"I know."

"How do you know so many things?"

She wrinkled up her face, held her hand to her forehead. "I just remembered—I have to be on tv tomorrow. Some news show with Esterbrook. I found out yesterday afternoon."

"Why didn't you say so?"

"I just remembered."

"Would you come if you didn't have to?"

"Jesus, Wiley." She looked up, stumped, turned a quarter-turn, looked at her feet. "Yeah, I'd come," she said quietly, looking up at him. The look she had given him when she had handed him the newspapers and the paperweight, a look that said: I mean this. "Yeah. I'd come in a minute."

"I'm afraid we're out of croissants, but I managed to round up another juice for you." He turned back the foil cover on the juice top, downed it in two swallows. He didn't know what had prompted him to ask Lexi to come with him—except that he wanted her to, and he was not used to wanting things, or maybe just not used to asking for them. Except in his work. There was almost nothing he wouldn't ask for in his work, ask of either his editors or his sources. That came with the territory: asking. For time, for information, for more information. But he wasn't used to asking for whatever it was Lexi could have given him. Her company. Whatever it was about her company that had acted on him, made him ask her to travel three thousand miles on the spur of the moment. He wasn't very good at understanding things like that, figuring out why he sometimes did things that were so different from everything else he did.

The pilot announced that they had just passed over the Continental Divide and were heading for the Texas Panhandle.

David was sitting on the aisle and couldn't see much out the windows, except to see that the sky was a brilliant blue. For a story once, when he was just starting out, he had flown in the cockpit of a 747. You could see forever from that little box, your line of vision seemed to be about two hundred and ten degrees. That must have been what made the job worth the tedium and worth the knowledge that the future of two-hundred-and-something lives depended on your reading of the mysterious notations on the radar screen. He suddenly remembered his daughter's prediction that the jumbo jet he was on was going to crash.

If he had not been so tired, he would have been more pissed off at Curtis for making Louise believe in Tarot cards. He couldn't believe a grown man, and a shrink no less, would spend his time doing something so ridiculous, and keep doing it and doing it. The way people played backgammon or video games. He couldn't believe that Gretchen fell for the Tarot cards. If he had not been so tired, he would have put his mind to thinking more coherently about the nature of predictions, what they meant to people, how much stock they put in what might happen, how much they needed to know whether the future would be worth the wait. It sold newspapers and visits to astrologers and boxes of Tarot cards. Predictions about who would win the election ten days from now clogged the pages of the newspapers Lexi had bought him. He shoved them into the pouch of the seat in front of him, with the air-sick bags. He was so tired of the news.

He pressed his seat back as far as it would go, closed his eyes and began to think of sleep, to think of Lexi's collarbone, thinking that the texture of the skin that covered her collarbone was as soft and delicate as an eyelid.

What she was thinking about as she looked through her refrigerator was David Wiley's attention. Her head ached and the roof of her mouth was as dry as sandpaper. In the vegetable bin were a bag of apples, a rotting head of lettuce, and a navel orange that rolled across the bin as she pushed it shut with her foot. He had asked so many questions. She stared at the almost empty shelves. A bag of flour tortillas, two bottles of hot sauce, a jar of mustard, a pint of milk, a bag of coffee. A glass container of orange juice, almost empty. She unscrewed the lid and drank from the bottle, hungrily, almost suckingly. It was so sweet, so cold. She wanted more. More juice, more questions, more him.

She opened the cabinet above the sink. A box of Triscuits, a box of Twining's Earl Grey, a plastic container of honey in the shape of a bear, a few spice jars. She took out the Triscuits and shut the cabinet door with extreme care. Wiley, ask me a question.

Are you all right?

Sort of.

Sort of?

My head hurts. I'm exhausted.

What can I do?

Take care of me.

The telephone rang. She listened to the next ring, to figure out where the phone was. She walked across the living room and found it underneath the coffee table. On the other end, Mark said, "I hope I didn't wake you."

"No, Mark."

"You sure?"

"I'm sure."

"I'm sorry to call so early. I tried you a few times last night. I'm leaving for New York in a few minutes and I wanted to be sure to get you before tomorrow. You got my message about the show Sunday with Esterbrook?"

"Emma told me yesterday."

"It's off. The producer called after you did and canceled. Esterbrook must have gotten a better offer. Or maybe he's tired of talking to you. Listen, how did the trial go?"

She swallowed hard, licked her lips. Her head hurt so much. "Bad. Young Garcia showed up late. And drunk."

"Jesus Christ."

"What's-his-name, the U.S. Attorney, had a picnic."

"How'd the father do?"

"He did great. Answered everything right."

"Any way you can declare a mistrial? Say the son was sick or something?"

"I don't know. I've been thinking about it."

"Listen, I'm going to be at this conference all of tomorrow in New York, but I can call you late and we can try to figure out what to do. You going to be around tomorrow night?"

"Yeah. Probably."

"Did you see the paper this morning?"

"Just the front page." Handing it to Wiley in the hotel lobby.

"Reagan reiterated his promise to destroy the Legal Services Corporation if he wins. They quoted some guy in his campaign who accused you and me personally of aiding and abetting illegal aliens in flouting immigration law. But he said 'flaunting' instead of 'flouting.'"

Her head hurt more when she laughed.

"Anyway, he's out to get us again. Listen, I've got to catch a plane. Sorry to call you so early. I asked Emma to call you later, but she was going away for the weekend."

"No problem."

She replaced the receiver in its cradle carefully. Everything hurt. She wanted more orange juice. She took the box of Triscuits with her into the bedroom, along with the telephone and the pile of mail that had come while she was away.

The clothes she took off were in a pile on the floor before she realized that the reason she had declined Wiley's invitation to New York was the television show with Esterbrook, and now that was off. She could have gone to New York after all. She put on a long T-shirt Nell had given her that said I ATE CHILI AT BARNEY'S BEANERY and decided that she would not have gone to New York anyway. Not with Wiley's plans to see his daughter. Lexi did not want to become, overnight, Daddy's Date or, worse, Daddy's New Girlfriend. It had been years since she had been anyone's Girlfriend. And she wasn't sure what she wanted to be in relation to Daddy, or what positions were available. She took the telephone, the Triscuits and her mail across the room to her bed, a mattress on the floor.

It was twilight in her bedroom, most of the Southern California sun barricaded at the window, prevented from entering by a dark-green U.S. Army blanket she kept pinned around the edges of the window frame with push-pins. Still, there were cracks of light where the blanket dragged on the push-pins, and the sun had its way in certain corners of the room. At high noon, even with the dark-green blanket covering the window, it was not completely dark inside. Now it was not noon, it was eight-thirty, according to the clock radio on the floor next to her bed, the bed bisected on the diagonal by a ray of sunlight that had crept in. The clock was fast, but she was not sure by how much. Maybe half an hour, maybe forty-five minutes. It kept her from being late in the mornings, or she pretended it did. So it was maybe eleven in New York. Lying on her side in her bed, she called information in New York to get Nell's brother's phone number. She had left her briefcase with the address book in it in the living room, or in the car.

Waiting for the operator to give her the number, she moved the mouthpiece away from her mouth and ate two Triscuits. Chewing crackers sounded like the end of the world on the other end of a phone. Nell's brother had an unlisted number. Paranoid New Yorkers. She slammed down the phone, and the back of her head throbbed. She ate another Triscuit. She lay down on her back and looked at the ceiling.

Tell me about your friend, the woman who wrote the story about gays.

We tell each other everything.

Will you tell her about me?

If her brother didn't have an unlisted number. If my head didn't hurt so much that I can't get up off the floor and look for my goddam address book.

What would you tell her?

Everything.

What's everything?

She pulled the summer blankets up to her neck and closed her eyes. Everything.

Nell would have her own questions.

So how was he in bed?

Well . . .

Not so hot?

That wasn't really the point.

Then what *was* the point?

She turned over and punched her pillow to increase the loft, give her head a fatter pile of feathers in which to rest.

The telephone rang and she reached across the bed to answer it. It had to be Nell. It was someone who asked for Hildy.

"Who?"

"Hildy. Hildy there?"

"You have the wrong number." She hung up.

A minute later it rang again. Without answering it, Lexi undid the clip at the base. Whoever wanted Hildy would get the point. And whoever else called her would think she wasn't home. All they would hear was a ring.

She turned and stretched under the covers. Her cheek touched the other pillow and upset the stack of mail she had rested on it. There was an envelope with her mother's handwriting on it.

Dear Lexi—

We were surprised to see your name in this article about illegal aliens (enclosed) in *Time*. Daddy says it's a wonder they're inclined to mention anyone who's not running for president or in a movie with one of those girls who's related to Hemingway.

Paul Jacobson has just left after a week with us and he's on his way to L.A. to give a lecture on photography at UCLA. He promised he'd call you, especially when he realized he hadn't seen you in 10 years. Since Berthe died he must have lost 30 pounds— about 20 too many. And his spirits have sunk as gravely. He says the only time he can forget is when he's working.

We voted absentee last week—the first presidential election we've been here for. A woman in our crowd whose husband was chairman of the Democratic National Committee said, "Just close your eyes

and vote for Carter." Everyone down here is sure
Reagan will win. Will that mean the end of your job?
                                    Love, Mother

She folded the letter and unfolded the *Time* article she had
enclosed. The usual black-and-white photograph of the hand-
cuffed Mexicans at the border detention site, in their American
clothes: striped cotton T-shirts, denim bellbottoms. Trim,
young, unshaven. Last year at the airport in Mexico City, on
her way to Cuernavaca to visit her parents, Lexi had seen a
family of men on their way from the terminal to the parking
lot, hauling their belongings in tattered liquor cartons tied
with string. Each of them, the one in his fifties down to the one
in his teens, wearing a ten-gallon hat, tight jeans, denim
jacket. Come home to show everyone that they'd made something of themselves, down to the tiny flap that said *Levi's* sewn
by the manufacturer to the back pocket of the pants. Waiting
for the VW van that would take her downtown and then
to the bus station that would take her to Cuernavaca, she
was filled with raw, dumb admiration for them, because what
they wanted was so simple and because they had achieved
it. The Texas hats, the Levi's, the pockets stuffed with dollars,
preening themselves in the airport parking lot like returning
war heroes, waving to the crowds from the mayor's lim-
ousine.
     What they had wanted was so simple, but it involved such
a risk. When she herself had only to buy a round-trip ticket on
AeroMexico and sit at her parents' poolside in Cuernavaca for
four days, the four days she had taken for vacation last year. Not
much of a risk, unless you count the change in altitude and the
change in the pace of her life for those four days. Waving her
foot for what seemed like hours at a time in the chlorinated
water, mesmerized by the tile design her parents had commis-
sioned a young Mexican artist to design and install on the floor
of the pool: a hundred shades of blue and green that the artist
called *Pesadilla del Mar*—Nightmare of the Sea. Even in their retirement her parents persevered in their search for "new talent,"
drawn to it like the tongue to a sore in the mouth. They weren't
afraid of the unpopular. They sought out and nurtured the un-
recognized.

They sought out their daughter when they found her name in *Time*. They introduced her to their friends, saying, "This is our Lexi." As if they had to remind themselves she was theirs. Though that was the way they talked about everything. Our art collection. Our artists. Our lovely house in the mountains. They were so charming and witty at cocktail parties. Kind to the help. Pleasant and uncomfortable with their daughter, perhaps because she was that way with them. They showed her off to their friends, like a new piece of sculpture. Our Lexi. Who defends poor Mexicans.

Paul Jacobson, one of their friends whom she had known since she was a child—one of the adults who had adored her for being, at age eight, such an adult herself—had always been unstintingly proud of her, unstintingly adoring. It had been friends of theirs like Paul who had given her a sense of herself, making up for her parents' preoccupation with their gallery, their artists, their new talent. But she had learned this from her parents: how to go after what you wanted. Even if it was a long shot. Especially if it was a long shot. Without their example she might not have made such a point of taking on windmills. Immigration law, police departments, the client who showed up drunk at the trial she had spent the last three weeks preparing for. She pulled the covers up around her. She tried to turn off her brain, turn off scenes from the trial that were going through her head. She tried to will away the rising knot in her throat.

She wanted to sleep so badly. And she wanted to stay awake so badly. She wanted to keep talking to David Wiley. Who had not been a creep in the morning. Who was not used to leaving women in hotel rooms. Who wanted something other than to get laid. She smiled, drew the covers tighter around her shoulders.

All right, so he wasn't so great in bed the first time. The question is: Can he be taught?

Well, there was this woman he told me about, something of a chippy, and she seemed to have gotten to him.

I've never known you to turn down a challenge.

Jesus, Nell.

She reached with her eyes closed to the box of Triscuits,

dug her hand in and pulled out a few. She felt the salt stick to her fingers as she ate them.

He's no Stephen Shipler. Doesn't walk into a room with his cock first.

That does get old, doesn't it? I mean, you'd think they'd get tired of that after about eleventh grade. You know that routine: A kiss isn't a kiss unless he's got one hand on your tit and the other in your pants.

She had expected the tiny kiss she had given Wiley in the lobby of the hotel to roll off his back. It had been practically the middle of the night. The bellboys and tour groups, lining up their luggage for the bus ride to Disneyland, weren't looking. She had expected him to be smoother, as improvident with himself as he had been with the company credit card at their dinner. Eighty-six dollars for drinks and salad. That had rolled off his back. Her plane fare to New York. That had rolled off his back. She had expected him to be easy, to swagger at dinner, in bed, the morning after. He had not. She had ended up swaggering enough for both of them. Until he invited her to New York, made her stammer in the lobby, "What?" "Are you serious?" "You've flipped." He might have been tired of her playing the shark. He might have wanted to see if he could trip her up, make her falter. But it was probably nothing so deliberate on his part. He was absolutely out of his element with her in the lobby, holding his newspapers and his snowing paperweight. Too out of sorts for contrivance.

She ate another Triscuit and turned over. She decided that you couldn't tell everything from one night, but you could tell a class act from a dog-and-pony show.

Still, there was geography to consider. New York was not exactly around the corner. Though he didn't seem to spend much time there. And she didn't spend much time in L.A. There were a hundred places around the country where they could meet. She had done the same for lesser men than David Wiley.

There was also this to consider: her feelings had been out of circulation for so long that she wasn't sure what she was supposed to do with the ones that seemed to be moving in her direction. Stalking her. Hovering close by. Slowly opening their arms to her. Our Lexi.

The pilot announced that the air traffic at Kennedy was unexpectedly heavy and they would have to circle for a while. He couldn't say yet how long before they would be able to land. David looked at his watch. Six o'clock. They should have landed ten minutes ago. The pilot began to make a right turn and everything tilted.

He took out his copy of *The Bald Soprano* from his briefcase and scanned it, looking for Louise's lines in a familiar but controlled panic, the way he felt looking through a legal brief the last minute before an interview, for the sections he knew he should know by heart. So he would be able to ask the best questions of the lawyer who wrote it. Save time. Look good. Look like you know what you're talking about. He usually did. With *The Bald Soprano* in his lap, he felt much less sure of himself— and it was not even his performance. Louise might flub her lines. She might appear on stage, about to say her first line, and then burst into tears. Stand there in front of hundreds of people, hands hiding her face, crying. As she had done that time in first grade when she had been selected to read the Christmas poem, and when she had gotten up in the front of the first- and second-graders, and the teachers and mothers—and her father, who usually didn't make it to anything—Louise Wiley had burst, quite suddenly, into tears.

Sitting in the second-to-last row with Gretchen that afternoon, David had panicked, felt himself about to jump up and rescue her, dash to the front of the auditorium and scoop her up and carry her away. But he didn't. He didn't move in his seat except to reach for Gretchen's hand, and the two of them sat like that, sweaty fingers entwined, afraid even to look at each other because they felt her humiliation and their helplessness so deeply. Sat there holding hands until Louise stopped crying and then, like a wounded soldier who keeps running, she recited the poem, with her nose horribly stuffed.

Now, with all of New York beneath him, the recollection brought with it a burst of the old shared shame but also a certain lightness. The tears on the stage had not brought lasting damage. They had been more like a fall on the playground: catastrophic at the time, barely remembered a week later. She got up the next semester and recited "She dwelt among the untrodden ways" by Wordsworth, flawlessly. And now she was to play Mr. and Mrs. Smith's maid in *The Bald Soprano*, had been chosen for the part, he reminded himself, over a girl two grades ahead of herself.

When her presence was close enough for him to feel, or to imagine feeling—as it was at this moment, with the plane circling over Queens, or that moment in the elementary-school auditorium—he responded to her accomplishments and failures alike with a primal feeling of identification. Not the stage-mother or Little League father crap: living through your kids. But actually feeling what it was to be her. What he had felt the moment she had begun to cry in the first grade was her public failure; he was up there with her, shuddering. And when she had told him recently that she had been chosen over the girl in the eleventh grade for the part of the maid, what he felt was something more than happiness for her, more than pride at being her father, something more than that the job had been well done. He had wanted to give her a slap on the back. You showed them, didn't you, kid. Jesus. Maybe he was a Little League father. Christ. Most of the time he wasn't any kind of father. Most of the time, when Louise's presence was beyond his reach, he didn't think about her at all.

The jumbo jet continued in its circle, the right wing pointing at an uncomfortable angle toward the ground. He didn't know which scared him more: the outside possibility of being a Little League father or the fact that he could go sometimes for days without so much as a passing thought of his daughter.

It occurred to him that the plane might keep circling and circling over the airport and that it might be too late before he got to the school auditorium to see Louise play Mr. and Mrs. Smith's maid. It occurred to him that if he missed the play, Louise would be crushed, notwithstanding her pleading with him the night before about the Tarot cards, the plane crashing, telling him he shouldn't come. Or maybe he wanted to think she would be heartbroken if he didn't make it. Or maybe it was he who would be heartbroken. He set the play aside, tightened his seatbelt and began to feel a cramp in his calf. He reached down to massage it.

Lexi was somewhere in his thoughts. Parts of her body, pieces of their conversation, a sudden start in his thoughts as he remembered the invitation to come to New York. Insane to have proposed it. Or maybe it only became insane because she had refused. Maybe the whole thing was insane. Still, it would have been wonderful to have her here, not for ornament's sake, the kind of thing Roger Gaston got off on. The beautiful starlet traveling with the crusty, overweight studio exec.

Lexi would have put them in their place. She would have been merciless about them and, the next moment, solicitous. Pulled another paperweight out of her purse, told him a story, startled him with an idea, a notion, an observation. She was not beautiful, not a head-turner—that was what he had thought during most of their dinner. A bit of a Bohemian in straight clothes. Her hair gave her away, the mounds of black hair that she pulled away from her face, haphazardly, with a barrette. It did not seem to matter a lot to her. She was not beautiful, but she was striking, and she had become more so as dinner went on. More striking still in bed, not because of the way she looked but because of the way she carried herself, some arousing mixture of self-confidence, daring and frailty that came across not in anything she said but in the way she held him.

She did not hold him the way he had thought the tough girl at dinner would have. Did not kiss the way the tough girl would have. Though it was not until late in their dinner that he had thought of kissing her. If he had not had so much to drink . . . He had not intended to sleep with her. It was not until after the cognac that he realized how much he wanted to. Wanted not to make love to her but to hold her. And when he finally did, he realized that she needed a hug more than she needed to make love. Almost everyone did. He himself—it had been a long time for him. There were women occasionally, ones he met when he traveled, a few he knew in New York, friends, friends of friends. Women who were unattached, or attached to little but their ambition, eager for the next byline, the next scoop. Pausing for a night and a morning for a little love. They talked shop with each other, they gossiped, they picked up their things in the morning and left. None of them startled him. That was what had been missing.

The pilot announced the beginning of the final descent.

David Wiley was the last one to file into the school auditorium. He took the first seat he could find, looking for Louise's name in the program as the lights went down.

There was an undercurrent of discomfort. Murmured, unintelligible strings of words fluttered in the audience. This had not been expected: Mr. and Mrs. Smith were dressed as punks. David was charmed.

The play opened with them sitting in overstuffed armchairs in what was supposed to be their plain English living room, she knitting, he reading the newspaper. They had done the scenery straight. Antimacassars on the arms of the chairs, obligatory bowler perched on the hatrack in the corner, mahogany coffee table between the Smiths, separating their fat, faded armchairs. Still knitting, Mrs. Smith spoke the opening lines:

> There, it's nine o'clock. We've drunk the soup, and eaten the fish and chips, and the English salad. The children have drunk English water. We've eaten well this evening. That's because we live in the suburbs of London and because our name is Smith.

The murmuring in the audience ceased, the result of either deference to the speech or the audience's growing admiration for the conceit. Mrs. Smith was a perfect punk: cropped hair streaked orange and slit-thin sunglasses with bright red frames. She was knitting a hot-pink scarf that was several feet long and draped over her lap, draped over her skin-tight black satin pants, touching the tight waist of the shiny purple-and-yellow satin baseball jacket that was zipped to the top of her neck. Mr. Smith, who showed himself every few minutes from behind his newspaper, was dressed identically to his wife, except that his hair was entirely bright blue and stood straight up, at ninety degrees, from his scalp. A Mohawk. It stuck up from behind the masthead of *The Times* of London that he was reading. He lowered the paper a few inches and said, "Here's a thing I don't understand. In the newspaper they always give the age of deceased persons but never the age of the newly born. That doesn't make sense." A few patches of polite laughter from the audience. Louise's entrance would be soon.

David noticed that his anticipation now was focused on what Louise's costume was going to be, more than on either the quality of her performance or his stake in it.

She appeared moments later in a tiger-skin jumpsuit with a red ostrich feather wrapped around her neck, draped over one shoulder, strutting like a vamp in spiked heels. The red of the ostrich feather clashed with her strawberry-blond hair. The orange in the tiger skin clashed with her hair. Her hair was thick and wavy, and as she strutted toward Mr. and Mrs. Smith she seemed to make a point of moving her head languidly so you were sure to see that the waves of her hair moved independently of her head when she walked. She gave herself a thick working-class English accent. Liza Doolittle before Henry Higgins got hold of her. She lost it every few lines, but it was not bad. Otherwise, she played the part straight, or as straight as it could be in that outfit. An occasional curtsy, head bent down in submission, cocked up again in humble protest. She was stealing the show. He was sure she was stealing the show. He was delighted with the pleasure he was taking in his daughter's performance. A new sensation for him, the delicious anguish of her public display. He wanted everyone else to think she was beautiful too. He looked to his left and his right for signs of a stranger's admiration. Impossible to tell. Too dark. What would it look like anyway? She exited stage left. He came back to himself suddenly when she left the stage. He decided to watch the play disinterestedly.

He decided it had a nice rhythm and that it was cleverly funny. More clever than funny. Dressing them up as punks gave the performance a twist that saved it from being outdated social satire. It may have been chic to parody the bourgeoisie fifteen years ago. Or maybe the bourgeoisie was always fair game. He wasn't sure. But he knew that he enjoyed the play more when Louise was on stage. Even dressed as a vampy maid.

Moments later she returned. She threw herself into the arms of the Fire Chief and said her line: "I'm your little fire-hose." The audience laughed. David did not laugh. He was too stunned by the wave of affection he felt at that moment for his daughter, and by his unworthiness to claim it.

At the end he applauded like a fool.

In the lobby of the school he waited with the other parents for their children to emerge from backstage. He had checked his coat, small suitcase and briefcase at the coat check on the other side of the lobby. His arms hung now, empty, at his sides. He shuffled a bit in place, put his hands in his pockets. Looked over the crowd. His instinct, as ever, was to categorize it, in preparation for writing about it. He caught himself. He didn't have to do that here. This wasn't an assignment, and he was just a member of the crowd, waiting, like all the others, for his kid to come out. He didn't know any of them. Couldn't remember the last time he'd been to the school. They were all well dressed, professional, white. Though a few, like him, dressed down: khakis, cords, turtlenecks. A few beards in the crowd, a few balding heads. Ten years ago they were young. He corrected himself: Ten years ago we were young. As young as Lexi is. She had been born in fifty-one, so that made her—

The girl who played Mrs. Smith brushed against him, en route to her parents. Three adults, actually. Probably a step-father. They hugged and kissed her all around. Her friends joined in the circle. He looked for Louise. He did not know what he was going to do with his arms when he saw her. What he wanted to do was to put them around her and hug her the way the other parents were hugging their kids. What he really wanted was for her to hug him back, the way the other kids were hugging their parents back, the way he was afraid she would not hug him. The last time he had seen her, at the end of the summer, her greeting had been aloof. "Hi, Dad, how you doing?" He had leaned down to kiss her cheek and it was not that he had felt her move away as his lips touched her cheek but that he had felt her not move at all: what it would be like to kiss a hatrack. It was the same when they parted, that visit—though during the time between the first kiss and the last she had been the same as always. The same as trying to hold the air in your hands.

He should have brought some flowers. It would have given him something to do with his hands while he waited in the lobby. Would have been something to put in her arms—a box of a dozen roses—that she would want to hold. David moved forward in the crowd, through clusters of grownups and teenagers, closer to the door that kids who had been in the play were coming out of. He made his way to the door itself and eased it open, uncertain of what was behind it. A long, empty hallway. It seemed to go nowhere, constructed parallel to the length of the auditorium, as antiseptic as an airport waiting room. She appeared suddenly at the farthest end of the corridor, in tiger-skin jumpsuit and—he made a point of looking—sneakers. She was short and thin, though she looked fuller, more curvy than the last time he had seen her. Though it might have been the suggestion in the jumpsuit. The tight waist, the padded shoulders, the extra height the heels had given her. He was leaning against the doorjamb, and, coming down the corridor in his direction, Louise didn't see him. Her step had changed, the stage strut taken out of it. Hands stuffed in the pockets of the jumpsuit, looking at the floor as she walked, scuffing her heels against it. Thinking about something, not thinking she was being watched.

"What happened to the red ostrich feather?" he said in a casual way, not raising his voice. The tone of her face changed immediately, from pensive to jubilant. Her eyes lit up. Like colored lights on a tree. They were so green. They walked toward one another and embraced. "You were terrific."

"I didn't think you'd come." They let go, walked out the door. She looped her arm through his.

"I told you I would. Anyway, you stole the show."

"You think so?" She was beaming. The color of excitement in her cheeks was so deep that it masked her freckles. Or maybe she was wearing makeup. "You want to go to a party?" she said. "The teacher who directed the play is having one."

"Sure."

"Here's his address." She reached into a pocket and handed him a slip of paper.

"Aren't you going?"

"Yeah, but—"

"Hey, Louise!" She spun around, away from David. A group of girls was waiting for her, with hugs and chatter. He stepped several steps back, away from the circle, and watched them. The bubbling, diminutive women. He felt like a man on the street with his nose against the Christmas window of a department store, the mechanical dolls and electric trains too well crafted, too beautiful, to be thought insipid. Touching scene, the one behind the window, but something you couldn't take home with you. You couldn't buy it even if you wanted to. Couldn't take Louise home with you even if you wanted to. Beyond tonight. Besides, he didn't have a home. Not even so much as an apartment right now. An occasional word from the growing huddle of teenage girls made its way to his ear: "Yeah." "Really funny." "Incredible accent." "Did you think he was?" "Oh no." "Really?" "Yeah." He looked at the piece of paper Louise had given him. Sean Carey. Spring Street. He didn't know that part of town. They would take a cab. He stuck his hands loosely in his side pockets and waited for the girls to disperse. He caught Louise's eye, raised his eyebrows. She imitated, smiling. Her mother's eyes were hazel and his were a cloudy blue—and somehow the combination had made hers as green as jade. She cut through the circle and approached him. She was holding something in her hand.

"Can you leave yet?" he said.

She shook her head. "I have to change and help clean up. I'll meet you there."

"How will you get there?"

"See that girl? Her stepmother, the one over there—she's the one who lent me the ostrich feather. Her name's Carol."

"The mother or the daughter?"

"The stepmother. The daughter's name is Jenny. Anyway, they're driving, but it's a two-seater. Her father's a psychiatrist and somebody flipped out tonight, so he couldn't come."

"So where will you sit if it's a two-seater?"

"There's always room for a kid in that space in the back. Would you take this with you? It won't fit in my purse."

She pressed what she had been holding into his left hand, smiled, said, "See you soon, David," and turned, heading for the door that led backstage. He looked down to see what she had given him. A box of Tarot cards. Larger and fatter than a box of playing cards. On one side was a reproduction of one of the cards: a drawing of a woman, naked except for a serpentine sheet draped around her like a banner, her body at the center of a wreath and flanked in the four corners by a man, an eagle, a lion and a bull. Beneath the picture were the words THE WORLD.

He collected his things from the coat check and dropped the box of cards into the deep pocket of his trenchcoat, tightening the belt as he left the school on his way toward Park Avenue to catch a cab. It was getting cold. He felt stung by Louise's plans to get a ride downtown. Though it shouldn't have been a big deal, the two of them going downtown together in a taxi. They might not have had anything to say to each other anyway. Maybe that was why she had made other plans. He held up his hand to hail a cab, thinking about the picture of the naked woman, the wreath and things in the corners. As a representation of the world, it could be interpreted a hundred ways. Not that any was more accurate, more true, than any other. The cards were nonsense anyway. A Checker cab stopped half a block ahead of him—stood waiting, obviously for him. You didn't need Tarot cards to know the world was a mess.

He shouted the address into the holes of the bulletproof partition. He had to say it three times. The driver had something in his ear: a hearing aid, or an earplug for a radio. David said, "One seven, not seven-oh" for the third time and moved forward in his seat, steadying himself on the jumpseat in front of him, in order to see what the driver had in his ear. A silver circle, the size of a half-dollar, with a narrow band of orange foam rubber around it. The center of the circle said SONY. It was attached to a silver-colored headband that was mostly hidden by his hair and his cabbie's cap. "Got that?" David shouted. The guy nodded. He kept nodding in time to music David couldn't hear. Couldn't have heard even if there weren't a partition. David had read about the thing he had in his ears, had read that the sound was supposed to be unbelievable. The whole thing no bigger than a transistor radio, but it sounded like Carnegie Hall when you put on the headphones. One of the ads he had read: *Better Sound in Your Little Ear than Most People Have in Their Whole House*.

The shock absorbers were shot. The potholes frequent, deep. Like driving on a dirt road in too high a gear, on the verge of being out of control. The city charged past him, unmistakably Eastern, old, industrial, even with all the new restaurants on Lexington, all the beautiful people waiting—and not waiting—to cross the streets. The streets in California were much more orderly. There, cars made left turns only from left-hand lanes; pedestrians waited for green lights to cross; the streets themselves were smoothly paved. Stopped for a light, David saw a man and a woman holding hands, crossing 37th Street against their own light. He couldn't believe it. Each was wearing a set of headphones like the cabbie's, and a hand-size cassette player was attached to the outside of her jacket. One player, it looked like, and two sets of headphones. You don't even have to talk to your girlfriend anymore.

In the school lobby Louise had called him David. Overnight she had gone from Daddy to David. Though he remembered now, skirting Gramercy Park, that she occasionally called him David. Usually imitating her mother, and in that same mock self-righteous tone: David, algebra is *such* a drag. This time, David, you've *got* to be kidding. David, you know I don't like asparagus. Louise's list of likes and dislikes was long and unequivocal and she tried to make him think that she was unforgiving about the ones he got wrong. But she was not completely unforgiving. She was about as forgiving as a raft.

He had once spent an evening in Truckee, California, at the foothills of the Sierras, with a man who had taken canoes, rafts and kayaks on every major river in the West and quite a few in South America. He had told David that rafts were more forgiving than canoes and canoes were more forgiving than kayaks. It had to do, the man said, with how much protection the boat offered you in the water, how much leeway it gave you in which to miscalculate. You had to know how to read the water, know which channel to take down a rapid, which way to paddle as you shot through it, when not to paddle at all. You were alone in a kayak, and when it tipped over, you tipped with it. When it rolled over a hundred and eighty degrees, you did too. Kayaks had no mercy, he had said. Canoes had a slight bit more, and you usually didn't take them in such difficult water. But rafts. The gentlest of river boats. A raft was like a voluptuous woman, a woman whose flesh protects you from everything. Of course, you still had to know how to read the water, and there was no guarantee that you'd get it right. But a raft was supple, the man in Truckee had said. It rode on the surface of the water, and when the water was too rough, you were thrown out of it. With any luck, you didn't land on a rock, head first. There were risks with a raft all right, but chances are that you and your raft will end up together at the end of the day, even if you've been bruised along the way.

Louise Wiley was as forgiving as a raft. She would give him the benefit of the doubt in some of his miscalculations. She would forgive him some, but not all, of his errors.

He looked at the cabbie with his Sony Walkman and thought that he would like to have one too. He'd like to listen to Berg's *Wozzeck* or something by Strauss, something loud and complicated that could drown out his thoughts, take him out of the world.

They had reached a part of town he wasn't familiar with. Warehouses, streets with no names, deserted, dark streets with wide sidewalks and no shops. Ten years ago, no one would have thought to live down here. Now it was as expensive as the rest of the city. It occurred to him that he didn't want to go to this party. He dreaded walking into that roomful of strangers. He had been to parties with ambassadors, senators, and movie stars, and it had never occurred to him to wonder what he would talk about with them. He was a reporter and they were people reporters wrote about. But tonight he was not a reporter and the people at the party he was going to did not care to be quoted, did not care to advance or deny a position. Tonight he was Louise Wiley's father and he was not sure he was up to the part.

Then it occurred to him what he would talk about with the people at the party. He would talk about what they were all going to be talking about, what parents everywhere talked about. They would talk about their kids. And they would talk about the election. Which was ten days away. They would, of course, be voting solidly Democratic even though—he could hear them now—they were disenchanted, the party was a mess, the Great Society had not lived up to its promise, et cetera, et cetera.

The cab driver's head rocked back and forth, like the head of a wooden doll with a spring for a neck. He took time out from rocking to stop the cab, click off the meter and shout, "This is it!" He was probably used to shouting, competing with the bulletproof partition and, now, the Walkman.

"Red meat's out. Chicken's out. This week, tuna's out too. But last weekend in Sag Harbor we had lobsters and clams for Jim's birthday, and she went through a dozen clams before you could even say the word vegetarian. There was a zucchini casserole for her in the oven and she didn't touch it. Do you have a light?"

David smiled as he walked past her, overhearing. The space in the loft was majestic and beginning to fill up. He stood on the sidelines, drinking club soda, watching the crowd. He moved back one step too many and his back brushed against something protruding from the hall. He turned around. A painting. Of sorts. A huge triangular pale-yellow canvas with a triangle cut out in the middle. He noticed then that there were four or five of them around the room, in different colors. Though it was not exactly a room, more like a great hall in a museum. Outlandishly high ceilings, vast floor space between facing walls. The huge colored canvases were practically lost in the space. A couple approached, the man holding out his hand. "Hi, I'm Sean Carey. This is my wife, Marie. Sorry we didn't see you on your way in. We must have—"

"No problem—" David stuck out his hand. "David Wiley. Louise's father." They shook hands. "Congratulations on the play. Great idea, the punk stuff." Sean Carey looked young and energetic, like a camp counselor. On the bland side, the one who would be a good swimming instructor but lousy at making up ghost stories. Didn't look like he had much of an imagination.

The wife said, "Your daughter was wonderful. Wherever did she learn that accent?"

"I don't know. It was the first time I'd heard it myself."

She turned a quarter-turn and said, "Would you excuse me, I think someone—"

"Of course."

Sean said, "Louise is really very good. She's got a lot of discipline too, especially with that accent. I guess it runs in the family—you're a psychologist, right?"

"That's her mother. I'm a reporter."

"I'm so sorry." His face was beginning to glow scarlet. David felt embarrassed for him. "Of course, the reporter. She talks about you. You live in California?"

"Seems like it sometimes. I travel a lot."

Sean's face turned a deeper shade of red.

"Don't worry about it," David said. "They don't pay you to keep track of all the parents. It would be a full-time job, especially with all the stepmothers and stepfathers." Sean smiled, probably not expecting a remark like that from one of the parents. "I was just admiring your place. You must have put a lot of work into it." Sean nodded. "Does one of you paint?"

"My wife. She did this—" pointing to the pale-yellow canvas—"and most of the others around here. She's got a show coming up at one of the women's co-ops down here. Can I get you a refill?"

They walked together across the room. On their way, Sean stopped to talk to some people. He introduced David. He went on about who David was, making up for his *faux pas* before. David said, "Would you excuse me? I think I see my daughter just coming in." He lied. He had not seen Louise. He just didn't want to talk to them. He didn't want to talk to anyone about the newspaper or the election or, for that matter, *The Bald Soprano*.

He had lied too about wanting a refill. He just wanted to move out of that spot next to the yellow canvas, and figured if he and Sean got moving, David would be able to drop off inconspicuously. Now he walked the length of the floor, away from the crowd. Thirty, forty, maybe fifty paces. Like walking around the block. The living room went on forever. He reached a mirror that was about eight feet high and fifteen feet long. In front of the mirror was a ballet bar. Two pairs of black ballet slippers tied together with string hung over the bar like clothes on a clothesline. He was surprised to see himself. Surprised, and not pleased.

He was everywhere he looked. The ballet bar bisected his body just below the waist. He lifted his glasses up off his nose and continued looking in the mirror, but without the glasses the image of himself was blurred, lacking definition. With his eyes out of commission, his ears seemed to pick up the slack. There was a speaker very close, a warbly woman's voice flowing out of it, singing: "Love is sweeping the country; waves are hugging the shore; all the sexes from Maine to Texas have never known such love before." He felt himself move, instinctively, a few steps forward, a few back, swaying his shoulders in time to the lazy beat. He thought of Lexi on Venice Beach at night, drunk, looking for her sneakers. Imagined her in bright white shorts and a white shirt, so she could be spotted in the dark, like a lighthouse or a buoy. And the rest of her, her black hair and dark skin, would blend in with the color of the night, so that all he saw, as he imagined her now—and imagined himself without glasses as he looked for her on the beach—were sails in the distance, wraithlike, moving in his direction. He wanted to save her. He felt drunk, which he wasn't at all, and silly, imagining the scene at the beach. Saving her. Saving *her*. He noticed he kept changing his weight from foot to foot, still moving his body like he was dancing, but in place. Then he imagined a scene she had not described: Lexi dancing around her living room in semi-darkness to disco music, alone, with Roger Gaston peering in at her, unseen, through a darkened window. Something about it aroused him. But he did not know whether it was the thought of himself in the room with her, dancing too—he never, ever danced—or the countervailing thought of himself peering in, unseen, with Roger. A feeling of weakness and desire, the body giving in to itself, not out of fatigue, began in his knees, began to spread upward to the inside of his thighs, as if a finger, not his own, were making a complicated path to his groin. The song ended and the sudden silence snapped him out of his reverie. He straightened his glasses and looked around quickly to see if he had been watched. No signs of surveillance. Timidly, he headed back to the party. He had frightened himself in front of the mirror.

"We went through the sixties thing with my oldest girl— she's an attorney in Atlanta now—and it never occurred to me that they'd come up with something even more outrageous fifteen years later. The boy who played Mr. Smith—his hair is really blue. That was *not* a costume."

"Amanda, he wasn't born with blue hair."

"Of course he wasn't born with blue hair. I wasn't suggesting that he was. I was merely pointing out that his hair was blue before he was picked for the part."

"Amanda, that's just type-casting."

Amanda turned slightly to her left and brushed against David Wiley's upper arm. "I'm sorry, I—we haven't—" She held out her hand. They introduced themselves. Her son, who was in the tenth grade, had done the sound for the play. David told her his daughter had been the maid. She was darling, Amanda said, absolutely darling. And that accent! Didn't he think the production had been ingenious? He did. And so clever. It had been. They'd seen it years ago, with their two oldest children, in Paris. In French, of course. Had he met her husband? She turned around for him and he was not there. Well, he's probably gone for a refill.

"Can I get you one?" David said. Please yes, he thought,

make her want a refill so I can get away gracefully. Even if I have to come back to deliver her drink.

"That would be lovely, David. Scotch and water. On the rocks."

David walked through the crowd and noticed his daughter far across the room, talking to a man. A man, not a boy. He squinted. It was Sean. She must just have arrived. She was wearing brown suede boots that went up to her knees and a narrow black sweater dress that went down as far as the middle of her thighs. He had forgotten short skirts were coming back. She held a small rectangular silver purse in one hand and with the other reached into a bowl by her side and dug out handfuls of cashews.

"So she said, Is he contagious? And I said, Contagious, he's been taking penicillin for twenty-five days. He pisses straight penicillin."

David turned around to see who was speaking. A woman behind the table that was being used for a bar. She was tall and blonde and nicely full. A woman who could not be knocked down. Her face was animated, laughing. Turned-up nose, blue eyes, strong jaw. She was talking to the woman who lived in the loft and who had painted the pictures on the walls. He couldn't remember her name. He approached the table. The blonde continued talking to the painter. "He'd been trying to get this job waiting tables at Barney's Beanery for two months, then he got sick and—" She suddenly noticed him standing across the table. She smiled. "What can I get you?"

He couldn't remember. He looked at his own glass, a piece of lime floating in the bubbly water. "Club soda," he said.

She looked over the table and made a "hmmm" sound. "I think we're out. Will Perrier do? You know, it's better for you—less salt than club soda."

"Sure." He was intrigued.

"I've been drinking it all day myself," she said and began to pour David a fresh glass. "Great for hangovers."

"I know the feeling."

"Lemon or lime?"

"Lime's fine." She handed him the glass. Then he remembered. "And a Scotch and water on the rocks."

"That's good for hangovers too."

"It's not for me."

"How 'bout a double?"

He gave up. "I didn't mean to eavesdrop. I heard you mention Barney's Beanery. Have you spent much time in L.A.?"

"I live there. What about you?"

"I go there on business sometimes. What do you do there?"

She handed him the double Scotch and water. "I'm between pictures. What about you?"

"Hey, David." Louise's voice. He turned and saw her, as if for the first time. Small and radiant. Arm curled around the small silver purse, held coyly against her chest like a fan against a woman's nose, concealing something important.

"Do you have the cards?"

"What cards?"

"The Tarot cards." Childishly impatient. A kid again. No coyness. No lace fan. But stunning. She held out her hand, palm up. He turned to the woman who had served him the drinks, met her eye and said, "Excuse me. I hope we can talk later." He walked away with Louise. "They're in my coat, in one of the bedrooms." He noticed the two drinks in his hands, looked around for the woman who wanted the Scotch. It would take an hour to find her. He planted her drink on the first table he found.

"So what do you think?" Louise said. They were headed for the bedroom where he had left his things.

"About what?"

"The loft."

"It's great. What do you think?"

"It's all right. *All* right. But the music they're playing sucks."

On their way to the bedroom Louise stopped and dipped a Ritz cracker into a bowl of beige dip. Someone behind him said, "Democratic, down the line. Even if the *Times* ends up endorsing some of the Republicans at the last minute."

He told Louise she could wait there and he would go and get the cards for her. She nodded, reaching into the bowl of carrot sticks.

His coat was at the bottom of the pile on the bed. He was not alone. About twenty feet across the room—this space too was enormous—a group of people was gathered in a huddle around something, something that was drawing them together. David found his coat and dug the box of Tarot cards out of the pocket. He went to see what was going on beyond the small circle of guests, mostly men. A boy about twelve and a girl about the same age were sitting on low stools in front of a television screen, playing a video game. Adults stood at their shoulders, mesmerized. The television screen was bright green, spotted with red and purple dots and squares moving in every direction. David spotted two white figures on the screen. One of them lunged forward, hitting a dotted white line. The second one touched the dotted line and the television made an electronic noise. A high octave bleep. The boy squealed. His point. Seconds later, another bleep. The noise that a box of cereal makes when the cashier at the supermarket runs it over the scanner. Bleep, bleep, bleep. The screen went wild. Game. The girl squealed now. Her game. She changed the channel and a different game came on the screen. The two players were blue ovals, the goalposts solid white lines. David had seen them in bars, but never in anyone's home. Bleep, bleep, bleep. "Zowee," the boy said. The man standing next to him said, "The future is now." Another said, "I've seen the future and it's electronic. It goes bleep." The first man said, "Crazy Eddie's got it made this Christmas." "Aw shit," the boy said. The score went up on the screen. David didn't like the noise it made, the bleep. He felt someone approaching him from behind, felt the movement of a body, the heat. "Hey," the voice coming from behind said. It was Louise. Of course. Looking for the cards. He was glad to see her, glad she was behind him and not in front of the television screen. "Got the cards?" She held out her hand.

"Smile for me." David held the box of cards at his side, feigning proprietorship. "Please," he said. She lowered her eyes, lowered her outstretched arm, tapped the silver purse against her hip. The smirk on her face melted slowly into a smile. She gave in, looked up at him. He held out the box of cards before she could even raise her hand to meet him halfway. She took the cards meekly, still smiling, and turned again and began the long walk across the room to the door through which she had come. Behind him the television went bleep, bleep, blip. A chorus of voices said, "Oh no." He turned and saw that the screen had gone blank, dark. The power had died. The man who had said, The future is now, said, "Is there a doctor in the house?"

When he returned to the living room he looked for Louise. It took a while to find her. She was hidden away, toward the back of the huge central room, in the kitchen. She was sitting on a stool at a counter top and across from her was the woman from California. A few of the Tarot cards were spread across the counter, but he couldn't tell yet which one of them was reading the cards. He drew closer. A few people were hovering over the counter, Louise and the other woman center stage, engrossed in the cards in front of them.

"The Juggler," the woman from California said. "The Juggler is in your past. He controls your originality, your spontaneity, your imagination." She slipped another card from her pack. "The present." She scrutinized the card in her hand. "Justice. Hmmm." She looked puzzled. "The present is marked by fairness, reasonableness, moderation." She looked up at Louise, looking for her response. Louise did not look pleased. Curious, not overwhelmed. She did not notice David behind her. Neither did the woman from California. He moved up a few inches. Neither of them budged, as entranced as the kids playing video games in the next room.

"Your future." The woman from California flipped up the next card in her deck. "The Ace of Batons." David moved a few steps to the left so he could see Louise's face.

"You're in luck. The Ace of Batons is it." She looked closer. Louise looked at her, trying to divine what was coming. "In the future card you can look forward to a period of creation, beginnings." She stopped, looked closer at the card. "Great personal gain and enterprise are about to come your way. Do you see the way the hand is holding the baton?—it's not really a baton, it looks like a clump of weeds to me. But weeds, they're—" She paused, as if in deep thought, and looked up at Louise. David looked at her too. Her face had gone pale suddenly. He touched her shoulder. "Louise." She turned to him. Her face was white as a sheet. "Are you—" She hopped off the bar stool and ran. The woman from California watched her. David watched her. She disappeared. David didn't know which way to go. "Where's the bathroom?" he said to the man next to him. The man shrugged. David bolted toward the bedroom where he'd left his coat, because it was the only direction he could think of. But there wasn't a bathroom in that bedroom. He looked for Sean. He couldn't find him.

"Have you seen a bathroom around here?" he asked the woman standing next to him. She pointed. He walked in the direction she pointed. Beyond the next doorway he found Louise, slumped over a toilet. He dashed to her, but stopped short a foot from her. She stood up, her hair all over her face, her face still colorless. She moaned. He touched her shoulder, then pulled back. "Are you all right?" She nodded meekly. She closed her eyes and he touched her shoulder again, to steady her, to make sure she wouldn't fall. She opened her eyes and nodded. "I didn't eat anything all day. Except those cashews." She reached to flush the toilet. The woman from California appeared at his side. "Is she all right?" Louise gripped the edge of the sink and nodded.

"Quite a reading," the woman said quietly, touching David's shoulder. "I didn't know I had such powers."

The address David gave to the cab driver was Gretchen's apartment on West End Avenue, where he used to live. If Louise had not been sick, he would have told the driver to take them to the St. Moritz, and if it had been booked they would have walked up the block to one of the other places on the Central Park South strip. They would have gotten two adjoining rooms, or a small suite, and had room service in the morning and a view of Central Park.

The last time he had planned to do that, early in the summer, he had blown it. He had caught a later plane back to New York than he told her he would and the traffic on the Long Island Expressway, even at that hour, had been murder. When he met Louise that night in the lobby of the building on West End Avenue, she had told him that no, she did not want to have dinner at eleven-thirty. He said he was very sorry. "You think all you have to do to be a father is take me to nice places. You don't even buy me anything because you don't have time to go to a store because you're always on an airplane. You're not normal. I hate you."

She had not stayed to hear his side. She had turned and walked across the lobby to the elevator, whose door was open, waiting for her. The elevator man had probably heard. It was just as well she had left because he did not know what he would have said to her if she had stayed. He did not have the energy or the inclination at that moment to defend himself, even if he had had the arguments. What she had said to him had barely touched him at the time—a pin prick in the finger instead of the knife to the heart she had intended. When he left the lobby, he had caught a cab to the Stanhope and slept, as if drugged, for twelve hours. He called her the next day at noon when he got up and she told him to go to hell and that she didn't want to see him again until she was fifteen.

Now she was fourteen and slept against his shoulder in the cab as it careened up Sixth Avenue. Her silver rectangular purse fell between them on the seat. He realized now that what she had wanted to hear that awful time in the lobby had not been his defense of himself, even if he had had one. What she had wanted to hear was something plain and unequivocal and parental. Something like: Even though I don't always show it, I love you. Even though you think sometimes that I must hate you, I love you. Even though you think that because I don't love your mother I don't love you, I love you.

"Wake up," he whispered fifteen blocks later. "We're here."

At first the doorman did not recognize him. Then he saw Louise on his arm. Then he apologized. The elevator man said,

"Good evening, Mr. Wiley. How are you tonight?" As if he saw him every night. The people who work in the building, like they say of servants, are not supposed to let on what they know. The good ones are not supposed to be surprised by anything they see.

David nodded. Fine thank you. And yourself.

Louise said, "Hi, Pat." She let go of David's arm, turned to speak to Pat.

"Hi, kiddo. How are you tonight?" The good ones were especially good with children.

"Drunk as a skunk."

"You gotta watch that stuff, Louise." The doors opened on the tenth floor. The elevator man said, "Watch your step," though there was no need to. David and Louise were alone now in the hallway, walking to the third door on the right. 10B. Louise opened her silver purse and pulled her housekeys out of it. "Why don't you let me?" he said.

"It'll take you forever." As if he had never opened a door before, much less that door.

She started with the top lock, worked her way down: third from the bottom, second from the bottom, the lock on the doorknob itself, moving from lock to lock instinctively, efficiently, the way a girl raised with horses knows exactly how to saddle one and mount it, can't imagine that anyone in the world doesn't. The door swung open.

Echo, the calico cat, rubbed against their feet as they walked through the foyer. Louise headed for the kitchen. David put down his bags and coat on the chair by the foyer table. Above the table was a poster from the New Orleans Jazz Festival. He remembered that he and Gretchen had bought it together, on the last trip they had taken there.

It was one of the vacations that were supposed to inaugurate their new life together. Which he knew, even at the time, would be short-lived. Though he had wanted something to change within him in New Orleans that trip. Had wanted to receive, not as a divine right but as an earned privilege, mastery over the impulses that hung him up: urge to travel, urge for adventure, urge to keep moving. All of those almost palpable urges in conflict with impulses that came from someplace like his heart. Story-book stuff that sometimes came true, and that he sometimes felt for his wife and child with an astonishing urgency. An urge to connect with something other than his own ambition, the satisfaction of a story well done, the pleasure, the inexplicable pleasure, of his byline.

He had felt something powerful for Gretchen that first night in bed at the Royal Sonesta. He had moved endlessly and without effort that night, had only to experience the sensations he allowed her to give him. A strange kind of mastery he had not sought, his stamina operating somehow in inverse proportion to his desire. Not his desire for his wife's body, but his desire for the placid domesticity she craved. Drinks before dinner, dinner at seven-thirty, tickets to the ballet, the theatre, the appearance and then the prompt resolution of family crises. Gretchen prided herself, with deserved acclaim, on her ability to solve personal problems. But, try as she did, he was one she could not solve. She had told him, sometime between New Orleans and Melissa deKalb, that he ought to see a therapist. "I'm married to one." "You're married to a newspaper."

He had known somehow, even that wonderful night at the Royal Sonesta, that their new life together would not last long. But still, the next day, or the day after that, they had bought the poster that Gretchen now kept in the foyer, displayed in a gold-colored frame, to celebrate a new life together that turned out to have lasted two-and-a-half days. He couldn't figure out why she had immortalized it. Maybe the same impulse that makes people save the ashes of the dead. Or maybe—he smiled as the thought formed—maybe she kept the poster up to remind herself of that night. Though it was not at all her style. But that night he had not been himself either.

He suddenly noticed the cat rubbing up against his foot, purring in the foyer. As if the cat were his cue, he went to look for Louise in the kitchen. "Can I get you something?" he said as he entered. Then shrank as he realized the absurdity of what he had said. There was nothing he could get for her in her own house.

"Mom left some chicken in the refrigerator." She opened the door and disappeared, crouching behind it.

"Cooked?" David straddled one of the high stools by the tall breakfast table.

"Of course. Want a piece?" she said. She sounded incredibly bored.

"Not right now." There was something different about the kitchen. The walls looked different, but he couldn't tell what had changed.

"Good. There's only one left." She closed the door and took her own stool, two seats away from him.

"It might upset your stomach."

"No, it's skinned. And she's into dill weed these days. It's very mild." She bit into a breast.

She chewed and tapped her foot against one of the lower rungs of the stool on which she sat, then kicked off her boots. The cat came and sniffed them. Louise stared blankly at the wall in front of them, above the toaster. It was covered with recipes torn out of the *Times.* Tomato aspic. Salmon *en croûte.* Crab Julienne. She stared at the wall and ate her chicken, as lifeless as a prisoner eating mush in his cell.

"The kitchen looks different. Did you get new wallpaper?"

"A long time ago," she said as if the next thing out of her mouth was going to be: Where have you been, Jack?

"I like it."

"We got new wallpaper in the bathrooms too."

"What kind?"

"What do you mean, what kind?"

"What's the design?"

"Why don't you take a look?" Now she sounded downright annoyed. He didn't know what he had done.

"Look," he said sharply. Too sharply. Her sudden coldness pissed him off.

She turned to him. "Look at what?" She could be so cutting, so cunning. Look at what I've done for you, dammit, he wanted to say. I gave your mother this apartment outright. I give her money every month to support you. I pay for your private school, your summer camps, your acting lessons. Look at me as if I'm not the stranger that I am. Would you look at me this way if we lived together? He had a fleeting thought of living with his daughter, just the two of them. But where? New York, in the apartment he did not have? He had to find a real place to live, a place where Louise could come and visit him. Instead of having to go to hotels, or to friends', or to her mother's.

Louise pulled a small chicken bone out of her mouth and stared at him blankly, waiting for him to speak. Suddenly something came to him, the way his thought to ask Lexi to go with him to New York had come to him that morning. He could not believe that it had been that morning. It seemed like days ago, weeks ago. Maybe he was ready now for another crazy idea; he seemed to be full of insanities today, full of sudden, outrageous propositions. Usually he had nothing up his sleeve. He rarely had anything to offer his daughter—or anything that she wanted. She might not want this either.

"Louise," he said. "What do you think about living in Los Angeles?"

"With you?"

He nodded.

"When?"

"I don't know. Soon. Maybe next semester  after Christmas break." He was making this up as he went along.

"Who'd take care of me?"

"What do you mean? You take care of yourself most of the time."

"Just on weekends sometimes."

"I would."

"How could you do that? You're never home."

She was right on that score. But the point of this, this fantasy, was to be home more. And there was only one way to do that.

"I'll get another job."

"Not at a newspaper?"

"Maybe not."

"But what else can you do?"

She was right on that score too. "I'd have to think about it. It might take some time."

"What would I do there?"

"Things kids do, things you do here. Go to school, take

lessons. You could go to the beach almost all year long. And bicycle along the beach. You could go to Disneyland."

"God, you think I still want to go to Disneyland?"

"You could go to rock concerts at the Hollywood Bowl."

"What if I didn't like it?"

"I guess you could come back. When the school year was over."

"What school would I go to?"

"I don't know yet, Louise. It would depend on where we lived."

"What does Mom think about it?"

"I haven't talked to her yet. The idea just came to me. I wanted to find out what you think before I talk to her."

"If I say yes and she says no, are you going to get a lawyer?"

"I hope not."

"This girl in my class, she lived with her mother, and then her father wanted her to live with him in Boston, and she wanted to, but the mother didn't want her to, so she got a lawyer, but then the father kidnapped her and took her to Boston, and so the mother went to court—"

"Stop right there. That's not going to happen. If you want to come, we'll try to work something out with Gretchen. If you don't want to come, you don't have to." He paused. "But I'd like it if you did. If I go."

"You know, she might want me to leave."

"What makes you think so?"

"I think she's going to marry Curtis."

"That doesn't mean she'd want you to leave."

"I might want to if she does."

"Did they tell you they're getting married?"

"No, but I can tell. They act real dumb together. And they fuck a lot."

"How do you know?"

"Well, first of all, he gave her this book about fucking for her birthday."

"In front of you?"

"No. I saw it in her suitcase after she came back from the country."

"What else?"

"What else what?"

"What else makes you think that they . . . ?"

"You càn just tell. They close the door all the time. I can hear them giggling. Especially Mom. That's why they go to the country every weekend. So they can fuck."

"I thought you go with them sometimes."

"They fuck then too."

"In front of you?"

"No, not in front of me, Daddy, but the walls are about this thin and you can hear everything."

"That must not be a lot of fun."

"Are you going to get married again?"

"I don't have any plans to."

"Do you have a girlfriend?"

"Maybe. A friend."

"That woman at the party?"

"What woman?"

"The one who read my Tarot cards."

"Not her."

"Did you like her?"

"Yeah."

"I did too. Would you like to go out with her?"

"I haven't given it much thought."

"Would you like to fuck her?"

"I don't know."

"I thought grownups just know if they want to fuck somebody right away."

"It takes time to figure out if you like someone."

"Like them enough to fuck them?"

"What is it with you and that word tonight? You've said it about thirty times in the last ten minutes."

"You think I don't know those words?"

"I'm sure you know them all."

"You know what a rim job is?"

He did. He hoped she did too, because he did not want to have to explain it. "Yes," he said.

"You think Tarot cards are bullshit, don't you?"

"Why do you think I think that?"

"Because you came to the play."

"And the plane didn't crash, did it?"

"That's what I mean, you think they're bullshit."

He didn't know how he was going to get out of this one. How long do you keep up the Santa Claus myth? But this one was different. This one had been her idea. The kid trying to pull one over on the parent, instead of the other way around.

"Well?" she said.

"I think there's a lot of room for interpretation." That at least was an honest answer.

"What's that supposed to mean?"

"It means that you read into the cards what you want to. You read them one way. Someone else might read them differently." He thought of the card on the cover of the box that was called THE WORLD. For a moment or two he had been taken in by that one. For a moment or two it had meant something to him.

"You can't even tell me you think they're bullshit."

"If I hadn't come to the play—would that have proved your point?"

"You don't understand anything. You never understand anything." She slid off the stool, began to walk to the door of the kitchen. He grabbed her arm as she went, grabbed it harder than he had intended to. "Get your hands off me, David." She wiggled out of his grip and stormed out of the room, toward the long hallway that led to her bedroom. She was livid.

It wasn't that he decided in so many words to let her cool down; it was that he didn't know what to do next. So he kept sitting on the high stool at the breakfast table where they had been talking about the two of them moving to Los Angeles together. She had slipped through his fingers like air. Again.

Fifteen minutes later her bedroom door was slightly ajar and the light was on. He knocked lightly, holding the door with his other hand so that it would not move as he knocked it. No answer. He waited a moment and pushed it open slowly, afraid that she had heard the knock and did not want to see him. Everything was quiet except the hinges on the door squeaking as he pushed it open. Ten steps beyond the door she lay in her bed under the covers with her eyes closed. The light on the night table next to the bed was on; the overhead light was on. The walls were painted a deep, muted pink, almost a purple, and were mostly covered with posters. He hadn't seen the room for a few years. When he came to the apartment, if he went upstairs at all, he confined himself to the foyer, the living room if he was invited in. Occasionally, he stayed for a drink. He and Gretchen conducted most of their business—the business of the child and the business of money—by phone. Now he leaned against the doorjamb. Louise turned in her sleep, away from him.

The clothes she had worn that night were strewn on the hardwood floor. The black sweater dress in a heap. Brown suede boots lying on their sides. White lace bra draped casually over the two boots, making a white lace bridge. White lace underpants left on the floor at the foot of the bed, the last thing she had taken off. And in them—he leaned closer but still in the doorway—something that horrified him, made him start for ten seconds, until he realized what it was: the crotch was smeared with blood. He thought, even when he realized what it was, that there was something he ought to do. Stop it, fix it, at the very least remove it. But of course there was nothing to do, nothing that needed to be done. Except to turn off the lights, quietly, so that he wouldn't wake her.

He walked back down the long corridor to the kitchen, to the liquor cabinet next to the refrigerator. Everything was exactly as he had left it, five going on six years ago. The Jack Daniel's. The Tanqueray. The Wild Turkey. Well, not everything. Not everything by any means. Maybe that's why she had been so bitchy before, not because he didn't believe in Tarot cards but because she had just gotten her period.

He poured himself a double shot of bourbon and went into the living room, heading for the bookcase that covered the farthest wall, beyond the couch and chairs. Instinctively he ran his forefinger over the bindings of a row of books, the way you run your finger over the keys as you walk past the piano. *The Lonely Crowd, Escape from Loneliness, Self-Analysis, Single Parenting,* Freud's *General Introduction to Psychoanalysis, Between Parent and Child, I'm OK, You're OK, The Complete Book of Running, Middlemarch.* Two shelves below was a hardcover copy of *Sexual Fulfillment.* That must have been the book Louise had been talking about. He pulled it out and flipped through it. The words Pickles and Relishes caught his eye. It was about adorning your se∷ with food. The idea did not appeal to him.

When he turned to look at the table of contents, he saw that there was an inscription on the inside front, practically illegible. Something about Gretchen, the Joy of My—he strained to make out the last word. Lite. Cite. Of course: Life. He tried to make out the signature. It didn't look anything like Curtis, but it didn't look like anything else either. Though maybe she had a pet name for him. Her pet name for David had been Dowich, pronounced Dow-itch. The way Louise said his name when she was learning to speak. She could say Dowich before she could say Daddy. Now sometimes she said David before she said Daddy. *Sexual Fulfillment* seemed to have been read and reread. The pages turned easily, fell flat. Gretchen must have studied it thoroughly. She had always been a good student, of whatever she undertook. Making up in enthusiasm what she lacked in imagination. Wholesome, ingenuous, even when she was supine. Or at least that was the image of her that came most easily to mind, a variant of the adoring college girl singing "My Guy" into his mouth back then. Even if now she wanted to be covered with fresh strawberries and whipped cream and eaten, like a Belgian waffle. It made him uneasy, even after all these years, to think about his wife in bed with another man. He slipped the book back into its space on the shelf, between *The Waning of the Middle Ages* and *Totem and Taboo*, and looked for his drink. It was on one of the middle shelves next to an abalone shell.

He heard the wind outside, whirring against the corner of the building. The temperature was supposed to drop about fifteen degrees that night—he had heard the radio report in the taxicab coming home. Winter was on its way, the disc jockey had said, and it was early this year. David wondered for a moment, crossing the living room that used to be his, about what was in all the psychology books on Gretchen's shelves. Whether they gave her the answers she wanted. Whether he would find answers in them for himself.

He slumped into a wing chair, tipped his head back and drank from the glass of bourbon. A grandfather clock across the room said it was five to one. He looked at his watch. It was still on California time. In California it was five to ten. He remembered that an hour before, he had been thinking of moving to Los Angeles. He had thought of giving up his job a hundred times, moving someplace far away, doing something completely different. Louise had been right when she had asked him what else he could do. He could probably do a lot of things. But he didn't want to think of what they were at the moment.

The last twenty-four hours had moved him to do things he did not usually think of doing. Who knows how many hours ago he had wanted Lexi to come to New York with him. Then he had wanted to stay longer with the woman who had read Louise's Tarot cars. Not a sexual impulse. More a curiosity. The same curiosity he had felt about Lexi until late in their dinner. It had had nothing to do with going to bed with her. But now he wanted to go to bed with her.

He closed his eyes and felt a rush of warmth from the bourbon spread to his face. He had been aroused by all of these women: Lexi, his daughter, the woman from California, all of these women including, he realized with a start, his ex-wife, whose bourbon he was drinking, in whose wing chair he felt himself grow heavy with fatigue and desire. The desire not directed at any one of the women but at himself. He wanted, for the first time in years, to change everything about his life, everything about himself. He tipped his head back and took a deep breath.

Because the phone was partially covered with a turned-down blanket on the bed, the ringing was unusually quiet. Still, she practically ran into the bedroom and dove for it so it wouldn't awaken Paul Jacobson, who had just fallen asleep on her couch.

It was Wiley. He wanted to know whether she was busy.

"Not exactly busy. I was just about to tuck someone in."

"You are busy. I'll talk to you some other time."

"No, wait. It's a friend of my parents. Hold on a minute. I'll be right back."

Paul Jacobson had come by a few hours ago, on his last night in L.A. Some people at UCLA had just given him a big dinner. He had eaten too much, drunk too much, and after he and Lexi had talked for a few hours, like someone with narcolepsy he had fallen asleep where he was sitting on the couch. And when Wiley called she had been about to cover him with a blanket. Some kind of respect for the elderly, or maybe just the sleeping. Hiding all of their floppy parts. Falling asleep while sitting up on someone's couch: a kind of incontinence. She draped the light blanket over his shoulders, put a pillow under his head and turned off the living-room lamp.

"I'm back. An old friend of my parents came by, someone I grew up with and hadn't seen in years. He'd had too much to drink and sort of passed out on the couch." She arranged herself cross-legged on the bed. "Where are you?"

"New York. At my ex-wife's."

"Is she there?"

"God, no. She's in the country with her boyfriend."

"Oh no."

"What?"

"I think there's someone at the door."

Boz was at the front door, his face lighted up starkly by the outside light. Boz, grinning and sunburned. "C'mon in," she whispered in the semi-darkness.

"What are you whispering for?"

She cocked her head in the direction of the couch.

"Who's he?"

"A friend of my parents. How was Mexico?"

"A bust. Except for this." He held out a large bottle of Kahlua. "You mind if I crash here?"

"You want to share the couch with him?"

"You got company?"

"I'm on the phone. Long distance. I'll talk to you later." She returned to her bedroom and closed the door behind her.

"It was an old friend on his way back from Mexico. To San Francisco."

"Tonight?"

"Tomorrow."

"Then I won't keep you."

"He's sleeping in the living room."

"With the guy who's passed out?" David laughed.

"Boz'll sleep on the floor."

"What kind of name is that?"

"Short for Bosworth. We went to law school together."

Boz knocked on the door and walked toward her, grinning suggestively and holding out a glass. He leaned down and handed it to her. "Kahlua on ice," he whispered. She took it. "You look like you've been getting some."

She moved the mouthpiece away from her mouth. "Does it show?"

David said, "What did you say?"

Boz nodded.

Lexi said, "Boz just brought me a glass of Kahlua from Mexico. He's on his way back to the living room."

As he closed the door he turned back and said, "Save one for me."

"Lexi?"

"I'm here. What time is it where you are?"

"Two-fifteen."

"You sound sad."

"I don't feel sad. I'm just tired. I wanted to talk to you. I didn't know you'd have a house full of guests."

"It doesn't happen often. All I need now is for Roger to come by to borrow a cup of sugar."

"Roger?"

"Your friend Roger. Remember? From next door?"

"I remember. I was thinking about him living next door to you tonight."

"What about it?"

"I don't know if I should tell you."

"Tell me. Please."

"It's strange. It's kind of kinky—"

"He's kind of—"

"I was at a party—"

"I thought you went to a play."

"I did. There was a party after the play."

"How was the play?"

"They made Ionesco look tame. They were all dressed as punks. Louise was wearing a tiger-skin jumpsuit and a red ostrich feather. And spikes. She looked about nineteen."

"So what happened?"

"At the play?"

"No, at the party, with Roger."

"I was thinking of him—he was standing outside your house, looking in through a window. And you were dancing. Disco dancing."

"Did he tell you he'd seen me?"

"No, this was what I was thinking. I was thinking that I was with him. We were both standing at your window watching you dance." He paused. "You think it's strange."

"Is that all there is?"

"Sort of. It was a turn-on."

"Which part?"

"The whole thing."

"Could you hear the music?"

"At the party?"

"No, the music I was dancing to."

"I don't think so."

"How could you tell it was disco?"

"By the way you moved."

"Was I wearing a tiger-skin jumpsuit?"

"You're making fun of me."

"Maybe a little. But I don't think it's strange. When I was in college I had a terrible crush on a guy and I figured out there was a classroom across from his room—he lived in the same building I did, a few floors down—and if I stood in the classroom I could see into his room."

"Did you?"

"Many times."

"And?"

"I saw him reading at his desk. And once I saw him pissing in the sink in his room. The man I loved pissed in his sink. It almost cured me." There was a knock at the door. "Come in."

"Did you smoke all the dope I left with you?"

"I think it's in my purse. Look on the floor next to the bookcase."

"The guy on the couch is snoring."

"Touch him on the shoulder. Gently."

"What do I do if he wakes up?"

"Introduce yourself."

He smirked. She smirked back. He closed the door as he left the room. "It was Boz again, but he's gone."

"Tell me something."

"Ask me a question."

"You think I ask too many questions?"

"Not enough. Never enough."

"What did you think about today?"

"Everything?"

"The top three."

She thought a moment. She didn't want to be flip, but she didn't want to be maudlin either. And she wanted, also, to be precise. The top three. "Love," she said. "Ambition." Another pause. Third place had taken up several hours of the day's thoughts: "What's going to happen to the Center if Reagan wins."

"If? He's going to clean up everywhere. He's like a fucking vacuum cleaner."

"I know."

"So what will you do?"

"Look for funding sources besides the government. If that doesn't work, I guess I'll look for a new job. Another cause. Though I would hate to desert my people."

"Your people?"

She laughed. "A few months ago a reporter mistook me for Chicana. He stuck a mike in my face and asked how 'my people' felt about something or other. I told him how they felt, but I made sure not to tell him they were mine."

"Why didn't you tell him?"

"What should I have said? 'Excuse me, they're not my people. I'm just a white girl who works in the struggle. Who goes back where she belongs every night after work.'"

David laughed. "Why do you do it?"

"Should I work for a downtown firm? Or maybe in the general counsel's office at McDonnell Douglas?"

"You could make a fortune."

"And be bored out of my mind."

"You really are a liberal."

"What about you? What are you?"

"I'm an objective observer. I report what I see. Just the facts."

"My ass. Reagan'll get you too if he's elected. Are you still hungover?"

"Not any more. Just tired. Tell me something, Lexi."

"What?"

"I don't know. Tell me how you ended up in L.A."

"I went to law school in San Francisco and Nell followed me there—"

"Nell?"

"The woman I told you about. She followed me there, lived there for a few years, got bored and moved to L.A. When I graduated from law school, I followed her here. I have a feeling we're going to keep following each other across the country."

"Sounds serious."

"It is. Serious and mysterious."

"Why mysterious?"

"Because the only person I've ever really been in love with is a woman."

"And you never slept together."

"I told you that four times."

"Have you talked about it with her?"

"Sure. We talk about everything."

"Everything?"

She had said too much. She didn't know how she was going to answer the question that was sure to follow.

"Did you tell her about me?"

"I haven't talked to her today." A moment's respite. The truth.

"But you'll tell her, won't you?"

"Probably. I'll say you asked me a lot of questions. That it was very sexy."

"Questions—sexy?"

"Sure. Don't you think so?"

"I never thought about it."

"Women adore it when men ask them questions. I think it's a sex-linked trait." David laughed. "And the other side is sex-linked too: that hardly any men ask enough questions. Although, of course, they love it when you ask *them* questions. But they think it only goes one way."

"What is it about questions? I don't understand what makes them sexy."

"It's a very focused kind of attention. A man who asks questions doesn't presume anything except that the answers may be worth listening to."

"What do the others presume?"

She thought about what Stephen Shipler had presumed: that she didn't mind the way he had pushed her head down. "All kinds of things," she said.

"Name three."

"Jesus, Wiley."

"I'm asking too many questions."

"No, you're not. It's just that—"

"Let's talk about something else. Where are you?"

"Home."

"Darling, I know you're home. I called you. But where?"

"Sitting on my bed."

"What are you wearing?"

"Shorts, and a T-shirt that says I ATE CHILI AT BARNEY'S BEANERY. Someone gave it to me."

"A man?"

"A woman."

"I talked to a woman tonight at this party about Barney's Beanery. She was telling a story—I don't remember much of it now. Something about penicillin. She was very funny. She read Louise's Tarot cards."

"Did she predict more plane crashes?"

"No, just mumbo-jumbo. I can't even remember. And when we got home—it was very strange—Louise talked a blue streak about fucking. About her mother fucking her boyfriend. She told me she hears them all the time. And she asked me if I knew what a rim job was."

"A what?"

"You don't know?"

"No. What is it?"

"I don't know if I can tell you. I think I'm embarrassed."

"That's sweet."

"Are you serious?"

"Of course. The things that embarrass people are very revealing. But since I don't know a rim job, I don't know what your embarrassment reveals. Except that you're capable of it."

"Why aren't you here?"

"Really?"

"Of course really."

"When I got home this morning, Mark called—"

"The guy you work for?"

"Yeah. He called to tell me the tv show tomorrow was canceled. I could've come with you."

"Would you have?"

"Your daughter made me uncomfortable. I thought she'd think I was Daddy's Date or Daddy's New Girlfriend." David laughed. "Wouldn't she have?"

"I suppose so. But she's used to all kinds of things. Probably things it would be better for her not to know."

"Like the way her mother sounds in bed?"

"Yeah, things like that. I suppose it bothers her more than she lets on. It bothers me and I don't even have to listen."

"Do you ever hear people in hotels?"

"All the time."

"Will we ever see each other somewhere besides a hotel?"

"What's the matter—don't you like hotels?" He sounded like he was looking for a laugh.

"I love hotels." She was playing along, but serious too.

"I used to love them. I hate them now. Hotels and airplanes and rented cars. I'm so tired of traveling. Of not living anywhere."

"What time is it?"

"Don't you have a clock in your room?"

"It's fast."

"How much?"

"I'm not sure. I just set it fast, without looking too carefully. It helps me get up in the morning—to think it's later than it is."

"It's five to three. What times does your clock say?"

"I can't see. It's too dark."

"You didn't tell me it was dark."

"It's not completely dark. There's a light on in the closet across the room."

"Are you under the covers?"

"No. Who's paying for this call?"

"My ex-wife."

"You're mean."

"You know what she does when I'm out of town? She waits until a minute after the cheapest rates begin and then she calls me."

"You're lucky she doesn't call you collect."

"She's tried it."

"You don't accept her calls?"

"Of course not."

"You are mean."

"She's a shrink. She makes twice as much money as I do."

"Did you take the tops to the pots too?"

"Is that a joke?"

"No, I knew a couple who got divorced and when the husband left he took the tops to the pots. Just to be a shit."

"I wasn't that much of a shit. Or maybe I was a different

kind. I just took the tv, which she was glad to be rid of. She hates tv."

"So do I."

"Oh no."

"What—the deal's off?"

"Maybe."

"What's your favorite show, *Meet the Press*?"

"God, no."

*"MacNeil-Lehrer?"*

"Lexi, please."

"Monday Night Football?"

"Sometimes."

"Hmmm."

"I guess it's best to find these things out at the beginning."

"Are you serious?"

"I'm always serious. Where did you learn to kiss?"

"Did I do something wrong?"

"Not at all."

"Reading *Peyton Place* when I was twelve. Someone said show me how to kiss and the other person said, just open your lips a little. It had never occurred to me."

"What do you think about fucking with food?"

"You mean something like chicken?"

"More like whipped cream."

"I think I pass. What do you think?"

"I don't know. I was looking at a book of Gretchen's tonight—apparently her boyfriend gave it to her—and there was a section on sex with food."

"Where'd you find the book?"

"In the bookcase in the living room, stuck in between the classics." He paused. "Tell me what you were thinking today about love and ambition."

"The one about love is sad. The one about ambition—"

"Tell me the one about love."

"The man in the living room, my parents' friend. I don't know if he's really passed out from drinking too much. I think he's just so depressed about everything that he sleeps a lot. He was married for forty years and his wife just died. He used to be vibrant and energetic, but he's like a vegetable now. He'd lost so much weight I barely recognized him. I think he's going to die."

"Of what?"

"Grief."

"People don't die of grief. That's a fairy tale."

"Haven't you read those articles about the husband dying two days after the wife and he wasn't even sick?"

"I always think there's something they haven't told you."

"You would think that. You think everyone's Jerry Falwell—a guy with a good PR person and a secret empire."

"What an ingenue you've become since last night."

"Last night? Is that when I saw you?"

"Don't you remember?"

"Of course I remember, but my sense of time is all screwed up. What did you think about today?"

"Talking to you."

"What else?"

"Making love with you."

"What else?"

"That took up a lot of time."

"Sounds very exciting."

"What's the last exciting thing that happened to you?"

She answered without thinking: "When you came to L.A."

He was quiet for a long time. She should have thought for longer before answering, she should have said something else. "What's the last exciting thing that happened to you?"

"When I came to L.A."

"Because you got to interview Cesar Chavez?"

"No."

"Because of the story you're writing about the election?"

"No."

"Because—"

He cut her off. "Why do you try so hard all the time?"

"At what?"

"Being cute. Being clever."

She didn't think he would notice. Or maybe she thought he would like it. "I don't know."

"You do know. You know that's what you do. This woman I met tonight at the party, the one who read Louise's cards, she was just like that too. She was wonderful, but she was *on* all the time. She was from California too."

"Maybe there's something in the air here."

"Stop it."

"I'm sorry."

"Lexi, don't be sorry."

"What should I be?"

"Be yourself."

"Thanks."

"I'm sorry. That was a stupid thing to say."

"It was. But so was mine."

"It's three-twenty-five here."

"Don't go yet."

"I'm not going. I thought you wanted to know what time it was."

"I wanted to know that half an hour ago."

"What do you want to know now?"

"If you're in bed."

"Yes."

"Whose?"

"My ex-wife's."

"Under the covers?"

"Yes."

"Are you thinking about making love with me?"

"No."

"No?"

"I'm thinking about a question I have to ask you. It's very serious."

"Okay."

"Don't laugh."

"I won't."

"Do you have a boyfriend?"

She hadn't meant to, but she couldn't help laughing.

"You said you wouldn't laugh."

"I tried very hard not to—but it was such a funny question. And you already know the answer. What did you want to know again for?"

"Just to put in the file."

"What—a girl in every port and you can't keep them straight?"

"Hardly."

"I have a question for you now," she said. "Did you want to sleep with the woman at the party you told me about, the one from California?"

"My daughter asked me that too."

"What made her ask?"

"She's nosey."

"Maybe she had a hunch."

"If she did, she knows something I don't know."

"If I hang up now, when will I talk to you again?"

"The day after tomorrow. Maybe the day after that. I have to tell you something. Don't say anything. Just think about it and tell me what you've thought the next time I talk to you. All right?"

"Okay."

"I was thinking tonight—I don't know if it'll happen—I was thinking of moving to L.A., with Louise. Sometime soon. Maybe after Christmas. If I can work things out." He stopped. She was speechless. "If I can work out a job and custody. Things like that."

"What do you want me to tell you?" She was trying to sound composed. She had not expected the stakes to change so quickly.

"I want to know if you'd like me to be there."

"How can you possibly, I mean, how—"

He cut her off. "You agreed you wouldn't say anything until the next time I talk to you."

"Why did you wait so long to tell me?"

"I'll tell you the day after tomorrow."

"Tell me now."

"I can't tell you now. I'm about to fall asleep."

"Don't go to sleep yet."

"I'll go to sleep after I hang up."

"David?" It sounded strange to call him David. She didn't want him to hang up. "David."

"What?"

"For the next time I talk to you, would you find out something for me from someone at your newspaper?"

"I'll try."

"Find out if you can really see the Great Wall of China from the moon."

"What do you want to know that for?"

"I can't tell you until the next time I talk to you."

"Damn you."

"Damn you too."

Love and
Ambition

Dear Lexi,

It started snowing 2 days ago and now Cincinnati is buried under 2 feet of it (& and I've tried calling you 4 ×—no answer). I'm supposed to be in Chicago t'mor to interview One More Single Woman, but at this rate, she'll be hitched by the time I can get there. The SW whose house I'm at now, Anne Cooper, keeps it together better than most of us. But one thing she said yesterday has been haunting me: "It didn't occur to me until this year that I would probably spend my life alone. It doesn't scare me as much as I always thought it would."

It's almost the same thing a handful of other SW's have told me in the last 2 months. A cultural phenomenon—not the being alone but the lack of fear, or maybe the lack of shame. Spinsterhood is moving uptown. But I'm beginning to think I don't want to be on that bus. How am I going to finish this book with an attitude like that?

We watched the inauguration yesterday. Anne, her brother Michael and I had to smoke a few joints before we could get up the courage to turn on the tube. Disadvantage of color: you can't mistake it for tv, it's definitely reality. Michael christened it Day

One of the Reagan Crisis. He lives in NYC and is stuck here in the snowstorm, expected back yesterday to cover Stock Exchange for some trade paper. Let me tell you about this boy from New York City, do-ah, do-ah, do-ah ditty: quite low-key and likable. And he knows his rock 'n roll. We were up talking till 3am. Who knows what'll happen if the snow keeps up.

Since you're practically cohabiting with D. Wiley, I'm sending this letter to your office. Pretty soon we won't even be able to talk on the phone for worrying about an audience. Still can't believe he's the same guy I met at my brother's. And that he's given up hot-shot reporting to write editorials in L.A. In the business they call that getting kicked upstairs, and usually save it for the old codgers who are so wrecked that about all they can do is pick up a telephone and hit a few keys on the typewriter. But all for a good cause: I myself moved across the country just to be with you.

Most love, N.

Two weeks into March, on Day Fifty-Six of the Reagan Crisis, Nell read the letter over again as the sat in Michael's living room on West 87th Street. She had forgotten to mail it, and in the meantime had been spending a lot of time in New York with Anne Cooper's brother, who, at the moment, was in the kitchen of his underheated, rent-controlled apartment, dishing out the Chinese food that had just been delivered. Minutes before, Nell had been rummaging through her suitcase for a hairclip and had found the outdated letter. As she folded it and stuck it back in the envelope, she realized it was another item on the list of things she had forgotten to mail, transcribe, deliver or remember in the past month.

Michael appeared in the living room with a tray of plates piled high with hot sesame noodles, chicken with ginger and double-sautéed sliced pork. Seeing him made her forget all the things she had forgotten to do.

"Hungry?" he said.

"I'm always hungry."

He was wearing a thick wool sweater and had a bath towel wrapped around his waist. They had been in the bathtub when the guy with the Chinese food had come. They hadn't been anywhere but the bed and the bathtub for the last three days; the only two warm places in the apartment. Michael handed her a plate and sat on the floor at her feet. She dug into the sesame noodles with chopsticks, mixing the bits of pork and chopped scallions into the gummy pasta. She was immensely happy. He kissed her bare knee, leaving a spicy mark as thick as a fresh coat of lipstick.

"I think I've lost a few hundred brain cells since I got here. I think I may never be able to walk again." She poked at the chicken ginger, gave him a lascivious look. "My head feels like a bag of marshmallows. Roasted marshmallows."

Another look, another bite of sliced pork. They couldn't go on like this. She had a book to write and he had a job, and this was the second day he had called in sick. At some point she also had to get back to L.A., but at the moment she wasn't sure why, except that Lexi was there and she hadn't talked to her in three days. She hugged his waist with her feet, covered up to her knees with thick knee socks that belonged to the woman who used to live here with him. She had moved out a year ago, leaving the complete works of Raymond Chandler, the *Nouveau Petit Larousse*, a ten-speed bicycle and a drawer full of clothes.

"Mine too," he said.

"Have we lost our touch with words of more than one syllable?"

"Double-sautéed sliced pork. It rolls right off my tongue. We've got nothing to worry about."

"So far." She was starting to get worried.

"What are you worried about?"

"My life, my book, my phone bill, how I'm going to pay for all these trips to New York." She was trying to decide whether to go for the chicken or the pork. "How I'm going to finish my book if I can't get out of bed long enough to brush my teeth. How I'm going to make a case for the joys of single-womanhood while I'm spending half my life in bed with you." She went for the pork. She was really starting to worry.

"Write a book about something else."

"That's the thing." She got stuck on a piece of fat, spat it into her hand. "The thing is that I don't think I'm up to writing a book about anything. It just so happens that the one I'm supposed to be writing is about single women, so I have an even better excuse for not writing it. I don't have the energy to write a book about anything."

"So don't write a book." He touched her leg. They had been through this ten times in the last three days, and he still hadn't lost his patience with her. "No one said you should write a book."

"At some point I said I should."

"And you changed your mind."

"But how could something so obvious be enough of a reason to just walk away from it? 'You changed your mind.' What kind of wimp goes around changing her mind in the middle of a life's ambition?"

"What life ambition? The publisher wanted you to write the book. They were the ones who called you."

"But I said yes."

"Half-heartedly." She liked it how he remembered things she had told him about what had happened to her before they met.

"They gave me an advance. I signed a goddam contract!"

"Calm down. Some people make a living figuring out how to break contracts. I bet one out of three contracts ends in divorce."

"I've got to get out of this thing. It's driving me crazy. I mean, I wish it were driving me crazy. All it does is make me want to go to sleep. But then I think about waking up and that makes me want to go to sleep again." Now nothing on her plate looked like it was worth eating. "I'm afraid to write a book because I'm afraid I'll fuck it up, and I'm afraid not to write a book because it'll mean—" she jabbed the noodles, twirled the chopsticks through them—"because I'm afraid it'll mean I've failed."

"Nell." He went to her, knelt on the floor, taking her plate off her lap so that he could hold her knees. "You're a star."

She shook her head.

"Yes you are. You're wonderful. If you don't write a book, you won't be any less wonderful."

"I'm an asshole. I can't write a book, I can't remember to mail a letter, I can't even remember to write down what day I get my period. If I had to plan to go to the bathroom, I'd end up pissing in my pants half the time."

"Baby." He stood up and leaned down, supporting himself by gripping the arms of the chair in which she sat. He rested his forehead against hers. "Come." He reached for her hands and stood up straight. He led her to the bedroom.

"The only thing I know how to do is screw," she said. "Screw and suck and eat Chinese food." She flopped onto the bed face down.

He lay down on his side next to her, stroking her head. "Let's read. I'll read you the rest of the story." She turned to face him. He dug his hand under her limp torso. "You're on the book," he said.

"I was wondering what that was." She rolled over onto her back and stared at the ceiling. "Did it ever occur to you that women spend more time looking at the ceiling than men do?" Out of the corner of her eye, she saw Michael looking through the book to find the place where they had stopped. "It may be one of those things that started out millions and millions of years ago as a passing thing, and now it's congenital. I mean, now if you're a woman and you don't look at the ceiling for a few hours every week, you're sure you're doing something wrong. You're betraying your body, you're betraying your race. That's why your basic woman doesn't like being on top."

He draped his leg over hers and propped himself up on his elbow, flipping through the book. She liked it that he knew when to ignore her babbling. She raised herself up on her elbow and looked at him, his eyes focused on the page. He had enormous powers of concentration; he could shut out whatever wasn't essential. "Okay," he said, "here it is." He looked up. "Ready?"

She nodded.

They had just started "In Dreams Begin Responsibilities" by Delmore Schwartz. The narrator is imagining that he is watching a movie of his parents' courtship at Coney Island in 1909. Michael read aloud: " 'My father thinks of my mother, of how nice it will be to introduce her to his family. But he is not yet sure that he wants to marry her, and once in a while he becomes panicky about the bond already established.' " Nell lay back, thinking about the bond already established. She had a twenty-one-day rule about relationships. All you got was twenty-one days with anyone. They could be all in a row or they could be spread out over a year, but that was all you got. She and Michael were on about the fifteenth day. " 'As the dinner is eaten, my father tells of his plans for the future, and my mother shows with expressive face how interested she is, and how impressed. . . . My father tells my mother that he is going to expand his business, for there is a great deal of money to be made. He wants to settle down.' " Maybe this was the sixteenth day. " 'After all, he is twenty-nine, he has lived by himself since he was thirteen, he is making more and more money, and he is envious of his married friends when he visits them in the cozy security of their homes, surrounded, it seems, by the calm domestic pleasures, and by delightful children.' " Nell was twenty-nine, she had lived alone for seven years, maybe eight years, but she couldn't relate to much of the other stuff the guy was going through. " 'Then with awful daring, then he asks my mother to marry him . . . and she, to make the whole business worse, begins to cry . . . and my mother says: "It's all I've wanted from the moment I saw you." ' " It had occurred to Nell a few days ago that Michael would last longer than twenty-one days.

In bed, they finished the Chinese food and drank flat champagne out of coffee mugs. They talked about their families. They talked about things they had in common. They had both been suspended from high school, she for editing an underground newspaper which slandered the vice principal, he for getting caught playing hookey, along with fifty other members of the junior class, to go to an anti-war demonstration. They had both lost their virginity in cars, she in the back seat, he in the front. They agreed that when she returned to L.A. four days from now they would miss each other a lot. They hugged. They warmed each other in the cold apartment. They agreed they could not keep this up for too much longer. For one thing, they couldn't afford it.

"I think you should move back to New York," he said.

"Do you? How come?" She nuzzled up to him. She liked hearing what she knew the answer would be. Just as important, the questions would bide some time. She had thought about moving back to New York too. But she had also been thinking about other things that were more difficult to explain to him.

He extolled her virtues. He was not at all shy, didn't mind repeating himself. But she needed to put another idea in his head, needed to break the dream in which he was speaking.

"Would you like to live in L.A.?" she said. That was not one of her dreams, but it might be a way to introduce another location into the conversation.

"I thought you hated L.A." He leaned back, rearranging pillows, drawing her with him, arms tight around her shoulders. His chest was warm. His feet were cold. She was frightened by all this comfort, afraid that it would be too hard to walk away from and do some of the other things she wanted to do.

"I do," she said. "I hate the way it's sunny all the time. And I hate the way when it isn't sunny it rains for days and days and days. And I hate my life there. I guess if I had a nicer life I wouldn't hate it so much, but I don't, so I do."

"So come to New York."

"And do what?"

"Live with me."

"And do what?"

"Have a life that you like more."

"What about work?"

"You might consider getting a job." He poked her in the side.

"What kind of a girl do you think I am?" They rolled over each other on the bed and pushed off the covers. "I'm cold. I'm freezing." He pulled the covers up around them. "Maybe I could drive a cab."

He shook his head. "Hours are too long. Not enough time for making love. Anyway, you might get shot." He pointed his finger at her head, sticking up his thumb.

"What do you think about Nepal?"

"The taxi commission would never go for it."

"I'm serious."

"So am I. There aren't enough digits on the meter. And it'd be hard to get a passenger for the return trip."

She waited a minute. This was probably as good a time as any. "I'd like to go there. I'd like to see Tibet."

"You can't see Tibet. No one's allowed in."

"But there's a ridge of the Himalayas with a great view. I've been reading about it."

"All right. Let's go. I'll call Pan Am." He started to get out of bed. She grabbed his leg. She kissed his thigh. "A little higher."

She pinched his ass. "That's all you ever think about."

"I learned it all from you."

"All of it?"

"Take it back. Maybe forty percent."

"Creep."

"You look so cute when you're angry."

"I don't want to look cute." She let go of his leg. "Cute is dumb. Cute is for little girls."

He looked at her. "That's not how I meant it. That's not what I meant at all." He kissed her forehead, held his lips there for a long time. She wrapped her arm around his waist. She really wanted to go to Nepal, she really wanted to see Tibet, she really wanted to live in the same city where Lexi lived. And the same city where Michael lived.

"I'm serious about going to Nepal." She pulled away.

"For how long?" He ran his fingers over her shoulder.

"I want to take a trip. I guess you'd call it a vacation, but that's not how I think of it. It feels like something I *have* to do, not something for R-and-R."

"I don't understand."

"I'm not sure if I do either. But it feels like a rite of passage. I feel like I've been around but I haven't really been anywhere.

I've never been abroad. I've never seen the world. Don't you feel like you have to do that?"

"Not with that kind of urgency. Anyway, what would you do for money?"

"I have some fuck-you money saved up."

"Some what?"

"Fuck-you money. It's the money you keep around so that you can say fuck you to whoever you want. Your boyfriend, your boss, whoever's paying the bills."

"Who've you said it to so far?"

"No one yet. But I think I'm getting ready to say it to Doubleday."

"You may have to use it to pay back the advance."

"I know. I was just thinking about that."

"Then how will you go to Nepal?"

"I don't know how I'm going to do it, but I know I want to. Would you like to go with me?"

"I'd love to go with you."

"You'd still like me if I gave up the book?"

He nodded.

"Less?"

"Maybe more. For one thing, we'd have something else to talk about."

"It's getting boring, isn't it?"

"Not at all. But I think you're going to need another crisis pretty soon. I think *you're* getting bored with this one."

"What about you? Tell me a crisis. I'm all ears."

He lay back, looked at the ceiling, looked like he was really trying to think of one. "The crisis is whether Nell is going to move to New York and if she doesn't what am I going to do." He looked at her. "How's that for a crisis?"

She reached to hug him. She held him tightly, to make up for not knowing what to say.

"Just tell me you want to be with me," he said. "Even if it doesn't happen."

"I do."

"Really?"

"Yes, really. Can't you tell?"

"Sometimes."

"I have to do better than that."

"You don't *have* to do anything."

The telephone rang in the next room. He didn't move. It rang three times. "It's Lexi," she said. Four times. Five times.

"How can you tell?"

"By the ring." Seven. Eight. This was getting more complicated than Nell could figure out on her own. But she couldn't talk to Lexi now.

"Are you serious?" He pulled away.

"Yes." The ringing stopped. "She just hung up. She could tell we were fucking."

He laughed. "When do I get to meet her?"

"Come to L.A."

"When?"

"Whenever you want."

"I've used up all my vacation until the end of the year. And I'm in the process of using up all my sick days."

"God, you look so sick. Have you seen a doctor?"

He shook his head.

"I just happen to have some medicine in my bag. I think it'll cure you."

"Then I'll have to go back to work. Forget it."

She wrapped her leg around his. "It's a very slow cure." She drew closer. "It sometimes takes days to take effect."

"How many?"

"Three or four, if you're lucky. But I should tell you." She leaned closer. "There are certain side effects. You may notice—" she looked into his eyes—"a tingling feeling all over. A lightness in the head. A kind of marshmallow feeling in the brain."

"Sounds wonderful." He kissed her. The phone rang. "Is that her again?"

"No. She'd give me at least half an hour."

As the wheels of the PSA 727 touched the runway at Los Angeles International Airport on the third Monday in March,

Lexi's newspaper slid off her lap. It was opened to the editorial page, folded so that the top editorial, REAGAN WRONG ON LEGAL SERVICES, was what she saw as she reached down to retrieve it. She had given Wiley the information a few weeks ago and wasn't sure what he would be able to do with it, whether it would fly with the rest of the editorial board. She had picked up a copy of the paper that morning in San Francisco and had been surprised to see his piece.

She added up the days since they had last spoken. Two nights and three days. Then the months they had been together in L.A. Going on three. The stewardess announced that they would be deplaning from the rear door. She smiled. David Wiley had her number. She undid her seatbelt and collected her things. Had her number down. As she left the plane, the stewardess smiled back at her. She headed for the airport bus that would take her downtown to her office, wondering as she walked through the terminal how long happiness was supposed to last.

Her office was one door down from the conference room, and at three o'clock that afternoon, going through her stack of mail and messages, she could hear the noise from a going-away party that had just begun. The second going-away party in the last two weeks. Around the office they called it Reaganomics at Work. She had spent the last three days in San Francisco meeting with people from all the other California centers, defense funds and institutes that he wanted to wipe out. There had been a lot of talk about strategizing and networking, preparing to slay the dragon.

Some people at the Center weren't waiting around to be laid off. Two weeks ago they had had a going-away party for an attorney and this week's was for Emma Sanchez, the secretary she and Mark shared. Through the open doors Lexi heard a bottle of champagne being opened, the cork hitting the ceiling as it flew across the room, and a chorus of exclamations. Isabel, in accounting, knocked on her open door and said, "Hey, *mujer*, there's a party going on."

"I'll be right in."

At the top of her in-box was a memo from Mark to the staff about cutting costs. Cut down on Xeroxing, cut down on long-distance phone calls. "If you call someone who has a Watts line, have him/her call you back," Mark wrote. "Make plane reservations as far in advance as possible in order to take advantage of special fares." They were going to slay the dragon with Super-Savers. Lexi threw the memo into the garbage can underneath her desk.

Next in the pile was a Xerox of David's editorial from the morning's paper, on the bottom of which Mark had written, "Did you have something to do with this?" She scribbled, "Who me?" under Mark's writing and put the piece of paper in her out-box.

Underneath the editorial was an announcement from the UCLA law-school personnel department. They were looking for someone to teach in their immigration clinic beginning in June. Responsibilities: supervise second- and third-year law students in cases involving deportation, asylum applications, and denial of rights to lawful and undocumented aliens; teach a seminar in interviewing and negotiating; write articles and model legislation on immigration law. She read it through twice, maybe three times, and sat, not quite reading it but looking at the piece of paper, with a fleeting image of herself in front of a roomful of students. Another of herself in a library at a university. Some shot from a movie: the woman professor working late, correcting papers, closing up the library. Or it could be a parody, the stereotype of the bilious, uptight law professor whom she mocked with her own performance. Though how would she perform? How did she perform now? There was one character she played around the office: a member of the family, often absent, though always in the line of duty. Another character in public: in court, during negotiations, in front of a microphone. The spokesperson. Cool, unflustered, even when she didn't know what she was going to say next.

She read the announcement once more, drew an arrow pointing to the name of the contact person, another pointing to the word University printed at the top of the page. She underlined it, circled it. She was at least three other characters: herself with Nell, herself with David, and herself with herself. An occasional fourth: herself with Louise. She drew some circles on the page.

Sometimes she thought of her life as a movie and herself as a character in it, taking directions from someone offstage. But more often she seemed to be giving them to others, because others were asking for them. Louise asked her for advice on things she wouldn't talk to her father about. And David had a steady supply of questions. It wasn't usually advice he was seeking but enlightenment. Explain yourself to me, he might say, in not so many words. Or, explain myself to me. His curiosity was disarming; it gave her an edge at the same time that it drew her to him, as if he were the one with the answers, the one with the edge. They seemed to pass the edge back and forth between themselves, the way two people collaborated on a writing project. Whoever had the latest draft got the last word—but it was always subject to revision. The point was not to win. The point was to keep going until you got it right. She folded the job announcement and slipped it into her purse.

Another cork from another bottle of champagne hit the wall in the room next door and Lexi's telephone rang. As she picked it up, an envelope in her in-box caught her eye. "Lexi you're going to miss the champagne," Mark said.

"I'll be right in." She hung up and fingered the envelope in her hand. The return address said only "Nell." She looked at the postmark. It had been sent four days ago from New York. The phone rang again. "Just calling to welcome you home," Nell said.

"You too, sugar. When did you get back from New York?" She slid her finger under the gummed flap and ripped the envelope open.

"Late Friday."

Lexi began to read the letter, got to the middle of the first paragraph before she went back and looked at the date on the top. "How come I just got a letter you wrote two months ago?"

"Because I just mailed it."

Lexi skipped to the last paragraph. "You really think writing editorials is like getting kicked upstairs?"

"Absolutely. Listen, he called me over the weekend and in-

vited me to dinner tonight at his place—I assume you're going
to be there."

"Yeah." Lexi swiveled in her swivel chair, skimming the
rest of the letter.

"Can you pick me up on your way over there? My car's
acting weird. I'm going to spend the afternoon working on it,
but I think there might be something wrong with the transmis-
sion. And I need to talk to you before we get there."

"What's wrong?"

"Nothing's wrong. Actually, everything's kind of wonderful."

"You're kidding." She swiveled the other way, fingered the
curly telephone cord, tossed the envelope onto her desk. "Are
you in love or something?"

"I think I might be."

"What about Michael?"

"He definitely is."

"Well, well." She heard another cork hit a wall in the conference room. "Is he going to move to L.A.?"

"I don't know."

"Don't tell me you're going to move to New York."

"It's come up once or twice. You know how people talk."

"Listen, I want a full report, but I have to go. Emma's leaving and there's a party for her that I'm already late for. I'll pick
you up about five-thirty. Okay?"

"I'll be here."

Lexi put Nell's letter into the pocket of her skirt, walked
down the hall and lingered at the conference-room door. Emma
was standing at the head of the table, opening presents and
drinking champagne. "Look at this, look at this!" She held up a
going-away card to the fifteen people crowded into the room.
"A going-away card from the President."

"The president of what?" someone called out.

"*Pendejo,* what do you think? The President of the United
States." She began to unwrap the package that came with the
card.

"You know what it is, don't you? A bus ticket to Tijuana," Edmundo Ramon called out.

"Yeah, one-way," someone else said.

Emma peeked into the book-size box and smiled. "Bus tickets for everyone," she said. "Even the Anglos." Then she picked up what was really inside the box, a lacy long white nightgown. *"¡Que linda!"* she squealed, holding it against herself, strutting in place, modeling. "But, you know, I'm not getting married."

"Not yet," someone called out.

"Wear it to work one day. You might get an offer."

"The handwriting on the card," Emma said, waiting for the noise to die down, "looks like Lexi's."

Everyone turned to Lexi. "Don't look at me, I've been in San Francisco since Friday."

"Let's have a toast—"

"Another one?"

"—to whoever goes next." A gallon jug of wine was passed around. Paper cups ascended.

"Not me," Edmundo said.

"Not yet, anyway. Give him two weeks. He's been taking long lunches—a sure sign of a man looking for a job."

"Or looking for something else," Edmundo said, rolling his eyes and raising his cup into the air.

"Good luck, with whatever you're doing at lunchtime."

"He'll never tell."

"Emma won't either." Everyone laughed. Emma knew everything that went on at the Center.

Mark said, "We're going to miss you, Emma."

"I second that," Edmundo said.

"Me too."

"Yeah."

The room grew quiet and everyone looked at Emma, who seemed uncharacteristically hesitant. "I just want to say—" she looked at Mark, and then at Lexi, and then around the room— "I just want to say I'll miss everyone too. Especially Mark, even though he worked me like a dog. Nights, Saturdays, Sundays. I used to wonder when he had time to sleep. And then I figured it out. He sleeps on airplanes."

"Not true!" Mark said.

"It is true," Lexi said. "I saw him sleeping on an airplane once. After he'd had about six beers."

"I confess," Mark said. "It as my handwriting on the card."

"Oo la la," someone called out.

"But my wife picked out the nightgown. I thought it was totally inappropriate, of course."

"Sure, Mark."

"I wanted to get you a Walkman, but Isabel—" Isabel, in accounting—"wouldn't let me. She said all we had enough money for was a nightgown."

"Mark," Emma said coyly, "I just want you to know I'll think of you whenever I wear it."

"Oh, Emma," Lexi said, "you can do better than that."

"Yeah," someone said from the back of the room. "You'll be meeting a lot of rich guys at your new job. They'll probably get you a Walkman when you leave. Unless Reagan sticks it to them too."

"Reagan's gonna stick it to everyone."

"Not me, man," Edmundo said.

"You're right, Ed, he'll deport you before he gets around to sticking it to you."

"Hey, I'm an American citizen."

"You don't look like one."

Everyone laughed.

"I'm genuine, man, I went to UCLA. I've got a driver's license and a mortgage. And I speak very fluent Spanish." He did his Stevie Wonder imitation for a few bars and danced in his place.

"Tell it to the judge, Ed."

"I do, every time I go in that place."

"And look where it's got you."

He shook his head. Lexi remembered suddenly that Nell had told her she was in love. She had said that before, about other men. But the other things she said about Michael had a different texture. For one thing, she didn't sound angry when she talked about him.

"Hey, Lexi," Edmundo said, "how was Frisco?"

"Frisco? That's what the sailors call it."

"I'd serve my country if they asked."

"San Francisco was really depressing. We just sat around in this hotel for three days trying to figure how to save Legal Services. And a bunch of hot-shots from Washington came in to tell us what to do. You're going to have to get your mother to write a lot of letters."

"My mother writes letters all the time. She's got letters from every congressman in Southern California. Even she knows they're bullshit and she barely speaks English."

"Tell her to get out the postcards."

"You just keep plugging, Lexi, you just keep telling all those assholes they're full of it. Man, I wouldn't want your job for a million bucks."

"I'm beginning to think I wouldn't either."

"I bet you're the next to go. I bet you're gonna go work for a big firm and make a pile of money. The hell with us Mexicans, right? I'm surprised you stuck around this long."

"I must like being exploited."

"You have to, to work here."

"Just between us, Ed—" she leaned forward—"what are you really doing at lunchtime?"

"Just between us?"

"Yeah."

He leaned closer to her and whispered, "One hot mama down the street. You know what she's called?"

Lexi shook her head.

"Pac-Man," he whispered and another champagne cork flew across the room.

She picked up Venice Boulevard at La Brea and fiddled with the knob on the radio. It was all news or all static. She turned it off and scouted ahead. The stoplights seemed to be out of synch and the traffic was thick. She was tired of driving, tired of being in motion, tired of thinking about the future of the

Legal Services Corporation and the future of her job. She thought about how many lives had been shuffled around during the last three months, how many definitions had changed: home, work, family, love, ambition. Her own ambition was spinning in its place, moving too fast to collect dust, but still not going anywhere. She did what she did pretty well, had most of her professional and public characters down pat. She had the form and the substance. Now she needed to figure out what to do with them, how they could be translated, parlayed into something else. Something larger. Something different. Maybe teaching at UCLA.

At the intersection of Venice and Sepulveda she stopped for a light and considered what Nell had said in her letter: that she and Wiley were practically cohabiting. It was hardly the case, though it must have seemed that way to Nell for the first month David had lived in L.A. For Nell, getting laid more than once a week was practically cohabiting. Though of the two of them, Nell, with all her time in New York, was closer to cohabiting than Lexi.

At Venice and Pacific Avenue she took a right.

The hood of Nell's VW was up, and Lexi honked her horn as she drove past her, pulling into the narrow driveway beyond Nell's house. She spun around as Lexi bolted out of her car. "My God, you're gorgeous!" Lexi said, kissing her on the cheek.

Nell tipped her head to the side and turned a full turn, showing off her new haircut. "Fifty dollars," she said. "Madison fucking Avenue. Can you believe they have the balls to charge that much for a haircut? They wanted me to come back in three weeks for a trim and I told them I didn't even have the bus fare to get across town. Do you think it makes me look like Meryl Streep?"

"She wasn't who I had in mind." Nell's hands were covered with grease, and there were smudges of it on her face. "How's your car?"

"Fucked. Completely and totally fucked. If I sold it for junk, I might get fifty dollars." She fiddled with some things under the hood, surveyed her work and slammed the hood shut. She leaned down to pick up her tool chest and lingered a minute by the left front wheel. "The hubcap's gone. The goddam hubcap's goddam gone."

"So? All the other hubcaps are gone too."

"Yeah, you're right." She picked up her tool chest, kicked the wheel and muttered, "You dumb wheel."

They went into Nell's house, talking, laughing, talking. They couldn't stop. Nell scrubbed her hands with Comet and a nailbrush. Lexi sat on the edge of the bathtub. "Something agrees with you besides the haircut," Lexi said.

"You think so?" Nell looked intently into the mirror above the sink and then stuck out her tongue, wiggled it around, made slurping sounds. Then she burped, a loud, cavernous burp.

Lexi collapsed with laughter. "Has Michael heard you do that?"

Nell wiped her hands and nodded. "He says it's getting so that he doesn't even notice it anymore."

They went into the bedroom. Nell took off her overalls and opened the closet door. "What should I wear?"

"Something tight and sexy." Lexi flopped onto Nell's bed and propped herself up on her elbows, watching Nell slip into a pair of khaki pants. She tried to imagine Nell in bed with Michael. Nell with her legs up or down or around. She used to try to imagine herself that way with Nell, and then try not to imagine it. Pretend it wasn't there. Think of all the reasons why they shouldn't. It was not just because they would have laughed. They would have had to look at each other the way lovers do, that sweet, conspiratorial meeting of eyes: we have a secret. The secret Nell had with Michael. The only one she and Lexi didn't have.

She couldn't take her eyes off the backs of Nell's legs as she rifled through the top drawer of her dresser. The khaki pants suddenly looked familiar. "Those are my pants," Lexi said.

"How can you tell?"

"The cuffs are coming undone." Nell looked down, unzipped the zipper, got out of the pants and left them in a heap on the floor. She turned back to the closet. "What the fuck am I going to wear?" She flipped through the hangers, talking to herself.

"So what's going on on the love front?"

Nell burped, slithered into a dress and turned around. "You think this is too short?"

"No. Short's in these days. Where've you been?"

Nell stooped down, butt in the air, and dug through a pile of shoes in the closet.

"Just don't do that in front of company. Your elastic is showing."

Nell sat on the floor and began to put her sneakers on. "What do you think about this: I might be going on the record with my life." She tied the laces.

"And?"

"He wants me to move to New York." She looked down and laced the other sneaker.

"And?"

"I'm not so sure I want to. But I'm not sure I want to stay here either. I don't know what to do." She sat cross-legged on the floor, looking up at Lexi. "And if it means moving to New York, I don't know what to do about us."

"Which us?"

"You and me, that us. I had a dream last night that we were supposed to go away together on an airplane, and we got to the airport, but it didn't look like an airport, it looked more like a train station, but I knew it was an airport." Her face wrinkled up. There was something she didn't want to say. "But when I got there you weren't there. I didn't know where you were and nobody else did either. I kept asking and asking—" she was speaking slowly, carefully, looking at Lexi and then looking away—"and then I woke up. I think I was shrieking, but I didn't know whether I was shrieking in the dream or shrieking in real life."

Lexi looked away, silent, embarrassed. She knew that if they were lovers she would have gone to her and hugged her, and that would have made them feel better, even if it only lasted a minute. Even if she decided to move to New York. Instead the two of them were silent, and the silence was unbearably awkward. Lexi sat up on the bed, as if movement of any kind could have the effect of reassuring words, or of an embrace.

"Are you serious?"

"About moving?"

"About him."

"I think so."

"What does it feel like?"

Nell was quiet for a while. She picked up a scarf from the floor and tied a few knots in it, her face contorted, uneasy. "It feels safe." She untied the knots she had tied. "I always felt like I was falling out of an airplane without a parachute. I was always terrified." She spoke slowly. "But I felt that way for so long that I thought that was what I was supposed to feel. I thought that's how I would always feel." She bit her lower lip, looked up. "I was getting so tired of being terrified—I mean, physically tired." She laid the scarf in her lap. "I don't feel that way anymore. I don't feel like I'm about to hit the ground from thirty thousand feet. You know what I'm talking about?"

Lexi nodded. "I think so."

"Is that what you feel too?"

"Not exactly. I don't feel so terrified anymore, but I keep thinking it won't last. I keep thinking someone'll tell me to jump soon—maybe not for a while, but there's going to be a time—"

"Because you'll get tired of him or he'll get tired of you?"

"Either. Both. I don't know. I just keep thinking that it won't last forever. I don't know whether I want it to and I don't know whether he wants it to. Or whether it's supposed to, or whether I should want something else, or whether there's anything else to want. Do you think about forever?"

Nell shook her head. "I don't think about forever, but I also don't think I'm about to get my head busted in. Jesus, I forgot to tell you. In New York last week I was walking down Broadway and there was this kid with a ghetto blaster and there was this song playing so loud you could hear it for twenty blocks, and the refrain was 'Love stinks.' They just kept shrieking, 'Love stinks, love stinks.' I was walking down Broadway, and what I thought for the first time in my life—I couldn't believe I thought this—is that it doesn't. I always used to think love was something they made up so they'd have something to write songs about."

"Can you believe this is us, talking about *love*?"

"No. Can you?"

"No."

Nell jumped up from the floor and said, "Then who are we? And who cares? Later for love. I'm really hungry. Let's go." She picked up her purse from the floor. "Is Wiley cooking?"

"Of course. He always cooks."

"That's adorable."

"Really? You think so?"

"Yeah, Michael cooks all the time too. Or he orders in. He's very good at it." Nell stopped in front of the full-length mirror propped against the wall and smoothed her dress. "The sneakers add a lot, don't they?"

"Yeah, but you should've shaved your legs."

"Should I change?"

"No, let's go."

As they walked through the living room, Nell said, "I'm going back to New York the day after tomorrow." She opened the front door and ushered Lexi out. "I've got to interview some people I couldn't reach last week."

"Why can't you talk to them on the phone?"

Nell shrugged. "Sometimes it's better when it's up close and personal."

They got into the car. Lexi said, "I'm going to Washington tomorrow night. Why don't you fly there, spend the day with me and then go to New York? It's only about fifty dollars more."

"Fifty dollars!"

"You just spent fifty dollars to get your hair cut." Lexi pulled out of the space, took a left at the corner.

"What are you going to do in Washington?"

"Testify on this Legal Services stuff. It'll take a few hours Thursday morning, and then we play. We haven't played in ages."

"I know."

"So you'll come?"

"I don't know. Probably not." Nell turned on the radio. "You'll be working."

"I'll be through by noon by Thursday."

"And you'll find out at quarter-to-twelve that someone's scheduled a press conference and a luncheon and debriefing. You'll be making lawyer talk until five." She turned the tuning knob. "This radio's really a piece of shit."

"It was fine until you started screwing around with it." She spoke harshly. She didn't want to hear complaints about the radio too.

"That's right," Nell said. "Blame me for everything. My first wife did that too." Maybe Nell hadn't heard the annoyance in her voice. Or maybe she had and she was trying to deflect it. "So did my second wife. Is it any wonder that I'm frigid? Is it any wonder that I can't get it up? Is it any wonder that I come so quickly?"

"You're sick. You're really sick." Lexi found a place to park across the street from David Wiley's high-rise at Marina del Rey. She reached into the back seat and dug her hand into the canvas bag she had taken to San Francisco.

"What are you looking for?"

"My diaphragm." She twisted in her seat, got up on her knees and dug deeper into the bag.

"I'd offer to lend you mine, but I left it in New York."

Lexi turned to her. "On purpose?"

Nell nodded.

"I see. Michael's now the keeper of the key."

"Yeah. And I figured it would keep me out of trouble too, in case temptation came my way."

"The sure sign of a woman going on the record. She leaves her diaphragm at her boyfriend's house. I'm impressed." Lexi got out of the car.

"Did you find it?"

Lexi shook her head. "I just remembered I didn't lose it." They walked across the street holding hands.

"Where is it?"

"I forgot to take it out."

Nell stopped abruptly at the curb. "Who did you fuck in San Francisco?"

"No one. I forgot to take it out last time I saw Wiley."

The doorman opened the big glass door for them and said, "Good evening." They said good evening back and kept walking. He knew who Lexi was, knew he did not have to announce her. In the elevator Nell punched the button for the fifteenth floor and said, "This place gives me the creeps."

"Me too."

"I hate doormen."

The elevator stopped at the seventh floor, but there was no one there.

Lexi pressed the CLOSE DOOR button. "So do I." She had grown up in buildings with doormen. They saw everything. They knew everyone's secrets.

"How come he lives here?"

The door opened on the fifteenth floor and they walked down the long, carpeted hallway. "Because he makes enough money to indulge his bourgeois tendencies, which, fortunately, neither of us will ever have to worry about." Lexi rang the doorbell. "And, to his credit, he really likes the view."

Nell whispered, "You know, if you marry this guy, you'll have to live here? Did you ever think of that? Did you? Can you imagine having some guy in a uniform know every time someone comes to visit—"

"Would you please shut up." They laughed as David opened the door.

"What's so funny?" He put his arm around Lexi. She reached up and kissed him.

"Hi, Wiley."

"Hi, Nell. How you doing?"

"Not bad. Smells great in her. What are you cooking?"

"Something with lots of garlic." They walked through the foyer to the living room. "We've got some company. An old friend and a new friend."

Roger Gaston and a woman were sitting on the couch, and beyond them, through the sliding glass door that led to the terrace, the sun was setting over the ocean in a spectacular burst of orange and blue. Roger got up and walked toward Lexi, holding out his hand. "Hiya," he said. She had never seen him here before. "I'd like you to meet a friend of mine." He turned back toward the couch and held out his hand. "Molly Compton, Lexi Steiner."

"How are you doing?" Molly said with a thick Southern drawl and held out her hand over the coffee table. Lexi took it. "Glad to meet you."

Molly was petite and blond and wore rose-tinted sunglasses, jeans and a hot-pink tank top.

"I'd like you to meet a friend of mine." Lexi introduced Nell to Roger and Molly.

"What can I get you to drink?" David moved toward the kitchen.

"I need a refill," Roger said and sat down next to Molly, who was working on a beer and smiling.

Nell sat down. "I'll take a beer."

"Me too." Lexi followed David to the kitchen. She touched his back as he opened the refrigerator and with the door open he turned around and put his arms around her.

"Do you mind?" he said.

"What?"

"Them?"

"No," she said, holding him, "not yet."

"He invited me to have dinner with them this morning, and I said yes, and about three o'clock I realized you and Nell were coming tonight. So I invited them both. She's new in town."

"So are you, sweet." They separated.

He handed her a beer.

"Opener?" she said.

"Just unscrew it."

She tried to unscrew it. "Are you sure?"

"Yes, I'm sure. Here." He took the bottle from her, undid the cap in an easy twist and handed it back to her.

"Where's Louise?"

"At Melinda's." David took a bottle of Scotch out of the cabinet next to the stove, opened the freezer and took a handful of ice out of the plastic bucket that was always full.

"Which one is she?"

"Beverly Hills. Father works at one of the studios. Swimming pool in the backyard. I think she's going to move in there. I'll be right back." He took the Scotch, the ice cubes and a beer for Nell into the living room. Lexi lifted the top to the big pot on the stove, and steam thick with basil and garlic flooded the small kitchen.

David returned. "How was San Francisco?"

"Depressing." She took a swig of beer. "I have to go to Washington tomorrow night to testify. Mark was going to go, but something came up early today. Actually, I think he's too busy writing memos about Super-Savers and Xeroxing. We just had the second going-away party in the last two weeks. The place is falling apart."

"Did you see the paper today?" David was stirring what was in the big pot.

"Yeah. It was great. Thanks."

"It wasn't great. It was just okay. They made me tone down a lot of stuff about Reagan."

"Why didn't you tell me it was going to run?"

"I didn't know until late yesterday. I didn't want to get you away from your meetings."

"Who's she?" Lexi cocked her head in the direction of the living room.

"A lawyer from Washington. I think she used to work on the Hill."

"I should go talk to them."

"Stay here and talk to me for a minute. Anyway, I think Nell can entertain them in your absence."

"Can I do something?"

"No."

"What's for dinner?"

"Mediterranean stew." He shook some cayenne pepper into the pot.

"What's that?"

"Sausages, spices and vegetables. Gretchen used to make it, but I think I've improved on the recipe." He shook some more spices into the pot. "Did you see Boz in San Francisco?"

"Yeah. I stayed at his house, but I only saw him once or twice. He's got a new girlfriend."

"Oh."

"Were you going to ask if we slept together?"

He moved some pots around on the stove. "Of course."

"Sorry, darling, I have nothing to report."

"Maybe next time."

"You'll be the first to know."

He turned to her. "After Nell." He smiled.

"That goes without saying." She smiled back. "You know, there are some things I don't tell her."

"Name one."

"I never told her what you like to do to my toes." He laughed. "I think I'm being rude to your guests," she said. "I'll be rude to you later."

As she passed him, she ran her hand across his back, stopped and hugged him hard. She didn't feel like she was going to hit the ground from thirty thousand feet anymore either. But what frightened her was that Nell was in love. What frightened her was that they might be drifting apart. Nell turning down her invitation to Washington so snottily. Nell leaving her diaphragm in New York. Not telling Lexi she was getting ready to make her next move. If she moved—that would feel like hitting the ground from thirty thousand feet. She held David tightly. He felt enormous with his arms around her. She wanted to ask him how someone so big could need someone as small as she felt next to him.

"So they were in the middle of marking up the bill," Molly was saying to Roger, "and someone said to Kennedy, 'Mr. Chairman, I've come to the conclusion that this is a waste of time,' and Kennedy said, 'I'm glad you've finally come around to my point of view,' and I thought, Holy Jesus, this *is* a waste of time, and a month later the whole fucking Senate agreed. I mean, they didn't have to agree, all the good guys just got wiped out. Phush. Boom. Strom fucking Thurmond, Chairman of the Judiciary Committee, overnight. Everyone in that office was catatonic for a week."

"She used to work for Kennedy," Roger said to Lexi. Nell and Lexi exchanged glances. Nell's look seemed to say: Ask me if I care. She didn't have to roll her eyes, she didn't have to scratch the tip of her nose. Their shorthand had become very, very short. Nell and Michael probably had their own shorthand. A different set of glances. More secrets. Lexi would never know what they were, even if she wanted to.

"He had to let go of about eighty people after the election," Molly said. "You've never seen so many Harvard lawyers out of work. Christ, everyone who works in the Senate these days went to Brigham Young. Undergrad *and* law school. Goddam Moonies." Molly's drawl was thick and crisp; Lexi couldn't place it.

"I'm surprised you two don't know each other," Roger said. "Molly did some immigration work for Kennedy. You've spent a fair amount of time in Washington, haven't you, Lexi?" Roger had some social skills that Lexi hadn't seen until now. Or maybe he needed someone he was trying to impress to bring them out.

"I think I've heard your name. I work at the Immigrant Service Center."

"Sure," Molly said. "I've talked to Mark Peyser a few times. How you folks doing these days? Has Reaganomics been good to you?" She laughed.

"Yeah, we're having a rent party next week."

"This'd be a great place to have it," Molly said. "This view is terrific. I don't think it's rained a day since I got here."

David came into the living room and took a seat across from Lexi, held a beer on his knee. "Nell, can I get you another?"

"Not yet."

"I learned everything I know about bartending from you."

"Don't remind me. Was anyone ever so hungover?"

"You or me?"

"All three of us," Lexi said.

Roger looked at the three of them, looking for an explanation.

"You had to be there," Lexi said.

"At least in spirit," Nell added. "Speaking of which, where's Louise?"

"She's doing Beverly Hills tonight," Lexi said.

"How nice for her. It's been *ages* since I've done Beverly Hills." Nell swigged her beer.

"How long have you been in town, Molly?" David said.

"A month and a half. This town is amazing. I'm going to get a convertible and an ice chest and kick back and watch the roller skaters until the rain comes."

"You and Wiley'd make a good pair," Roger said. Lexi looked at David, who was looking at Roger. "I've known this guy for about ten years and I've never seen him so laid back. I think all he does is read the food section of the paper and spend his afternoons buying groceries and cooking."

"Not exactly, Roger." He was not amused.

"You've got to admit, Wiley, you've been taking it easy."

"Yeah, I have."

"And you love it."

"I like it."

"Honey," Molly said to no one in particular, "I *love* it. You couldn't get me back to Washington for all the pecans in Georgia."

"Is that where you're from?"

"Hell, no, only time I ever set foot in Georgia was on my way to D.C., and I'm sure not going to take that trip again."

"Where from?"

"New Orleans. I used to wonder why I ever left there, but now I know. It was so I could end up here." She guzzled her beer and looked at the sunset.

"I thought you went to Yale Law School," Roger said. He had probably been figuring out how to work that into the conversation since Lexi arrived.

"That was the first mistake," Molly said. "Washington was the second."

"I'll agree with you on that," David said. "Washington—not Yale."

"Just take my word about Yale—if you have any mind to apply."

"No chance of that."

"What are you working on these days, Roger?" Lexi said. "I haven't seen your name in the paper lately." Lexi knew that was like accusing him of not being able to get it up anymore.

"They've taken me off immigration and got me working on some Mafia stuff, which I'm not at liberty to talk about, even among friends." He looked at David. "Or colleagues. We could have a good time with this one, Wiley. Too bad you're not doing news anymore. I mean, real news."

Kicked upstairs. That was how Nell had put it in her letter. David shrugged. Lexi knew he missed it. She knew he had taken the job only because it gave him something like regular hours, and that was Gretchen's condition for his custody of Louise. Roger probably knew it too, which did not explain why he was rubbing it in, except to show off for Molly, who seemed as impressed with him as she had been with Yale.

"I'm getting used to pontificating in print," David said. "In fact, I think I've taken to it quite nicely." He stood up. "I think dinner's about ready."

"It makes perfect sense," Roger was saying as he ate his salad. "California was developed by entrepreneurs, by outcasts, Jews, Italians, renegades, all the people they wouldn't let into Harvard and the Athletic Club in 1900. They all just said fuck that stuff and came here. And three months ago they all left and went to Washington. They don't give a damn for tradition, whether it's the Ivy League tradition or the Great Society tradition. They just want to blow all the rules out of the water. They want to run the country the way they ran California. They built the dams so that there'd be water for L.A., and they couldn't give a damn about the rest of the state, couldn't give a damn about the rest of the West. They take care of their own, and that's where it ends."

Roger was drunk, but he was making sense. They were all a little drunk.

"You think they really buy all that Moral Majority crap about abortions and marijuana and gays? Hell, no. All they want is cheap labor, defense contracts and segregated swimming pools."

"What about killing Legal Services?" Lexi said. "Where's that on your spectrum?"

"It's the underpinning of the whole theory," David said. "Social Darwinism, Horatio Alger, whatever you want to call it. What it comes down to is, if you can't afford a lawyer, you don't deserve one. If you can't afford a swimming pool, you shouldn't swim. If you're poor, it's just because you're too lazy to be rich." David uncorked another bottle of wine. "What we're going to do about it is another question."

"What do you mean, what are *we* going to do?" Roger said. "We're sitting here having dinner in Marina del Rey—an excellent dinner, by the way, Wiley—"

"So you said."

"—drinking expensive wine, with a first-rate view of the Pacific Ocean, and all of us except Molly Compton here are gainfully employed, and *she* is unemployed by choice."

Molly shot a surprised look his way.

"I think he means that three out of five of us are gainfully employed," Nell said.

"You're not exactly employed, but you're writing a book," David said.

"After a fashion."

"What's your book about?" Molly said.

Nell cleared her throat, reached for her wine. "Single women." She finished what was in her glass, put it down and licked her lips.

"What about them?" Roger said.

"All kinds of things about them." She reached across the table for the wine and refilled her glass.

"Got a publisher?" Roger said.

Nell nodded.

"New York? L.A.? Boston?"

"New York."

"I could tell you were a class act, Nell."

"Thanks."

Roger turned to Molly. "But you had job offers after the election, didn't you?" Roger said.

"Up to my ears. After the election, Kennedy called up Sargent Shriver's law firm and said, 'How many do you want?' Twenty people from our office must have gotten jobs with that phone call."

"Did they offer you one?" Roger said.

"Sure they did, and I said, 'Hell, no, I'm getting out of here on the next plane.'" The doorbell rang and David got up to answer it. Molly turned to Roger and said, "You ought to take cooking lessons from David, honey."

"David's got all the time in the world these days. Not to mention all those housewifely instincts. I think Lexi lucked out."

Nell kicked Lexi under the table. It was almost time to tell Roger to shove it, and if Lexi didn't, Nell would.

David appeared with Louise at his side and introduced her to Roger and Molly. Louise was in a punk phase these days, her thick strawberry-blonde hair was cut almost to a butch, and she was wearing a black satin baseball jacket, tight white pants, and red lipstick on her eyelids. She stood awkwardly at the head of the table. David said, "Would you like to have dessert with us?"

"What is it?"

"Rhubarb pie and fruit."

"Christ, Wiley, so that's what you were doing all afternoon, making a goddamn pie," Roger said.

"I bought it."

"I'm on a diet," Louise said. "What kind of fruit?"

"Mandarin oranges."

"Yuk. I'll just have a Tab."

David went into the kitchen.

"Hi, Louise," Lexi said from across the table.

"Hi, Lex."

"Hi, Louise."

"Hi, Nell."

"Pull up a chair."

"I have to make a phone call. I'll be right back." She headed for her bedroom and called out, "David, what did you do with the phone?"

"I don't remember," he called back. "Look around."

"How old is she?" Roger said.

"Fifteen," Lexi said.

"How come she's up so late on a school night?"

David came back with her Tab, the pie and a bowl of oranges and began to serve.

"Roger wants to know why Louise is up so late," Lexi said.

"She goes to bed when she wants to." David began to pass around the plates of pie.

"What if she wants to stay up all night?"

"You go to bed when you want to and you know better than to stay up all night."

"But she's just a kid."

"Honey," Molly said, "these days kids are not kids anymore."

"What are you going to do when she's sixteen, Wiley? I guess you'll have to buy her a car," Roger said.

"She's going back to live with her mother in New York after the summer."

"For good?"

"For a year. And then back here. I guess I'll have to get her a car then. She's got a friend here who's sixteen and who drives, the girl who drove her home."

"Aren't you worried—her driving around with a sixteen-year-old?"

"I try not to think about it." He finished off the wine in his glass.

"I'm trying to figure out how you all know each other," Molly said.

Nell said, "Why don't you take this one, Lexi."

Lexi marshaled her thoughts for a moment. "It's kind of a long story, Molly. Roger and I live next door to each other in Venice. And he always used to see Nell at my house. And for some reason, which is beyond me, he got it into his head that we were, how you say, a little strange." The silence was absolute. "To make a long story short, he told David that that was his take on the situation, and David invited me out to dinner to find out if we were. Or if I was."

"Not exactly," David said and smiled at her. She smiled back. They gave each other a lot of slack. Nell laughed.

"Roger, couldn't you have found out for yourself?" Molly said.

"Roger's one of those men who thinks that if a woman doesn't sleep with him, it's because she's a lesbian," Lexi said. Shove it, Roger. David laughed.

"That's not the reason you think *I* don't sleep with you, is it, honey?" Molly said.

Louise walked across the living room and toward the table with Walkman headphones covering her ears, the wire leading into one of the pockets of her black satin jacket. She picked up her can of Tab, flipped the top off and sat down between Lexi and Nell.

"Please take that off if you want to sit at the table," David said.

"What?"

"You heard me."

"What's the big deal—you can't hear it."

He looked sharply at her and she reluctantly pulled off the headphones and put them on the table.

"The Tab is warm," she said.

"There's ice in the freezer." David began to peel an orange.

"Aw, it's all right." She took a swig from the pink can and looked bored.

"How's school?" Lexi said.

"All right."

"Did you finish the paper you were working on last week?"

"Yeah. Now I've got to do another one. I think David can help me this time. It's about the election. Who cares about the election, anyway?"

"I helped you with the last one."

"You just read it and told me the grammar was wrong."

"I told you how to make it right."

"Yeah, but you didn't know anything about the French Revolution."

"Is that what they're teaching kids in L.A. these days?" Roger said, finishing off his pie. "Why aren't they teaching you how to run computers?"

"They are," Louise said. "It's the worst class. The computers are always breaking and the guy who teaches it is a moron. Every time a computer breaks he says, how long is it going to take you to learn how to do this right. But it's not our fault, it's the computer's fault." She took another gulp of Tab. "Computers suck."

"From the mouths of babes," Roger said.

"Who's a babe?" Louise said.

"Just a figure of speech, Louise."

"You looking forward to going to New York?" Lexi said.

"Sort of," Louise said.

"When are you going?" Nell said.

"Wednesday. Day after tomorrow."

"Me too," Nell said. "When's your flight?"

"I forget. When is it?"

"Ten-fifteen," David said. "P.M."

"Mine too. United?"

He nodded.

"Good deal," Nell said. "We can share a set of headphones. I hate to give those guys more money than I have to." Louise looked at her, beginning to smile. "It works like this," Nell said and picked up the headphones to the Walkman. "You take one ear, I'll take the other. The only thing is that we'll have to sit real close together." She leaned close and held one headphone up to her ear.

"What if they say we can't use the same one?" Louise said.

"They can't say that."

"They probably can," Roger said.

"Then we just won't let them know what we're doing," Nell said and turned to Louise. "Right, Louise?"

Louise said, "Yeah" and grinned triumphantly.

As Roger left, he turned to David. "You outdid yourself with that meal, Wiley. I didn't know you had it in you."

"Thanks, Roger."

He left with Molly. Nell stayed. Louise continued to drink Tab and play with her Walkman.

"What were you listening to?" Lexi said.

"The Germs."

"Are they any good?"

"They're great. I got the tape from Melinda. You want to listen?"

"It might piss David off."

"You're a grownup, you can do whatever you want."

"I know, and I don't think I want to piss him off right now."

"Come in my room later. I have to ask you something."

"What about?"

"I'll tell you later." She must have learned how to say that, Lexi thought, from her father: I'll tell you later. That, that baiting, pissed her off. Though Louise had an excuse, had two excuses: one, her age; two, her father's example. He returned to the dining room with a bottle of cognac and three glasses.

Louise said, "How can you drink that stuff?"

"How can you drink that stuff?" David said.

"It doesn't have any calories."

"It tastes like it." He smiled, waiting for her smile, which did not come. He pulled the cork out of the cognac and poured out a shot. "Nell?" He handed her the first glass.

She shook her head. "If I have anything else to drink, I'm going to pass out. Or vomit."

Louise laughed.

"Isn't Nell a cut-up?" Lexi said.

"She's funnier than you guys any day."

"There's nothing funny about passing out or vomiting, I can assure you."

"What did you do at Melinda's?" David passed Lexi a glass across the table.

"Watched a movie with The Who. Her father just brought it home from work. They have a really big screen attached to their television. It's almost as big as a movie theatre. Then we watched part of a movie with Kristy McNichol, but I can't remember the name of it. It was pretty good."

"What about your homework?"

"I did that before I went. You always ask me the same thing and I always tell you the same thing."

"That's my prerogative."

"What's a prerogative?"

"A right. As your father, I have the right to ask you about your homework."

"It's so boring."

"What is?"

"Everything."

"I thought you had a great time at Melinda's."

"I did, but girls are so boring sometimes. I want a boy-friend."

"Men can be boring too," Nell said.

"At least they're different."

"They're necessary," Nell said, "but not sufficient."

"What's that mean?"

"I think it might be too late to try to explain it tonight. Will you take a rain check?"

"I guess so."

"Unless you want to give it a stab, Wiley."

"I think it's out of my depth."

"Folks, I hate to eat and run, but I'm about to fall asleep." Nell got up. "Or, like I said, vomit." She held out her hand to Lexi. "Can I take your car? I'll bring it back first thing in the morning."

"Sure."

Nell turned to David. "Great dinner, Wiley." She stuck out her hand. "Didn't know you had it in you—" She made her voice go very deep, imitating Roger. David took her hand. "You closet queen. Har, har." She winked at him.

"Thanks, I needed that."

"Isn't Roger an asshole?" she said in her own voice.

"I think he is," Louise said.

"Really, Wiley, the dinner was excellent."

"Thanks."

"Good night, folks." She walked to the front door, turned back and looked at David. "I guess I'll be seeing you around the baths, huh?"

"And at the airport," Louise called out. "Remember? We're going to New York."

Lexi and Louise sat at the dining-room table. "I think she's really funny," Louise said. "*Really* funny."

"I think she is too."

"I want to be like her when I grow up. How old is she?"

"Twenty-nine. Hey, Wiley, let me do the dishes," she called into the kitchen.

He called back, "No one's doing them tonight. I'm just putting some things away." He returned and picked up his glass of cognac from the table. "I think I'm going to turn in."

"I'll be in soon." He stood at the head of the table, leaning against the chair in front of him, snifter of cognac at his side. The benevolent patriarch, winging it with some newfangled idea of home and family. So many definitions had changed. Lexi wondered if it ever frightened him.

"Good night, my love," he said.

Louise looked up. "Me or her?"

"You."

"Oh. Yeah." She looked down again at her soda. "Yeah, g'night."

Lexi waited to hear the sound of David's bedroom door closing. "What did you want to talk about?"

"Come in my room."

They went into her room. Louise sat on her bed and told Lexi to pull a chair up close to the bed so he wouldn't hear. "You promise you won't tell him?" She leaned close.

Lexi nodded.

"You sure?"

"Yes." She could keep secrets as well as any doorman.

"Can you die from taking birth-control pills?"

"You mean take one and die?"

"No, take them for a week and die."

"No. That's not what happens. Are you taking them?"
Louise nodded.

"What for?"

"I sort of have a boyfriend."

"Are you sleeping with him?"

"No. I mean, we're not *doing* it."

"Then why are you taking birth-control pills?"

"Because we're going to."

"When?"

"I'm not sure."

"Does David know him?"

"No, he'd have a fit. You can't tell him, either. You promised."

"I know, I won't. Who is he?"

"That's what he'll have a fit about."

"Who is it?"

"This guy I met at Melinda's. His name's Bliss."

"Bliss? First or last?"

"First. But the thing is that he's eighteen. He plays the drums in a group. He doesn't go to college either. He was going to, but then he decided it was bullshit."

"How long have you known him?" Lexi was trying to sound cool. David would have a fit.

"You're going to tell him, I can tell."

"I'm not going to tell him." It helped to say it aloud, because it would be an effort not to.

"Two weeks. I've only seen him a few times, but I think he's really neat. *Really* neat. We haven't done a whole lot of things, I mean, you know—" She moved her hand in circles through the air, looking, but not really looking, for words.

"Besides dying from birth-control pills, which you won't do, what is it you want to know?"

"Whether I should."

"Should what? Sleep with him?"

"Whether I should keep going out with him. Whether I should tell David. I don't know. Everything."

"I think you're in over your head."

"What do you mean?"

"What's this guy got going for him, besides being in a band?"

"He's cute. He's got a motorcycle."

"Jesus, Louise."

"You're going to tell him!" she said in a loud whisper.

"I'm not!" Lexi whispered back. She sat back, changed gears. "What I meant by your being in over your head is that you're doing things you're not sure you're ready for. With people you're not sure you want to be hanging out with."

"*I* like him, it's just that I know David won't. He'll kill me."

"He won't kill you, don't be ridiculous."

"Well, he won't let me go out with him. He practically freaks every time Melinda drives me somewhere, and she's a really good driver. She took driver's ed and her father got her a driving teacher. I even told him that, and he still freaks."

"He doesn't freak. He's just concerned."

"I used to take the subway all the time and he didn't care. What's the big deal about a car?"

"This guy doesn't have a car, he has a motorcycle."

"Lots of people have motorcycles."

"Is that where you were tonight?"

"No, I was really at Melinda's. And he wasn't there. You don't believe me, do you?"

"Yes, I believe you."

"What should I do?"

"When are you going to see him again?"

"Maybe tomorrow. Definitely when I get back from New York."

"Where'd you get the pills?"

"From Melinda."

"Why didn't you go to a doctor?"

"I don't know who to go to."

"What about Melinda's?"

"He costs seventy-five dollars."

Lexi looked around the room, looking for something to say. Louise was not the only one in over her head.

"She's lucky," Louise said. "Her father doesn't care what she does."

The only thing that came to Lexi were platitudes: she's not lucky; in five years you'll understand that; when you're my age you'll understand. She couldn't bring herself to say them, and they wouldn't have helped anyway.

"You really think I'm in over my head?"

Lexi looked at her and nodded. Way over, and Lexi had no idea how to bail her out—and she sounded like she wanted to be bailed out.

"Let me sleep on it," Lexi said. "Maybe we can get together tomorrow night and talk more about it."

"Not here."

"You can come to my house. I'll have a few hours before I leave for Washington."

"Okay."

"Nell might be around too," Lexi said. "She's always got advice for the lovelorn." Louise looked up. "And she can read your Tarot cards."

"Jesus, Lexi. Tarot cards are bullshit. Complete bullshit."

"You didn't used to think so."

"Yeah, well, now I know better."

"Yeah, well, now I'm going to sleep." Lexi got up.

"No you're not, you're going to bed. With you-know-who."

Lexi stood at the foot of Louise's bed and the choices raced through her head. She could admit it, deny it, make a joke of it, let it pass. She knew she was dealing with dynamite.

"Well, aren't you going?" Louise said.

She nodded and said, "I'll see you in the morning." Louise reached for her Walkman and slipped the headphones over her ears. She lay back on her bed, fully clothed, and closed her eyes. She had gotten the last word without yet understanding the exact nature of the competition.

The door to his room down the hall was closed and Lexi paused as she reached to open it, standing in the hallway between the jealous daughter and the father, who would be jealous if he knew what Lexi knew about Bliss. She touched the doorknob, contemplating her entrance. She had stood this way at the doors to who knows how many hotel rooms, when what was waiting for her inside was something illicit. It had given her such a complicated, lustful rush back then. But in their own way those entrances had been easier than this one. The only secrets she had had to keep back then were her own. A trade-off she had not expected: I'll keep you from hitting the ground from thirty thousand feet if you help me take care of my daughter. There was a time when she would not have considered the deal. She turned the knob.

"Is that you?" David said. She opened the door and saw him under the covers, behind a paperback. She grabbed his feet and shook them.

"What are you reading?" She crawled onto the bed.

"A book about computers." She lay close to him and looked over his shoulder. "I'm thinking about buying one."

"What for?"

"So I can write a book." He closed the book and put it on the night table.

"About what?"

"I'm not sure yet." He kissed her nose.

"You made a great dinner."

"Maybe I'll write a cookbook."

"I can't believe what an asshole Roger is. Doesn't it bother you?"

"I've known him for ten years. Most of the time it rolls off my back."

"You think they're really not sleeping together?"

"They probably are. Everyone does."

"Did you like Molly?"

"Yeah, she was great."

"Would you like to sleep with her?"

"I'd like to sleep with you." He began to unbutton her blouse.

"How come you want to write a book?"

"I want a project. I'm bored."

She undid the rest of the buttons herself and went on to the zipper on her skirt.

"I'm so full I don't know if I can do it." Lexi tossed her clothes to the floor. David laughed. "I saw a record a Boz's house, a forty-five called 'Too Drunk to Fuck.' One of those punk British imports. Can you believe it?"

"Are you?" he said.

"No, are you?"

"No." He kissed her breasts. "Where's your diaphragm?"

"Here." She held his hand between her legs.

"When did you put it in?" He touched her closer.

"I forgot to take it out last week."

She rolled on top of him, disengaging his hand, and reached into the drawer in his night table. "I need new stuff. I'll be right back." She got up and walked across the room to the bathroom.

"What were you and Louise talking about?"

She squatted in the bathtub and turned on the water. "Girl talk."

"Like what?"

"Wait till I turn off the water." She reached inside herself, took the diaphragm out and got it ready. She could do it with her eyes closed. She had done it with her eyes closed. When Louise got tired of worrying about dying from birth-control pills, she had all this to look forward to. Lexi wiped her hands on a towel and turned off the bathroom light.

She stood at the edge of the bed. "Boys," she said.

"What about them?" He lifted the covers, inviting her in.

"How you'd feel if she had a boyfriend."

"Does she have one?"

"No." She wrapped her arms around him, thinking that you can sometimes forget you're lying when you're making love.

"How does she think I'll feel?" He held her tightly.

"She thinks you'll freak. I think you might too."

"What makes you so sure?"

"You're supposed to. You're the father of a daughter."

"Did your father freak?"

"Quietly. Not so that anyone would notice. He might not have noticed himself."

"Maybe I'll be quiet about it too. What else did you talk about?"

"Different things."

"Like what?"

"Just stuff girls talk about."

"How come I think there's something you don't want to tell me?"

"Because it's true." She kissed his neck, buried her face in it.

He pulled away.

"I can't tell you what it was. She swore me to secrecy."

"Is it bad?"

"No."

"You're lying."

"She's worried about things fifteen-year-old girls are worried about."

"And you won't tell me?"

"I can't. I promised I wouldn't." More platitudes came to her: don't worry, she'll get over it, it's just a phase. They wouldn't be any more comforting to him than they would have been to Louise. She knew there was a lesson here. "She's going to come to my house tomorrow night before I go to Washington and we're going to talk some more. She just needs someone to talk to. A woman."

"What on earth do women talk about all the time?"

"Men."

"All the time?"

"Most of the time."

"What do you and Nell talk about?"

"Men. All the time." Lexi laughed.

"That's reassuring."

"Not just you, darling."

"You talk about your other men?"

"I don't have any other men."

"Not now, but you might get bored sometime and go prowling. You and Nell, like the old days."

"We never went prowling. Not together, anyway."

"What do you think about the three of us? You and me and Nell."

"Are you trying to tell me you want to sleep with Nell?"

"Not Nell. *You* and Nell."

"I went out with someone once who wanted to do the same thing, the three of us. He said that fucking Nell would be a way of fucking me more completely."

"Maybe he was right."

"What do you mean?"

"It's like you're fourteen and you've got a crush on each other and you don't know what to do about it. With all your phone calls and secrets and giggling. It intrigues the hell out of me."

"That doesn't mean we should all sleep together."

"But do you see why it appeals to me?"

"I think you like the idea of it. If she and I said yes, I bet you wouldn't show up."

"I would too. You're the one who wouldn't."

"You're right. That would make it a pretty dull orgy. Nell all by herself."

"You're the one who wanted to sleep with her."

"I used to want to do a lot of things."

"Name one."

She moved away from him, propped herself on her elbow, hand against her cheek. "Sleep with men I didn't care about."

"I don't think you ever wanted that, really wanted it." He turned and faced her. "I think what you wanted was to be hugged, and that was the *quid pro quo*: if I screw you, you'll hug me."

"You think so?"

"I do."

She moved closer. "Hug me."

He opened his arms to her, pulled her close. "I'm hugging you."

"Don't stop."

"Ever?"

"Let go in the morning."

"How long are you going to be in Washington?"

"Until late Thursday. I think my plane gets in at nine."

"Why don't we go away for the weekend? Can you do that?"

"Sure. Where should we go?"

"I don't know. Someplace far away. Maybe Mexico."

"What about Louise?"

"She's going to New York Wednesday. Have you ever been to Cabo San Lucas?"

"No. It's pretty far away for a weekend."

"That's the point. You have to go somewhere far away so you know you've been away."

"But there's never anything to do in those resort places."

"But I'll be there." He kissed her forehead. "Anyway, you should do nothing for a few days."

"I'd like to do nothing for a long time." She ran her lips against his shoulder. "Maybe a week."

"You sound like me five years ago."

"Is that a compliment or an insult?"

"Neither."

"I might stop sounding like you pretty soon. I think I'm going to apply for a job at UCLA. They have an opening in their immigration clinic. Starting in June."

He loosened his grip, moved to look at her. "Part-time?"

"Full-time."

"What about the Center?"

"The Center may not be around in June."

"Won't you miss it?"

"Of course. But maybe it's time to do something else. Do something I don't know how to do as well. Is that why you want to write a book?"

"I hadn't thought about it that way, but maybe. Come here." He held her closer. She wanted to tell him that Nell was in love, but she also wanted not to think about what that might mean. She wanted not to think about all the things women talked about, Louise's secrets, the ones she had appropriated. He kissed her.

The water level fell. Here, this minute, she wasn't in over

her head. He cupped her face in his hands. He grew hard against her thigh, pressed himself against her. She pulled the covers off of them and lay on top of him. He wrapped his arms around her and he rubbed himself against her. "Not yet." "I won't." She reached behind her and gripped his wrists, and he let her take them and press them against the bed. "Press back." He pressed back. "Harder." Effortlessly, smiling, watching her, he lifted his arms an inch off the bed as she bore down with all her strength. They looked at each other and laughed. He let up. "It's genetic," she said and shifted her strength from her shoulders to her hips. "It's no contest," he said. "Kiss me." He kissed her, his eyes still open, and she let go of his wrists and closed her eyes at the moment he came into her, her mouth and her cunt suddenly full of him, the separate sensations spreading and meeting in the small of her back, as if that place too were being filled, as if it could be. "Don't move," he said. He laid his palms lightly on her back. She relaxed her grip, let her legs hang limply against his closed thighs, let him move under her in smooth, slow circles, carefully tantalizing her dead weight, bringing it slowly, slowly back to life. "Not yet," he said. "When?" "Soon." "Now." "No." "Yes." She felt him shaking his head. He was saying no. "Yes." As she began to come, in the corner of her mind she thought of Louise two rooms away, Louise, then David, then of nothing except how hard he was suddenly, seconds before he came, when the sensation and also the idea of his coming pulled her sharply, as if a thick cord between them had snapped and released her, over the edge.

"How long have you been thinking of it?" she asked. It was dark in the room, the expanse of sky through the big windows dark too.

"A few weeks. Maybe a little longer than that."

"It sounds like deciding to get married before you know who you want to marry. Planning the wedding before you know who the bride'll be."

"It's not that I don't have any ideas. It's just that I haven't

hit on the right one yet. I don't even know if it'll be a book.
Maybe I'll just write a long article, or a movie script. There's a
guy at the paper working on a movie script about some drug
smugglers who do runs between South America and here."

"True?"

"Yeah, but the movie's more about one of the smugglers'
families, stuff about his wife not knowing exactly what he does.
She thinks he works for the CIA or that he's got a girlfriend in
Colombia, something like that."

"Do you want to work with him on it?"

"He hasn't asked me to, but it's given me some ideas about
how to start, what to look for in a story. The formula."

"I like the idea of innocent people getting involved, inex-
tricably involved, without even knowing what's happening to
them. Hitchcock does that a lot."

"Maybe I'll rent some movies. Get one of those machines,
like Melinda's father has."

"You're going Hollywood, honey."

"No I'm not. I'm just looking for something to write that's
longer than a fucking editorial."

She laughed.

"Maybe we could rent dirty movies."

"You would think of that, Wiley."

"Lots of innocent people getting involved in weird things."

She turned over, her back to him. "I'm going to be a professor and you want to watch dirty movies."

"Maybe I'll write a dirty movie." He curled up against her
back.

"It wouldn't be too hard."

"You could help."

"Go to sleep."

"Lexi."

"What now?" She reached for his thigh.

"You want to get married?"

"In general?"

"No, not in general."

"Are you serious?"

"Of course."

"How long have you been thinking of it?"

"Since about two minutes ago. And a few times before to-night."

"How come you never said anything?"

"Stop asking questions. Talk to me."

She rolled onto her back, moving closer to him. Moving but not speaking. Her thoughts were coming to her in sputters. Images, words, phrases, nothing that could be said. But she had to say something. "Tell me what we would do if we were married."

"Do? The same things we do now."

"You think we'd fight more?"

"I didn't think we fought now."

"You think we'd be any good at it?"

"Jesus, Lexi."

"Say something about me that you don't like."

"Your hair."

"What about it?"

"I don't know. It just hangs."

"How should I wear it?"

"Differently, away from your face more. Go to some fancy place and have them do it, or just fool around with it. Brush it differently."

"What else?"

"Nell."

"You don't like her?"

"I like her a lot. I have a feeling she doesn't like me. She's polite, she tolerates me. But we've never really had a conversation. Just chit-chat. I have a feeling she doesn't feel comfortable in the same room with me unless you're there."

"It's not that," Lexi said. "I think it's territorial imperatives. But I think the territories might be changing. She's in love with that guy in New York. She hasn't said so, but I have a feeling she's thinking about moving to New York."

"When?"

"I don't know."

"Would you go with her?"

She turned to him. "It hadn't occurred to me."

"Why not?"

"First of all, she hasn't decided yet. Second of all—" she slid her leg across the bed, held it against his—"this is where I live. And this is where you live. And you just moved here from there."

"You haven't said anything yet about getting married."

"It seems like we always do this: talk about our lives as if it's a business proposition, and everything comes down to saying yes or no to some monumental plan, like your moving to L.A. or living together or getting married. We don't talk about feelings, we talk about situations."

"All right. Let's talk about feelings."

"You go first."

"I love you."

"What does that mean?"

"Why don't you stop thinking about what things mean for a minute?" He took a deep breath. "You make everything so complicated. Your mind goes right past whatever you're feeling. You're the one who's thinking about the situations instead of the feelings."

"But marriage is the ultimate situation."

"And the reason you do it," he said, as if he were patiently explaining something to Louise, "is because you have certain feelings for someone. And because someone, I think, has certain feelings for you. But at the moment, I'm not sure."

She went to him, felt him stiffen as she moved closer. "I have them." She touched his cheek. He did not open his eyes. "I just don't know what to do with them sometimes." He yawned, pulled the covers tighter around his shoulders. "Doesn't it scare you?"

He curled his hand under his face. "What's it?"

She sighed deeply. She had lost her breath for a moment. She felt ashamed, paltry next to his willingness. He had asked her to marry him and she had turned it into a parody, a sit-com. She couldn't even tell him back that she loved him. "I don't know what it is," she said finally. She reached for his hand and held it tightly, as if to steady herself, thinking about the intimacy of this otherwise innocent gesture, how much more intimate it was to reach for his hand than to have reached earlier for his penis. She was often startled by how little obstruction there seemed to be between his heart and his head. "I was just thinking," she said and leaned closer to him, "I was thinking that—" She touched her nose to his forehead, and then drew back, relieved. He had given her a respite for the night. One of the rewards for the simple-hearted: they could fall asleep when they were tired.

She got up and put on the shirt of his that was hanging on the doorknob of the bathroom, rolling the long sleeves up to her elbows, buttoning only two buttons beneath her breasts. The tail of the shirt trailed to the top of her thighs, and she walked through the dark apartment to the kitchen to wash the dishes.

They were stacked in the sink, waiting to be put in the dishwasher. She wanted instead to wash them by hand, one by one, watch, in the faint light from the window above the sink, the caked-on food disappear. She squirted a dot of Joy in the center of a plate and rubbed it clean with a scrub brush. All the lights in the building across the way were out.

She slipped the clean plate into the dish drainer and remembered a favorite history teacher in high school who had a husband and child and seemed to everyone immensely happy, content with her life. Lexi had asked a friend, "You think she's happy all the time?" "No," her friend answered, "she saves all her unhappiness up for the middle of the night, for when no one's looking."

Holding a handful of forks under the spray of the faucet, Lexi thought that there had to be something more than this, more than whatever love was, more than whatever ambition was. More than washing the dishes in the middle of the night in the home of a man who wanted to marry her. She slipped the forks into the utensil drainer and wiped her hands against the shirt he had worn all day, holding the damp cotton cloth for longer than she had to. She put her elbows on the edge of the sink and rested her head on her fists and looked at the twenty-story building across the way.

Maybe, though, this was all there was. Maybe the trick was not to want more but to accept what you had, the love and the ambition, the dinner parties, the going-away parties. Maybe there was for everyone an empty, private space that neither love nor ambition could fill. Maybe there were for everyone moments of terror in the middle of the night. Even for the history teacher who looked happy all the time.

He wanted to get married and she knew she had never before had to decide whether to give her energy to something as large.

She had given it to Nell once, so effortlessly that she had not even been aware she had been handing anything over. Now they were going their separate ways. They might not keep following each other across the country.

A light went on in the building across the way, a few floors down from where she stood. Another nighttime wanderer. Poor thing. Poor thing, she said aloud, all by yourself in that big, rich building. You think no one's watching you. Drops of semen trickled down the inside of her thigh, semen and stuff and her own fluids. She held her legs tightly together and cried into her open hands.

"You didn't say yes, did you?"

Lexi shook her head. At eight-thirty that morning they were driving north on Pacific, Nell driving Lexi's car, Lexi in the seat next to her, so tired that her head ached. "I can't remember exactly what I said, but it didn't go over very well. He ended up saying I didn't pay attention to my feelings, that I made everything too complicated."

Nell stopped for a stop sign. "Of course you do. That's why he's in love with you." She put the car into first gear. "That's why I'm in love with you. Jesus." She sped away. "Pass me another donut."

Lexi dug her hand into the bag. "What kind?"

"Glazed."

"And catch this: Louise is taking birth-control pills because she might have a boyfriend. She got them from Melinda and she swore me not to tell David."

"Did you tell him?"

"Of course not."

"That kid must love you."

"Except that I'm sleeping with her father. We had words about that too."

"I didn't think things could have gotten worse once Roger left."

Nell pulled up in front of her own house, got out of the car and stood at the door of the driver's seat. Lexi took her seat and looked up at Nell through the window. "Tell me one thing: do you think we have what we always said we wanted—I mean, love and ambition?"

Nell wrinkled up her face, dug her hand into her shoulder bag and pulled out her house keys. "I'm not sure about ambition anymore. I think you got more of that than I did."

"What about love?"

"It doesn't stink anymore, but I don't know what it does instead."

Instead of going to lunch that noon, Lexi rewrote her ré-sumé and called a guy she knew who taught in the clinical program at UCLA to ask him what it was like to work there. "Crazy," he said, "and nowhere near as stodgy as the law school itself, if that's what you're worried about." That was one of the things she was worried about. Another was not having the teaching experience that would make her application be considered seriously. "It's mostly patience that you need," her friend said. "Most of the students need to have their hands held more than they need to know what the law is. They can read a book for that." She thought of Louise, who knew what the law was and who needed to have her hand held. "You've got a pretty good shot at it," he said. "You're practically a celebrity." She had no idea what she was going to say to Louise that evening.

"Yeah, a star in the most unpopular cause in the country."

"Don't knock notoriety. Anyway, I think you should go for it."

She looked through her wallet for a stamp so she could mail the résumé. "I think I will." Between her library card and her driver's license she found a commemorative stamp with a drawing of Kitty Hawk above the words THE SPIRIT OF FLIGHT. She hung up the phone and looked from the stamp to the plane ticket that lay on her desk. It was impossible to predict which single-minded inventor, which homemade flying machine, would alter the course of history. She was thinking of her own history, and David Wiley, an inventor of another sort. All he had done was take her out to dinner.

Louise wasn't home when Lexi called her at five-thirty to say that she was on her way. At five-forty Louise walked into her office with her Walkman headphones on, said, "Hi" and flopped into the armchair that faced her desk as if she did this every day, as if there were a reason for her casual boredom. To-day she was wearing black pants and her black satin baseball jacket.

"How'd you get downtown?"

"I got a ride."

"Who with?"

"Bliss."

"What are you listening to?"

"Nothing. Why?"

Lexi touched her hands to her own head and Louise did the same, coming up against the headphones she had forgotten she was wearing. She pulled them off and said, "He's going to Alaska on Saturday. I'm really upset."

"For how long?"

"I think forever." She tapped her foot against the desk. "He's sick of playing the drums, but I think the reason is that he has another girlfriend." Louise stuck her hands into the pockets of her baseball jacket and looked down at her lap. She tapped her foot harder against the desk. "I sort of knew about her be-fore, but Melinda told me she was in Alaska." She looked up.

"Who ever heard of anyone who lives in Alaska? And besides that, she's nineteen."

When you're as old as I am you'll barely remember any of this. Instead Lexi said and said so that Louise would understand that she meant it: "Sometimes love really stinks."

"You just heard that song, Lexi." She was really angry. "You don't really think that, you think love is all mushy and you never want to do anything that makes David mad. And I bet he wouldn't get mad at you anyway. And I bet you told him everything last night."

"I didn't, Louise. I told you I wouldn't."

"Yeah, well, it doesn't matter anyway now."

You don't even have to wait until you're as old as I am. In six months you won't remember his last name—though who could ever forget his first name? In a few years she'd laugh at that. "I'm really sorry it didn't work out the way you wanted it to."

The telephone rang. It was David, who wanted to know when she was going to see Louise. He had tried calling Louise to ask her, but there was no answer.

"She's sitting right here."

"Doing what?"

"I don't know. What are you doing, Louise?"

"Who is it?"

"Your ace."

"My what?"

"Let me talk to her."

Lexi reached across the desk to give the receiver to Louise, who took one hand out of the pocket of her baseball jacket so that she could talk to whoever her ace was.

As Louise spoke to her father, Lexi's eyes wandered to the map of the United States on the wall behind Louise, moving from New York to Alaska to New York to Los Angeles. She was counting miles, thinking about the spirit of flight, thinking: Take me somewhere, take me away. I want to go too.

"Lexi. David wants to know what time you're going to the airport and if you want a ride." She handed the phone back. They agreed to meet at nine, and hung up.

Louise took her Walkman out of her pocket and pressed a

button. The cassette tape popped up. She turned it over and put it back in, and then put the Walkman back in her pocket.

"Should we go?" Lexi said.

"I guess so." Louise stuck her hands in her pockets and looked around the office.

"By the way, what are you going to do with your birth-control pills?" Lexi filled up her briefcase with things she needed to take to Washington. Out of the corner of her eye, she saw Louise shrug.

"I guess I'll throw them away. Unless you want them."

When he got to the end of the paragraph, David Wiley hit the key that said LOG, then the key that said OFF and then the key that said EXECUTE. Within seconds all the green letters on the screen disappeared, except for those at the top which said SAVING STORY: JUVJUSTICE. The telephone rang. He picked it up and said, "Wiley."

"How come you always say that?" Louise said. "Why don't you just say hello?"

"Hello." The cursor flashed in the corner of the screen. He smiled.

"Hi."

"I was just about to leave. Are you packed?"

"Almost, except that I was just looking for my Walkman and I couldn't find it and I might have left it at Lexi's last night, so I was wondering if you could stop there on your way home, because I'm *definitely* going to die if I have to take a plane all the way to New York without it."

"What a horrible way to die."

"So will you pick it up?"

"I think I might be able to."

"If I could drive, I could do it myself."

"If you had a car."

"But if I could drive, you'd get me a car, wouldn't you?"

"Let's talk about something else. How much packing do you have left to do?"

"Just some things."

"Get them all together and I'll be home soon with the Walkman. What do you want for dinner?"

"Nothing. I'm on a diet."

Half an hour later he unlocked the door to Lexi's small house, stepped three steps into the dark living room and almost tripped over the phone, knocking the receiver out of its cradle. He put it back, turned on the first light he could find and scanned the room for the Walkman. He continued through the cluttered rooms, turning over books, magazines, knee socks, sweaters, three telephone books, a bag on the bathroom floor from Bullock's that contained—he couldn't resist—some pantyhose, a pair of tweezers, a bra and a plastic bottle of something that said CAMOMILE on it. He looked closer; bath oil. He loved the things women had, all the odd, sweet-smelling containers, the underthings, the things like tweezers that they used, usually when you weren't around, to make themselves look ever so slightly different.

He found the Walkman on the desk in the bedroom, between a stack of magazines and a stack of legal pads. As he reached to pick it up, the corner of an envelope sticking out of a magazine caught his eye. Not the envelope so much as the name written on the paper triangle that protruded out of the *California Law Review*: Nell.

He picked up the review and let it fall open to the place where the envelope was. It was addressed to Lexi at her office and marked—he picked up the envelope to read the postmark—March 20. New York. He turned it over a few times, fingered the stamp, the flap on the back. He looked again at the handwriting, as if it might tell him what was written inside so that he wouldn't have to read it. Have to read it. He did not have to read it. But he had to.

He read it. He read the last paragraph three times: "Given up hot-shot reporting to write editorials in L.A. In the business they call that getting kicked upstairs, and usually save it for the old codgers who are so wrecked that about all they can do is pick up a telephone and hit a few keys on the typewriter."

Suddenly there was a noise in the next room, someone at the front door, trying to get in. He stuck the envelope back into the review and listened hard. The noise kept on. He put down the review and picked up the Walkman—a weapon. He slithered across the room, gripped the Walkman tighter and peeked out the bedroom door. Across the living room, just as surprised to see him as he was to see her, was Nell.

"You scared the hell out of me," she said.

"You scared the hell out of me too. Do you have a key?"

"Yeah. I didn't know you did too." They stood across the room from one another. He shrugged.

"Executive privilege, huh?" she said.

"Something like that." Executive—the word was loaded. He could never think of what to say to her anyway.

"Is there a party going on?"

He shook his head. "Louise was here last night before Lexi went to Washington. She left this." He held up the Walkman. "I was just on my way out. What about you?"

"I've got to pick up some clothes. For New York." Nell walked past him on her way to the bedroom. He followed her.

She opened the closet door and began sifting through Lexi's clothes. "Your clothes or hers?" he said.

"Who knows anymore?" He didn't want her to see him smile. He wanted to trip her up. "How's the masterpiece on single women coming along?"

"China's still a long way off."

"What?"

"Never mind." She pulled out a black blazer and held it up. "You think she'll miss this for a few days?"

David shrugged. "Are you going to see your new boy-friend in New York?"

She nodded, flicking a speck of lint from the collar. She hung the blazer on the closet doorknob and went to the dresser, opening the second drawer down. She knew her way around Lexi's things. She pulled out a blue turtleneck sweater and gray crewneck sweater. "Which do you think?" She held them up for him, and then something caught her eye. She put down the blue one and looked at the elbow on the gray one, shaking her head.

"She never darns anything. Look at this." There was a hole in the elbow. He couldn't tell whether she was putting on this routine. It didn't fit with the rest of her. She shoved it back in the drawer. "I'll fix it when I get back." Damn her butting in, David thought, fixing other people's clothes, when Lexi couldn't care less about the hole in the elbow of her sweater. And damn her for thinking I've been kicked upstairs. Executive privilege.

"Lexi said your boyfriend's a reporter."

She nodded, closing the drawer.

"A trade paper, right?"

"Yeah."

"Has he been there long?"

"A year and a half."

"So he hasn't exactly made a career of it?"

"What, reporting?"

"Reporting for a trade."

Nell looked at him sharply. She knew what he was talking about. Trades were the bottom of the heap, usually in bed with whatever industry they covered. "I guess he's working his way up to the big time," she said. "Some of us start there and some of us have to work up to it." She picked up the turtleneck and the blazer from the doorknob.

"I have some friends in New York, if he ever decides to—"

"He's got his own friends." She brushed against his elbow as she huffed past him, through the bedroom door and, within seconds, out the front door, slamming the flimsy screen door behind her.

He stood in the bedroom doorway holding the Walkman, stunned by her whirlwind exit, stunned too by his own performance. He had not meant to keep going that way. Of course he had. She was probably on the phone to Lexi this minute, reporting it all. He stalked through the living room, and as he reached the front door, the phone rang. Another chance to look into her life when she wasn't around. He didn't want to know who it was. Though at least it wouldn't be Nell. It kept ringing. It occurred to him that it might be Louise. He turned and stooped down to pick it up. Whoever it was had hung up.

Louise was not packing. She was lying on her side on the couch, her face to the wall, and talking on the telephone. She did not move as he walked across the room to her, probably because she could not hear him, because the song on the stereo, one of whose speakers was several feet from her head, blasted "All dressed up and no place to go, we just wanna dance" repeatedly through the apartment. When he lowered the volume on the amplifier, she rolled over and said to the person she was talking to, "I couldn't believe he said that. I mean, I thought I was going to *die*."

"Louise."

"Hold on a sec, my father's here." She covered the mouthpiece with her hand and said, "Yeah."

"Are you packed?"

"Almost."

"We're leaving here in exactly twenty-five minutes."

"It won't take me that long."

"Please get off the phone."

"I told you it wouldn't take me that long."

"I told you I want you to get off the phone. Now."

She rolled her eyes and exhaled theatrically. She spoke into the receiver: "Melinda. I think I have to go." David turned and as he walked toward the kitchen he thought he heard something funny coming from the stereo. He listened closely and thought it was just the way the song went. But after the sixth or seventh time he realized the needle was stuck in the groove and if he did not do something about it, the song would not stop by itself and he would have to listen all night to some girls singing "wanna dance wanna dance wanna dance wanna dance." Louise hung up the phone and lay on the couch looking up at the ceiling. David poured himself a shot of Jack Daniel's.

The phone rang. Louise picked it up before the first ring was over. A moment later she called into the kitchen, "It's for you. It's your girlfriend."

He went into the living room, took the receiver and covered the mouthpiece with his hand. "You have some things to do," he said to Louise. She swung her legs off the couch and strutted across the room toward her bedroom.

"Wiley?"

"Hi."

"I've been thinking about you. How are you?"

"I've been better." This was not the time to confess, and as long as he was on the phone with Lexi, Nell wouldn't be able to get through. Though she might have talked to her already. Lexi might be calling to find out his version.

"What's wrong?"

"Just more of the same. You know how it is with newspaper executives. Fancy offices, secretaries, someone to screen your calls." He wasn't going to confess, but he wasn't going to lie down either.

"Sounds like Roger's been giving you a hard time."

"Not exactly."

"What do you mean?"

"I'll tell you sometime." Maybe he would. "Did you testify yet?"

"Tomorrow morning. I spent the day at hearings and re-writing the testimony."

"By yourself?"

"Mostly with this guy from a law firm who's doing some work for us, and a few other people in the struggle." She laughed.

"And you're all staying at the Mayflower, right?"

"The Best Western."

"Nervous about tomorrow?"

"No. I thought I would be, but not after seeing these guys operate all day. The senators and their minions. In their penny loafers. Jesus. Answer me this, Wiley: how can you take anyone seriously who's wearing penny loafers? It's the last quarter of the twentieth century and grown men are wearing shoes with little slots in them for pennies—and some of them even have pennies in their slots. They're running the fucking country in their loafers."

"What is this—the Nell school of political commentary?"

"She's not that far off. Are we still going away on Friday?"

"We have plane reservations for Cabo. Do you still want to go?"

"Of course. Where are we staying?"

"I don't know yet. I was going to make some calls tomorrow."

"Not a Hyatt or a Hilton. Some place with a little character."

"Maybe we could rent a cottage or a house or something." He thought about her house. "What about a funky cottage? Could you handle that?"

"Not too funky."

He laughed. "I'll ask around. People at the paper might have some ideas."

"I wish you were here."

"Not Washington."

"Then I wish I were there."

"Me too." It was almost not a lie.

"You sound better."

"Than what?"

"Than when I called."

"I feel better. But I have to go. Louise's plane leaves at ten and she seems to be having trouble packing."

"Are you taking Nell to the airport?"

"What for?"

"I thought she and Louise were on the same flight."

He had forgotten. "I just ran into her. We arranged to meet at the airport." Lexi would find out the truth soon enough—if she hadn't heard already.

"Where did you run into her?"

"Your house. Louise left her Walkman there last night. Nell came by to pick up some of your clothes. Or some of hers. I don't think she has it straight."

"I'll call you Thursday night when I get in," Lexi said. "And we'll go away Friday."

"Good. Good luck tomorrow. Just remember that you have the truth on your side."

"That doesn't seem to count for too much here."

When he hung up, he went into Louise's room and watched as she languidly went through her drawers. "I forgot to tell you. We're meeting Nell at the airport."

"I know."

"How do you know?"

"She called before you got home."

"What did she say?"

"She said, I'll meet you at the airport." Louise stuffed some shirts into her canvas bag.

"Anything else?"

"No."

"She didn't say anything about me?"

"Why would she say anything about you?"

"Just asking."

Louise bent down to zip her bag and, with her back to him, she said, "I bet you think everyone wants to be your girlfriend."

In the car at a stoplight Louise pointed to the stick shift. "Which gear are we in?"

"Neutral. That's what you're in when you're not moving."

They began to move. "What about now?"

"First." She leaned down and peered at his feet. "Second," he said as he let up on the clutch.

She sat up and looked at the stick as he shifted from second to third. "Can you go from second to fourth if you want to?"

"It's not a good idea. You double-shift more when you're down-shifting." He pulled the stick back to fourth.

"When are you going to teach me how to drive?"

"I'm teaching you right now."

"When are you going to let me drive?"

"When you get your learner's permit."

"Melinda didn't have to wait until then."

"In case you haven't noticed, they do things differently at Melinda's."

"That's for sure." She turned on the radio. It occurred to him at that moment that she might want to stay in New York, that she might not want to come back. In the fast lane of the San

Diego Freeway he slipped the car into fifth, was tempted to tell her what he was doing: this is fifth, this is overdrive. And he would have to explain to her what that was. There was really nothing to be afraid of, but still, all of a sudden, he was afraid. But she had to, had to come back—if only because it was the middle of the semester. If only because of Melinda.

"Maybe Curtis'll let me drive."

"In the city?"

"No, in the country, David. Remember?"

He remembered that Curtis had a house in the country, and it made him sad that she called him David all the time. "In the Berkshires, right?"

"Yeah."

"What else are you going to do in New York?"

"See Jennifer, see Blake, see Alicia, see Emily—maybe see Suzanne. Maybe meet some boys. And Gretchen got tickets to this show on Broadway I never heard of."

"When you come back, do you want to start taking acting lessons?"

She shrugged. David took the exit for the airport.

"I don't know if I want to be an actress anymore."

"What do you want to be?"

"Why do I have to be something? All you guys talk about is what you are. I think it's really boring. Maybe I won't be anything." She didn't sound angry. She sounded like she just wanted to let him know what her plans were.

He headed for the short-term parking. The disc jockey was talking about the Dodgers, the Rams and Nancy Reagan's wardrobe. They found a space. Louise watched his hand as it moved the stick shift. "Which one's that?" she said.

"Reverse." He turned off the engine.

"I thought it has to be in neutral when you're not moving."

"It should be, but you should park it in gear."

"How come?"

He reached into the back seat for her bag. "I'll explain it to you on the way. Let's go."

"I bet I'll know how to drive by the time I come back here. And then how could you stop me if I already know?" As he turned to look at her, she let herself out of the car. He reached to lock the door behind her and saw she had left something on her seat. Astonishing she could have forgotten about it for a minute. The goddam Walkman. He stuck it into the side pocket of the canvas bag she was taking to New York. Of course she would come back. This was where she lived now—this year anyway. "United's that way," she said and pointed across the parking lot, over thousands of cars. He locked his door, and as they walked, a smile came over her face. "I just realized I'm going to New York. With Nell. I'm really going, right now." Her pace picked up. "I wish I was already there."

At the newsstand in the terminal she bought three packs of sugarless bubble gum, *Rolling Stone*, *People* with a picture of David Bowie on the cover, and a *National Enquirer* with the headline: YOKO WANTED DIVORCE FROM JOHN BEFORE HIS MURDER.

"Got everything?" David said. They were in the United waiting area.

"I think so." She had the magazines under her arm, the canvas bag strap over her shoulder and her ticket in her hand. He wished she hadn't cut off all of her hair. He wished she cared the way girls were supposed to about getting some color. His daughter had to be the only teenage girl in Southern California who didn't cultivate her tan. Gretchen would think he wasn't taking care of her properly. She would think he was too permissive. But what could you do if she came home one day with her hair cut off?

"I gave you money for a cab, didn't I?"

"Yes, David."

"Make sure you let him know you're from New York, so he doesn't take you for a ride."

She rolled her eyes. "You think I don't know that?" A

voice came on with the second or third boarding announcement.

"What happened to Nell?" Louise's eyes darted around the
waiting area.

"She'll be here any minute."

"But we won't be able to sit together."

"You can trade seats with someone."

"What if she had an accident?"

"She's fine. She's just late."

Still looking around the terminal, Louise unwrapped a
pack of gum and, without looking at him, handed him the
wrapper. He stuck it in his jacket pocket. He watched her chew.
Chewing for her life. Another boarding announcement came
over the P.A.

"Maybe you should get on the plane. There won't be any
place left to put your luggage if you're the last one on. I'll wait
here for Nell. I'll tell her what seat you're in." She looked up at
him, chewing hard. "Come on." He took a step, hoping she
would follow.

She didn't move. She turned and looked at the line she was
about to join, then looked back again at him. "David?"

"What is it?"

"What if the plane crashes?"

"It won't. I promise." He touched her cheek. "You know
how many planes I've taken in my life?" She nodded. "I'm still
here. And I'll be here when you get back. Okay?"

"I guess so."

"In five hours you'll be in New York." He thought of the
plane doors closing, locking up tight like a vault. He touched
her shoulder to get her moving. She didn't move. He took her
bag from her and walked with her to the end of the line of
people who were on their way to New York. It was as simple as
that: the doors would close in Los Angeles and open five hours
later in New York. In the air they would eat a meal and watch a
movie. It happened thousands of times a day. There was nothing, absolutely nothing to be afraid of. This is what he thought
but did not say to her. He turned the canvas bag over to her and
met her terrified glance. "There's nothing to worry about. I

promise." He leaned down to kiss her, and as his lips touched her cheek, she nodded and turned to take her place on the line.

A moment later she handed her boarding pass to the man at the door. He watched as she walked down the long ramp that led to the plane. She looked back three or four times. Looking straight past him. Looking, of course, for Nell. As he braced himself to look for her too, she walked quickly past him and on down the ramp, so fast that she might not have seen him. She had probably been on the phone with Lexi all this time.

Lexi was right. If she and Nell said yes, he would lose his nerve. He had just lost what was left of his curiosity.

On his way out of the terminal, he passed the strip of rent-a-car desks, the bank of telephones, the hot lines to the local hotels. That used to be me, he thought. Picking up the bright-red phones, looking for a place to stay at the last minute. He didn't miss that life at all. But this new life offered more occasions for terror than he could ever have anticipated. He stepped onto the rubber mat that made the door open in front of him. His daughter was having problems she wouldn't tell him about. Just things fifteen-year-old girls were worried about—that was how Lexi had put it. He didn't know what fifteen-year-old girls worried about. Except boys. Clothes. School. She didn't seem worried about school. But still, he wanted to know what it was that troubled her, even if it was only something that fifteen-year-old girls are worried about. He walked across the lot. He wanted to be the one she told. There was a silver Jaguar with a license plate that said 9 INCHES. Then there was an old Mustang with a license plate that said NOT RICH. California was full of crazies. The sky was full of jumbo jets, taking people to places he had already been. The dark green Saab he thought was his was not his. He headed for the next aisle over.

He took so much for granted: flight itself, the arrival of this plane and every other plane his daughter would take in her life. But still, he was afraid. He was afraid, for a moment, that her plane would crash. And afraid that whatever her secret from him was was something serious. He got into his car and turned on the ignition. The radio blared. He turned it off and pulled out of the space.

Women and their secrets. The things they told each other when you were in the next room. The things they wrote in letters they never expected you to read. He stopped at the booth and paid for the forty-five minutes his car had spent in the lot. It was really true. They talked about men, all the damn time. When the brainiest women in the world got together, they probably talked about men. Lexi had gotten a full report by now. He had been a shit. He had pulled rank on her, on her boyfriend. He turned onto Century and tried to imagine the phone call, the two of them giggling. Trashing him. He wanted to know how much Lexi had told Nell about fucking him. He wanted to know, as he took the right for the San Diego Freeway North, if there was a point at which loyalty to a man, maybe love for a man, superseded gossip. If you could call it gossip. If you could call what she felt for him love.

He hesitated at the end of the on-ramp as the freeway opened into five lanes. She hesitated about love, marriage. He was going to lie low, he was going to give her time. He accelerated hard. It surprised him that he enjoyed the challenge, the anticipation that he could make her come around. As if he were on the verge of getting a story, on the verge of figuring it out. He just needed a little more time, a little more information. For the moment, he relished the uncertainty of her affection. And the prospect of a night without her. Without Louise. Without Nell. A night of his own.

Lexi said, "Yes." She would accept the collect call.

"Did I wake you?" Nell said.

"I'm getting dressed. I've got to testify at ten. Where are you?"

Nell cleared her throat and didn't answer.

"Nell? Are you all right?"

"Uh-huh."

"Where are you?"

"You'll never guess."

"It sounds like I'm going to have to."

"Louise and I had a lovely flight. Perfectly delightful." She cleared her throat again.

Lexi was silent for a moment. "Oh no. You're at Gretchen's."

"They're in the other room. I told them I had to make a few phone calls."

"What's she like?"

"You expect me to talk about her in her own house?" Nell whispered. "She could pick up the extension any minute."

"How did you end up there?"

"The plane was late, I left my keys to Michael's in L.A., by the time we got to the city he'd already left for work, but he isn't there yet. So I figured I'd come here until I could get in touch with him." She paused and leaned against the desk in the corner of the room. " And I have to tell you something."

"I have to tell you something too. I called you last night, but your line was busy. For two hours."

"Yeah, I was talking to Michael. Listen, I went to your house last night to pick up some clothes—" she spoke softly, directly into the mouthpiece— "and found Wiley in the living room with some story about Louise's Walkman. And he went into this totally unsolicited rap about Michael working for a trade paper. Out of the fucking blue."

"What did he say?"

"Hold on a second. It sounds like someone's at the door. Talk for a while."

"The reason I called you last night is because I'd just gotten back from having dinner with—guess who?"

"Henry Kissinger."

"Stephen Shipler."

"Did you have something more than dinner?"

"He offered me a job."

"Really? On his desk?"

"In his firm."

"In his firm what? Or I should say, on his firm what?" Nell

walked across the room and opened the door to see if there was anyone on the other side of it.

"Forty-eight thousand bucks a year."

The long hallway was empty. She closed the door. "I trust you told him to blow it out his ass," Nell whispered.

"Not in so many words. No one in Washington ever says what they really think."

She went back to her place, leaning against the desk. "Maybe that's Shipler's problem. No one ever told him what an asshole he is."

"What does she look like?"

"Very Upper West Side." She spoke softly. "Long brown hair. Little on the skinny side." She paused. "Nothing to write home about, if that's what's worrying you."

"I'm not worried. Just curious. What exactly did Wiley say to you last night?"

"Something like if Michael ever wanted to get a real news job, he had some friends. I said he had his own friends, asshole. Then I left."

"You called him an asshole?"

"No, but I should have."

"Did you say something to provoke him?"

"Are you kidding? I walked in and he attacked me."

"Was he serious?"

"Serious? He was vicious. Hold on. Someone's here."

Louise came in. "Gretchen wants to know how you want your eggs."

"However you're having them."

"I'm not having any. I'm having a croissant. About this big." She opened her hands as if she were holding a cantaloupe.

"I'll have one of those."

"She has bagels too."

"I'll have whatever she's serving."

"She's serving eggs. Do you want an omelet? I'll tell her to make an omelet if you want one."

"Louise. I'll eat whatever she's making. Anything." Louise looked like she was not going to leave until she got a better answer. "Scrambled," Nell said. "I'll be there in a few minutes."

Louise closed the door behind her. Nell listened for the clap of her steps down the hallway.

"She's making you breakfast?" Lexi said. "Does she know who you are?"

"You think she wouldn't if she knew? These guys have been divorced for a hundred years. Anyway, I think there's some guy who lives with her. Louise told me she used to hear them fuck all the time."

"Did she say she hears Wiley and me?"

"No. But she did say that she thought you told him about Bliss. Did you?"

"No. I told her I wouldn't."

"I think she wants him to know. Mostly to see how he'll respond. Or if he'll respond."

"He'd respond plenty."

"I'm not so sure he's capable of it."

Lexi let it pass. "What were you talking to Michael about for two hours?"

"All kinds of things." All kinds of things she didn't want to talk to Lexi about.

"Where are you?"

"I told you."

"Which room?"

Nell looked around. "It looks like a combination study and bedroom. Lots of books and a bunch of diplomas. What is she, a professor?"

"A shrink."

Nell looked closer at the bindings of the books. "Yeah, looks like shrink books."

"What about your book? Who are you going to interview in New York?"

Nell sat down at the desk chair. She needed to sit down for this. "My editor."

"Why her? Is she single?"

Nell took a deep breath. Deep enough for Lexi to hear. "I have to ask her what happens when I break the contract."

She had expected the silence on Lexi's end. But had not expected it to last so long. "Are you there?" Nell said.

"Are you serious?"

"Yeah." She had never assented to anything so quietly.

"What happened?"

Nell shrugged. If Lexi could have seen the shrug, she might have understood. Maybe she wouldn't have. Nell wasn't sure what Lexi knew about turning back before you got where you said you were going to go.

"Nell?"

"Yeah."

"It's just a book. I guess it wasn't the right one for you to do."

"I thought you'd be disappointed, my ambition going down the tubes and all."

"It's not your ambition, it's just this project. Maybe you should write a book about something else."

Nell crossed her legs and looked down at her lap instead of at the wall of books. "It's not the project and it's not the book. It's my ambition. It's the thing itself. I don't know where it went." She had not intended to get into this on the phone. It was just as well Lexi couldn't see her. Just as well she didn't have to meet Lexi's eye. Her silence on the other end of the phone was bad enough.

"You know how it is," Lexi said finally, "when you haven't gotten laid in longer than you care to think about and you think it means you never will again? You're absolutely convinced your fucking days are over. And then someone comes along and overnight you just can't get enough. I mean, you can't believe you ever did without it. Maybe ambition's like that too. You just need a taste of it to get you going, and then you take off."

"Are you making this up?"

"What do you mean?"

"Do you really think that's how it works?"

"I don't know for sure. But I know it doesn't just die." Maybe she knew more than Nell gave her credit for. But Lexi still hadn't said what Michael had said. She hadn't said: I'll love you anyway. You're still a star. She could ask her, but it didn't mean the same thing when you had to ask. Even if it was Lexi you were asking and you were pretty sure what the answer was. "Nell?"

"Yes."

"I know my timing isn't very good, but I have to go. I'm meeting Stephen downstairs in five minutes and all I've got on is pantyhose."

"Shipler? I thought you told him to shove it."

"He's working on the Legal Services stuff. I've been hanging out with him since I got here."

"Does Wiley know?"

"No. I talked to him last night and kind of glossed over the cast of characters. Otherwise, he would have asked me thirty-five questions."

"Does Wiley think you're still sleeping with him?"

"No. He just likes to play reporter."

"Yeah. Now that all he's doing is writing editorials. I guess he wants to keep in shape by badgering you."

"He doesn't badger me."

"You just said he did."

"I don't think of it as badgering. I just didn't feel like talking to him about Shipler for half an hour."

"I don't know about this guy, Lexi. I don't think he's anywhere near up to you."

"Can we talk about this some other time? I'm half naked, I spent the night having bad dreams about congressmen and illegal aliens, I've got to testify in forty-five minutes, I'm—"

"All right, all right. I just thought you'd want to know what happened."

"I did. I do. I don't know what to say. I'll find out what was on his mind."

"You're going to tell him I told you?"

"Of course I'm going to tell him. You want me to, don't you?"

"Christ. We sound like Louise. Did I tell you she offered me her birth-control pills?"

"Me too."

"Aren't you glad you're not fifteen anymore?"

"Nell, I have to go."

"Just one more thing. Would you come to New York when you're through and meet Michael?"

"We're going to Mexico tomorrow. Didn't I tell you?"

"No."

"We'll be back late Sunday. I'll call you in New York. Shit, there's someone knocking at my door. I've got to get dressed."

"Don't answer it until you are."

"Thanks, Nell."

"Any time." Nell listened until she heard Lexi hang up the phone. She sat in the chair in Gretchen's study and tried to imagine Lexi as she scrambled to get dressed, to answer the door, to testify. Lexi in a suit and high heels, toting around her briefcase, her principles. On her endless, effortless voyage to China. When she herself couldn't even remember to bring the keys to Michael's apartment.

She looked up at the wall of books, the diplomas, the framed baby pictures. Her ambition had fizzled, spent itself. She was tired of trying to figure out where it had gone. When it might come back. What she would do in the meantime. She couldn't spend all her time being in love.

She picked up the phone and dialed Michael's office. He would tell her not to worry. He would tell her she was till a star. If she heard it enough times, she might begin to believe it. The line was busy. She hung up and a minute later she tried the number again, thinking as she listened to the busy signal that it was just as well Lexi had gotten off the phone when she had. If they had been on for another ten minutes, Nell might have found the courage to tell her that she had decided last night, during Louise's blow-by-blow account of how Bliss had broken her heart, that she was going to move to New York.

"Nell!" Louise was shouting from the other end of the apartment. "Breakfast!"

The ocean floor off the shore at Cabo San Lucas was thick with brightly colored coral, sea fans, anemones, thousands of strands of things Lexi didn't know the names of, swaying, fluttering, dancing beneath the surface of the aquamarine water, landmarks and hiding places for the purple-and-green-striped fish, the black fish with rainbow tails longer than their bodies, the schools of tiny iridescent minnows strong enough to swim against the undertow, and, shooting out in front of her, something long and yellow diving behind a moss-covered rock, the moss so green that it might have been lighted from within by electric lights instead of by the noon sun in this spot a few degrees south of the Tropic of Cancer, in the shallow clear blue Gulf of California where she and David were snorkeling.

He waved to her underwater, pointing to the shoreline. She shook her head. She was not ready to get out. She did not want to stop feeling the sun's heat on her almost bare back as she waved her feet through the calm water. The children's question: If you could be an animal, what animal would you be? Almost all of them had said a bird. Underwater she watched David swim to shore and then lost sight of him as he walked out of the water. She swam out toward the coral reef, breathing through the plastic tube in her mouth, her breathing more regular than it had been on dry land for years.

As she approached the reef, the water grew darker, the colors of the sea plants deeper shades of purple and pink. She dove for a shell shaped like the wing of an angel in a fourteenth-century Flemish painting.

Swimming back to shore, she pulled off her face mask and snorkel. She stood on the sandy sea floor and tipped her head back into the water to guide her hair away from her face. As she walked to the kiosk to return the rented gear, her hair felt soaked and heavy, plastered to her back. She laid the flippers, the face mask and the snorkel on the sandy counter top, said a few words to the boy behind the counter. She withdrew and scanned the beach for David. Beyond the kiosk toward the road were a concession stand and a collection of garden tables covered with umbrellas. He was sitting at one of them, talking to a woman sitting across from him, her face shielded by a white straw hat with a wide brim, a colorful scarf wrapped around the base.

He looked up as he saw her approach, lifted his hand in

greeting, his eyes hidden behind sunglasses, head covered with a cheap straw hat he had bought the day before. The woman looked up too, her face framed with thick blonde hair that fell on her shoulders, big sunglasses with white frames, a lacy white jacket over her bikini.

Lexi walked to the edge of the table, touching her knee against David's outstretched leg. He said, "Lexi Steiner, Melissa deKalb." As Melissa reached out her hand for Lexi to shake, she said, "Melissa Owens." David said, "Sorry." As they shook hands she turned to him and said, "No problem. It was good running into you." She stood up, moving away from the table into the sunlight, swinging a white straw bag over her shoulder. "If you two want to have dinner some night, you know where we're staying."

"Probably not," David said. Lexi took Melissa's seat and looked from David to Melissa, looking for whatever might be hidden behind their sunglasses. "We're just here till tomorrow night. Thanks anyway."

"Maybe some other time." Melissa smiled. Teeth as white as everything else about her, except her skin, which was deeply tanned. "Good to meet you," she said. Lexi nodded. David said, "Congratulations again." Melissa tipped her head to the side, shrugged her shoulders. "We'll see," she said and walked away in the direction of the concession stand. She looped arms with a man standing at the counter and reached her other arm back to keep her hat from blowing off her head in a sudden gust of warm wind. She had terrific legs.

"An old friend. I was just sitting here and she walked up to me. I barely recognized her. She just got married. She's on her honeymoon."

"So I gathered." Lexi reached for the bottle of Coke at David's place.

"You want some lunch?"

"Do you?"

"Sure. How was your swim?"

"Okay." There was more she had wanted to say, but she didn't want to give him that now. "How was yours?"

"It was wonderful."

"How come you got out so soon?"

"To get out of the sun. My back was starting to fry."

"Getting smaller all the time, isn't it?"

"What?"

"The world. In the middle of nowhere, one of the great lays of your life shows up." She took a swig of Coke and felt her possessiveness assume a frightening, unexpected shape.

"I never said that."

"You're right. You were more genteel about it."

"I never told you the whole story."

"She was better than you said?" The shape was the shape of a tantrum, with words instead of limbs flailing.

"No, there's another part to the story."

"What's that?"

"I don't know if I can tell you."

"You always do that, Wiley. 'I don't know if I can tell you.' 'I'll tell you tomorrow.' 'I'll tell you some other time.' What are you waiting for? And do me a favor, take off your sunglasses." She had not expected to enjoy her tantrum so much.

"Why?"

"Because I feel like I'm talking to you through a one-way mirror. You can see me, but I can't see you."

He took them off. "Better?" He spoke softly; he meant to please. She did not. He reached into his shirt pocket and put on his regular glasses.

She nodded. He averted his eyes, looked at his lap. "I don't know why I do that. No one ever called me on it before." He looked up at her. "Why do you think I do?" He sounded diffident. He was handing back the edge, maybe without knowing that a transaction was taking place.

"It's a tease. Making me wait. You want me to keep coming back for more." She finished off the Coke. "Not realizing that I will anyway."

She had not intended to give in so quickly. She wasn't giving in. She was just taking a break. "I brought you something." She held up the shell she had plucked from the floor of the ocean. She leaned toward him and placed it on his sunburned thigh. "Congratulations. You're a winner."

"What do I win?"

"A moment's peace."

He smiled.

She sat back in her seat. He didn't know that the moment was almost up. "You think I should wear my hair like hers?"

"How was she wearing it?"

"You know, lots of body." She drew a wave with her hand a few inches from the side of her head.

"Your hair wouldn't do that. It's too frizzy."

"I could get a perm."

"Perms are dumb. Women who get perms are dumb."

"So what should I do with it?" Now she asked in earnest.

"I like it the way it is now. Away from your face."

"I shouldn't go to a beauty parlor?"

"No, just get a barrette or one of those things they used to wear." He made a broad U shape with his thumb and forefinger and clamped his spread fingers on top of his head.

"A headband?"

"Yeah."

"Early American Bandstand. Good beat, easy to dance to—" She cocked her head in Melissa's direction. "You think she has good legs?"

"I didn't notice."

"How could you miss them?"

"I was too busy looking at her ass." He was not often as sarcastic, or as quick. She was impressed.

"I thought it was too big."

"I thought it was just right."

She kicked him in the shin with her bare foot, gently but at an angle which made the shell fly off his thigh and land on the cement patio, breaking into three neat pieces. She hoped that didn't mean there was one for each of them.

He looked down. "Your poor shell." The edge in his voice was gone. "You broke it." He reached down to pick up the pieces. As he raised his hand to offer them to her, she lowered her eyes, suddenly, acutely, ashamed of herself. She held open her hands to receive the broken shell, as white against her palms as Melissa had been next to her. There was a woman somewhere who would have a tantrum like this one if Lexi showed up unexpectedly, one of the great lays of someone else's past. She did not want to be that woman anymore. That as much as anything else accounted for her shame, and maybe for her tantrum. He leaned forward and touched her knee. "Let's stop. Please."

Late in the afternoon they rented bicycles and rode north against the light wind on the main road toward San José del Cabo. The air was moist, salty, intoxicating. Grass grew tall out of the sand dunes on both sides of the road. Nothing but sky as far as they could see, but in the distance, it grew thick with deep gray clouds. They had miscalculated: they were riding right into the afternoon shower. They were miles from where they had started. The rain would catch up with them one way or another.

They took turns going fast, silent as they passed each other, the only sign of recognition in either of them this bit of competition on the bicycles. Though it was hardly a contest. She really had to work to catch up with him, and as she did, his pace slackened. He didn't mind not being the front runner for long stretches of highway. But then he would surprise her, shoot out of nowhere and overtake her, the tails of his shirt fluttering in the wind as he passed her. Maybe this was what it was to be married: unspoken accommodation, not without a spin. They were aware of each other at every moment, aware that there were things one of them did not do as well as the other and that allowances had to be made. But still, could you go on like this forever? David appeared at her right, pedaling along, suddenly all innocence on a rented bicycle that matched her own. They would have appeared to anyone passing by as The Happy Couple on Vacation. The four-color ad that makes you want to go to Bermuda with the one you love, that makes love look perpetually carefree and suntanned, till death do you part.

The temperature dropped suddenly. The wind picked up. It began to drizzle.

"Hey, slow down." She pedaled harder. "What do we do now?"

"Look for shelter."

They rode next to each other against the wind.

"I read there was a restaurant somewhere out here," Lexi
said. "Maybe that's it up ahead."

"It looks like a shack."

"Were you expecting Golden Arches?"

The sky rumbled and moments later the afternoon storm
was in full swing.

The shack was called Las Palmas and outside there was a
big metal sign that said COCA-COLA swinging from a wooden
beam that supported the thatched roof. They parked their bicycles against the hut and went into the dark bar. "Hi, hi," the man
behind the bar said, with a thick accent. "How are you?"
Speaking his resort English happily. The place was empty and
chilly as a cavern. A few gas lights hung from the beams. The
windows were sealed tight with dark wooden boards; the
clumsy afternoon ritual for when the rain came. They wiped
their faces, necks and shoulders with paper napkins.

"*Mojada,*" Lexi said to the proprietor. They were drenched,
chilled. There were four or five tables and in the corner a jukebox.

"*No mojados,*" the man said with emphasis, smiling. They
weren't wetbacks, he was saying. She explained to David.

"You want a beer?" she said.

"Sure." David sat down.

"What kind?"

"Dos Equis."

She ordered two of them.

"I can't believe they have a jukebox," she said. "Do you
have a quarter?"

"You think a Mexican jukebox takes quarters?"

"It was a joke."

He reached into the pocket of his damp shorts and pulled
out a handful of coins. "See if any of this works."

"Any requests?"

"No Donna Summer."

She ran her hand across his back as she passed him.

The beer came and, in competition with the thunder, Stevie Wonder sang, "Here I am baby, signed, sealed, delivered, I'm yours."

"Tell me something," he said. He sounded sad, or just serious. The music didn't make him feel the way it made her feel: happy the way The Happy Couple is happy. It may not last much longer than the song itself. But for those few minutes all you really want is to be lightheaded and dumb. And in love.

"What?" she said.

"Anything."

"Your nose is going to start peeling in about three days."

"Tell me something that's not obvious."

"You tell me something that's not obvious. Tell me about Melissa."

He shook his head, bemused. "She just got married to a guy who runs a computer store in San Francisco." He laughed. "A fucking computer store."

"I don't get it."

Then he told her the story he hadn't told her before, the sequel to the story he had told her the first night they had spent together: what happened after the most exotic sexual experience he had ever had. The beginning of the end of his marriage. The phone calls in the middle of the night, the second one of which he was not home to take. "Gretchen made up her mind the next day. I guess I'd made up mine too."

"You make it sound so easy."

"It wasn't, but I didn't know what else I could do. We'd gone through, I don't know, a hundred rounds. She wanted me and I wanted the news. I wanted adventures I couldn't have on West End Avenue."

"Did you want Melissa too?"

"Maybe in the same way you wanted the men you've told me about. I wanted her to be off the record. She belonged in a hotel room, but not anywhere else in my life."

"What about now?" She took a swig of beer.

He looked hard at her. "You know the answer to that."

"You're making do without."

"Without Melissa?"

"No, without the news. You've still got your finger in the pie, but sometimes you wish you had your whole hand in it." He smiled. "And you've got Louise, whom you adore even though she won't let you." He nodded. "And you've got a view of the ocean and a hankering to write something longer than an editorial." He kept listening. "And you want to marry me."

"Whom I adore even though she won't let me."

"Even though I was such a bitch about Melissa?" She knew the answer to that too, and knew that she was hiding behind the question. It was easier to talk about Melissa than about herself.

"It was kind of endearing," he said, "watching you get all worked up. I didn't know you had it in you."

"I thought you did pretty well yourself. You're not usually so sarcastic."

"I'm not usually so provoked."

"Except by Roger."

"He's not the only one."

"Who else?"

"Nell." He lifted his empty bottle off the table, tipped it. "You want another?" She nodded. He raised his hand to catch the waiter's attention and held up two fingers.

"Well?"

"The other night when you were in Washington and I was at your house, she came over—"

"I know. And you had words."

"She told you?"

"Of course she told me."

"I knew she would."

"I was going to ask you what happened."

"I was waiting for you to. I didn't know what I was going to say." He paused, touched the beer bottle with both hands, rolled it between his palms a few times. "Before she got there, there was a letter—" he rolled it some more; she let him talk— "on your desk. Next to Louise's Walkman. Not exactly next to it. Inside a magazine, sticking out of a magazine." He shrugged, looked up at her.

"And you read it." It was not a question. He did not nod. "About your getting kicked upstairs." He nodded. "I see. And that's why you were snotty to her about Michael's job." The second round of beer arrived. They were silent as the waiter took the empties and surveyed the table for debris. He removed the napkins they had used to wipe the rain off their chins.

"How come?" she said.

He drank some beer. "I was curious. I still can't figure you two out. I keep thinking there's something you're not telling me, and if you told me, I would understand you better." He rolled the bottle between his hands. "But I don't even know what the question is that would elicit the information. I guess that's why."

"What did you find out?"

"That you'll always have your secrets."

"Not if you keep reading my mail."

"Are you pissed off that I did?"

"I don't think so." She raised the bottle to her lips. "But I'm not sure why I'm not. I probably should be." She wasn't teasing him; she was just trying to figure out what it was. "Maybe I wanted you to see a part of me that I didn't show you myself. There's something appealing about being watched when you don't know anyone's watching. About having a part of yourself revealed unwittingly."

"You wanted me to watch."

"It wasn't what I had in mind, but now that you have—"

"Did you leave it there for me to read?"

"If I'd wanted you to read it, darling, I wouldn't have put it in a magazine in my house when I didn't think you'd be there. And I'd have left something juicier for you."

"Like what?"

"I don't know. A letter I was writing. Or a journal. Nell did that to me once in college. Left out a page from her journal specifically so that I would read it when she wasn't there—all of which I found out later. I guess I never told you this story."

"No, but it sounds like a good one."

"It's one of our best." She began to peel the label off the beer bottle. "She had a lover in college, a music teacher who was married to a woman who taught at Barnard. There was a party one night in the apartment building where we lived, and he and I were both a little tight—more than a little—and I ended up dancing with him for what seemed like hours. Dancing with this guy was not casual. It was more like fucking. We weren't boisterous about it, we were just dancing very slowly, close together." She continued to pick at the label, rolling each shred between her thumb and forefinger, dropping them on the table. "I knew that I should stop, but I couldn't. Or I didn't want to badly enough. I hadn't touched anyone in months—" she looked up at David, smiled— "but I don't know what *his* excuse was. Anyway, I finally tore myself away and left, went back to our apartment and went to sleep. When I got up in the morning, Nell was gone but there was a light on above her typewriter and a piece of paper sticking out of it. I started to read it and got the point after the first few lines. All I remember is 'I can't believe they danced to every song.' She told me later she'd left it out for me to read."

"Did she ever even the score?"

"What? Dance with one of my boyfriends?"

"Whatever."

"She slept with Boz once, but that was different. They both asked my permission, independently—it was kind of touching. But things with Boz were casual in the extreme. Everyone more or less fucked everyone. It wasn't the summer of peace and love, but it was San Francisco and we were all trying not to get too ruffled about things like that."

"But you'd be ruffled now."

She looked up suddenly. "If you dance with her, I'll kill you."

He laughed. "In case you haven't noticed, I don't dance with anyone."

"We should dance sometime."

"Can you imagine me disco dancing?"

"We'll dance slow." She touched his leg under the table and winked. He scowled. She scowled back "It's like making love. All you have to do is take the first step and a higher power does the rest for you. It's easy." He scowled again. "Don't pretend not to be intrigued, Wiley."

"I'm not pretending."

"Just you wait. One night the urge will overcome you."

He shook his head, smiled. "But there is something that still intrigues me."

She rolled her eyes. "Still?"

"Not that. All I want to know is why you didn't sleep with her when you wanted to so much. What held you back?"

"Unmitigated terror." She took a swig of beer. "And I was sure we would laugh, I mean, laugh hysterically at some crucial moment. We can't even have a decent fight without laughing. It's all over when we realize we're acting like people who've been married for thirty years. It's hard to keep up your anger when you start to sound like someone you're not."

"Then how come you didn't laugh when you were going on about Melissa?"

"That was me," she said. " I was pissed off."

"I don't understand why. I slept with her once, twice, and haven't seen her in six or seven years."

"I just didn't think you would be attracted to someone who was beautiful and dumb."

"I wasn't in love with her."

"I didn't say my anger made sense. I was just trying to explain."

"What about that guy of yours? The one you picked up and went to the ten-dollar hotel with. He wasn't any Rhodes Scholar."

"It might bend your nose out of joint if we ran into him."

"It might. It might not." He took a long swallow of beer. "Would you have gone with me to a ten-dollar hotel that night? The first night?"

"You'd never go to a place like that."

"But would you have?"

"Would you have wanted to sleep with me in a flea bag?"

"So it wasn't me. It was my hotel."

"I was intrigued by the package."

"Jesus. You make it sound like Club Med."

"You were supposed to be off the record. But you asked too many questions, for someone who just wanted to get laid."

"I didn't want to get laid."

"I know. You wanted to find out if I was gay."

"That was at the bottom of the list of things I wanted to find out."

"What was at the top?"

"Strictly business."

"Darling, where was your sense of adventure? Where was your desire for a turn of events?"

"Getting laid isn't usually my idea of an adventure. Getting laid is so—predictable."

"Then what's an adventure?"

"All the other things that happen that you don't expect. The things where you don't know beforehand what the ending is going to be."

"What about me?" She touched his leg under the table. "Was I an adventure?"

He looked at her closely and shook his head. "You sound just like Nell. Flip and casual. You must think I find it charming. Or sexy. Or something." He finished off his beer and put the bottle on the table with emphasis. The clap of glass against wood was the only sound in the place. "Let's get out of here." He stood up, took some money out of his pocket and put it on the table. He looked down at her for a moment and then turned and stood in place, waiting for her to get up.

Even if she had known what to say, she would have been afraid to speak.

She followed him outside. It was not until he wiped his wet bicycle seat off with his shirt sleeve that she remembered it had been raining.

"David." After she said it, she realized she never called him that. To call him David was to be not flip, not casual. Not Nell. A peace offering.

"What?" He turned to her and folded his arms. He was waiting for her to speak.

"What do you think? That all you are to me is an adventure?"

"That's the way it sounds sometimes."

She moved closer, shook her head and draped her arms around his neck. He did not hold her back. She tipped her head back to look at him. "You changed my life." She reached for his arm and put it around her back. "You took my breath away." She took his other arm and put it on her waist. "Hug me." He moved closer. "Harder." He tightened his grip. "Don't let go. Even in the morning."

They returned from Mexico late Sunday night, and on David's way to work the following morning the regular news was interrupted with a bulletin. The President had just been shot outside the Washington Hilton. His condition was uncertain. Several others had also been struck. The assailant had been apprehended at the scene of the crime. His identity was, at this time, unknown. The Washington correspondent was on the scene to cover the latest developments.

The airwaves were jammed with the news. The freeway itself seemed to be alive with it. David saw, or imagined he saw, the faces of alarm, bewilderment behind the windshields. Everyone wanted to know more. Even when they came to know everything there was to know, they would still want to know more, because most of them would never know what it felt like to be shot, and none of them would know what it felt like to be the President of the United States and be shot. He was getting in the mood to write an editorial.

The newsroom was jumping. More phones ringing than there were people to answer them. He stopped to look at what was coming off the wire. There was no other news in the world but this. He stopped to talk to a guy he knew on the national desk. Brady got it too, and a Secret Service agent. Reagan's still alive. Son of a bitch. Can you believe this. It's getting to be the national pastime. Hold on—he picked up the phone, said his name, cupped his hand over the receiver—it's Berman in Washington. Jesus. He listened to Berman. What else? Where'd he get hit? A Saturday-night special? White or black? Thank Christ for that. Where's he from? When'll they know? If it's L.A., we'll have our hands full. I'll be right here. He hung up. Jesus. How's this for a Monday morning, Wiley? What do you think those bastards at the NRA are going to do with this one? Have you seen that bumper sticker: GUNS DON'T KILL PEOPLE, BULLETS DO. Shit. Catch you later. Both of his phones were ringing.

The receptionist in the editorial department told David to head right to the meeting in the conference room. He passed his office, passed the five open doors that lined the hallway. All the offices were empty. All the phones were ringing. Unlikely he'd get a crack at the editorial on gun control, a plum that the editor of the page would probably take. They were all sitting around the conference table. He took a seat, took his notebook and pen out of his jacket pocket. They were smoking and drinking coffee in Styrofoam cups, trading predictions. The possibilities raced through his head: gun control, international stability, national security, the madness of the world. If Reagan kicked, it would be wide open. Even if he didn't. This thing could go on for weeks. Not bad for a Monday morning. Even though his sunburned shoulders hurt like hell. Even though all he was doing was writing editorials.

Early in the afternoon Louise called from New York. "What do you think?" she said. "Did you see it on tv?"

"Yeah." There were three televisions in the conference room, with replays on every network, sometimes in unison.

"You're not going to write some bullshit about how sad it was he got shot, are you?"

"No." He laughed quietly. "Someone else is writing that."

"You told them you wouldn't, right? You told them he was such an asshole you didn't care, right?"

"Not exactly." He tried not to laugh.

"I told everyone that's what you'd say."

"That's not the kind of thing you can say around here."

"But that's what you think, isn't it? Everyone thinks that."

"I think you're right. How are you doing otherwise? What's going on there?" He hadn't talked to her since she had left.

"Nothing."

"What's wrong?"

"I want to come home."

"How come?"

"Did Gretchen tell you she was going to get married?"

"No."

"Well, she did. Last weekend, before I got here. And you know what? I have a new grandmother, and she wants me to call her Grandma, and she has blue hair."

"Like that guy in *The Bald Soprano*?"

"No, like an old lady." She practically spat.

"It doesn't mean Gretchen doesn't love you. We both do."

"Curtis is an asshole. I hate him."

"What did he do?"

"He told Gretchen California's a weird place to bring up a kid and he doesn't think I should live there anymore."

"He said that in front of you?"

"No. He was in the bedroom and I was in the bathroom, but I had the door open and he thought I had the door closed and he had the door open. Last night. I called you, but you weren't home. Lexi wasn't either."

"We were on our way back from Mexico. We got you something."

"What?"

"A surprise."

"Tell me."

"Then it won't be a surprise."

"I don't care."

"I do." Then what she had told him came back, full blown. "What did Gretchen say when Curtis said you shouldn't live in California?"

"I didn't hear that part."

"Did you ask her later?"

"No. She went to sleep. Then she went to work. Are you going to get a lawyer?"

"I'm going to talk to her."

"What are you going to say?"

"I'll tell her what we agreed, that you'd be with me this year and with her next year."

"If she says I have to move now, will you get a lawyer?"

"You can't move now. It's the middle of the semester. She understands that. Curtis does too."

"I bet he doesn't. He's such a jerk. And I'm not going to live here with him. I'm going to stay with you. Next year too. If you get a lawyer, I won't have to move. Melinda's father got a lawyer so she could live with him."

"I don't think we can decide anything right now." The first two paragraphs of an editorial on the National Rifle Association were displayed on the screen in front of him. He had an hour to finish the first draft. An hour before he could call Gretchen. "Louise, I know you're upset, but this isn't a good time for me to talk. I'll call you tonight."

"I won't be here. We're going to see my new *grandma* tonight. She lives in Great Neck."

"Call me when you get back."

"What if it's late?"

"It's three hours earlier here. I'll be up. I won't go to sleep till you call."

"Will you be home?"

"Of course I'll be home."

"Okay."

"Have a good time in Great Neck."

"Puke Neck."

"You'll survive."

"I might not."

"I promise you will. I really have to go."

"All right. Bye."

"Bye, love." He listened until he heard the click of the phone across the country. He turned forty-five degrees to his video display terminal and saw the name John Hinckley in the center of the screen, in bright green letters.

"So you know what Mark said? He said, 'The bullet bounced off his heart and landed in his lung,'" Lexi said. David howled. They were eating dinner that night, sitting on the cheap lawn chairs on David's fifteenth-floor terrace. "Too bad you can't put that in the paper." She was talking with her mouth full of chicken he had barbecued on the small grill at the edge of the terrace. "Is there any white meat left?"

He poked around on the serving plate in the semi-darkness. The two pieces of chicken left were both grilled black. "Try this." He forked one, reached across to the plate she held out.

"I'm starved," she said. "What's for dessert?"

"I didn't get anything."

"You know what I ate today? An egg sandwich and home fries for breakfast, a tuna sandwich, coleslaw and two bags of potato chips for lunch, M&M's at three and a bag of peanuts on my way here. I mean, a big bag of peanuts."

"Are you getting your period?"

"Tomorrow. God, this is delicious." The grease on her lips shone peculiarly in the shadow in which she sat eating his chicken. "You know what I want? Ice cream. Can we go to Seven-Eleven?"

"Sure. But I have to watch the news at eleven." He looked at his watch, tilted his hand toward the light coming from the living room. "It's nine-forty-five." After midnight in New York and Louise hadn't called yet.

Lexi sat back in her seat. She inhaled deeply and looked at him. "Serious question, Wiley." She rested her bare foot on his knee, the leg she had kicked the other day when she was pissed off about Melissa's ass. The guy who ran the computer store could have Melissa's ass. "Are you happy?" She curled her toes around his bent knee.

"Yeah." He felt himself smile, as uncontrollable as a twitch. "Very happy. Are you?" He reached to touch her foot, lifted it off his knee and cupped the heel in his palm.

"Yes. Can't you tell?"

He nodded.

"You couldn't tell the other day."

"I could." He stroked her arch. "I just wanted you to say so."

"Is that your phone?"

David let her foot down and headed for the kitchen. It was long distance. It was Nell calling from New York.

"Wiley, how the hell are you? Could you believe that about Reagan?" Reagan getting shot had put everyone in a good mood; even Nell had warmed up to him. "I hope you're going to write the shit out of it."

"I did my best. Did you hear this? The bullet bounced off his heart and landed in his lung." Nell laughed. "Lexi just told me that."

"Is she there?"

"Yeah, hold on."

He went back to the terrace. "It's for you."

"Who is it?"

"Guess."

Lexi jumped up. David stayed where he was, doused the charcoals with what was left of a beer, leaned against the terrace railing and looked at the ocean. Gretchen had been with a patient when he had called her and she hadn't called back. He didn't know what he was going to say to her or to Louise. He knew that he wanted Louise to stay, but he knew that wasn't the agreement. Curtis wasn't part of the agreement either. Married to Gretchen for a week and he's trying to run the show. David winced at the thought of lawyers and courtrooms. He felt Lexi coming up to him from behind.

"Hey." She put her arms around him, leaned against his back.

"That didn't take long." He turned around, held her.

"Were you listening?"

"No. I just read letters when no one's looking."

"She's going to do it. She decided." She spoke softly, her cheek against his chest.

"What?"

"Move to New York."

"She called to tell you that?"

"No, she called to ask if I'd pick her up at the airport tomorrow. I asked her if she'd made up her mind about moving to New York and she said she'd talk to me tomorrow. That means yes."

"I didn't know it was this serious."

"I didn't either. I mean, I did, but I never thought she'd actually go through with it." She looked up at him. "Do you know how many things we said we were going to do that we never did? I thought moving to New York would be one of those."

He leaned against the railing, took her with him. He kept holding her, stroking her head.

She was quiet for a long time. "She took my breath away too."

"I know."

"It took more than a night, it took, I don't know, a few months. But it felt the same way as if it had happened in a night. It felt that way for years. It still does."

"I know." But he still didn't really know about the two of them.

He held her tighter and thought: If only everyone didn't keep moving across the country. If they could just stay put for a while. That would be something. Something quite different from what he had always thought he wanted.

# Everywhere Around the World

$\mathcal{E}$ight weeks and five days later, on the last Friday in May, David had some people over to celebrate, or at least acknowledge, two life-changing experiences. There was a third that he was unaware of, one that had not been positively confirmed. For the moment, exactly half an hour before the guests were expected—David making margaritas in the blender, Nell mashing avocados for guacamole, and Lexi in the dining room, arranging forks and cocktail napkins around the bowls of vegetables and dip—knowledge of the unconfirmed life changing experience was shared only by Lexi and Nell. Lexi spread the forks in a row and ate a handful of sliced zucchini.

On the radio the disc jockey announced that a woman in West Covina had just won a trip to New York for two. Lexi heard Nell say, "Where's Louise?"

The blender roared for a moment, crushing ice cubes in a mixture of tequila and Rose's Lime Extract. The noise stopped. "What?" David said.

"Where's Louise?"

"She's got a date." He turned on the blender again. Lexi ate more zucchini. "She said she'd be back about nine."

"She'd better be," Nell said. "I've got a present for her." Nell also had a one-way ticket to New York, and her plane was leaving in four hours, which was one of the two commonly known reasons for this get-together. The other was that Lexi had gotten the job teaching at UCLA and today had been her last day at the Center. She moved the wheel of Brie to make room for the guacamole, sliced off a chunk and popped it into her mouth. The blender went off and on, off and on, sporadically silencing the radio. If you had the right bumper sticker on your car, you could win a free trip for two to New York, or a hundred-and-four dollars' worth of groceries at Von's. That was only one reason to keep your radio dial exactly where it was. This was also the beginning of a dynamite oldies weekend. The disc jockey's voice faded. Every guy grab a girl, everywhere around the world. The forced rhyme, like everything else this week, made Lexi feel unsteady and nostalgic.

"Any job prospects yet?" David asked Nell. Fifteen feet away from them, Lexi strained to hear Nell's answer. She had been listening closely for the last two months to Nell's every word on the subject of her ambition, or lack of it. If Lexi could have, she would have given Nell some of her own ambition. There was more than enough to go around, more than she needed. She moved closer, leaned against the open swinging door to the kitchen. David poured the margaritas from the blender into a glass pitcher.

"If I knew what I wanted to do, I'd have an idea of where to go for a job." Nell shook a bottle of hot sauce over the bowl of mashed avocados.

"So what's your plan?" David lifted the bottle of tequila to see how much was left. "Another book?" He opened a cabinet, took out another bottle and twisted off the sealed cap.

"I don't think so, unless—" she looked across the kitchen at him, at Lexi—"unless there's a market for books that are thirty pages long. I think that's about all my attention span could bear. I don't know, maybe I'll get a job as an editor and mess around with what other people write. Or maybe I'll write some articles about my thirties crisis."

"You won't turn thirty for six months," Lexi said.

"I know, but I feel it coming. You know, when there's a hurricane in the Caribbean, it rains like a son of a bitch in Florida so they know it's coming? I feel like I'm Florida and it's only a matter of time before I get ravaged."

"Take it from me, it's not that bad," David said. "You'll survive. It's forty I'm starting to worry about."

"You've got a few years," Lexi said.

"Jesus, who ever thought we'd get old?" Nell said. "I mean, your parents get old, your uncles get old, your teachers—"

"Twenty-nine isn't exactly the end of the line," David said. "Neither is thirty."

"But forty might be." Lexi poked him in the arm.

"Yeah, and when I'm forty, Louise'll be—eighteen."

"She's been eighteen for years. She was born eighteen."

"No, I think she was born twenty-eight and she's been working her way down," David said.

"That's what growing up in New York does to you," Nell said. "I think Lexi was born twenty-eight too. Now she's older than both of us. Shit, she's going to be a professor in three weeks. She'll be one of those people—what do you call people in their eighties?"

"Octogenarians," David said.

"Yeah, she'll be one of those. A professor emeritus."

"I'm not going to be a professor, I'm just going to be a teacher."

"But you should make them call you professor anyway. That's what I'm going to call you from now on," Nell said and dipped her finger in the guacamole. She licked her finger and shook her head. "I thought this hot sauce was supposed to burn the roof off your mouth." She picked up the bottle and looked at the label. There was a drawing of a thermometer on the side and the red mark, indicating the level of hotness, went almost to the top of it. She shook in a few more drops.

"Maybe you should think about having a kid, Nell," David said. "Take time out between careers. That seems to be the thing to do these days."

"Yeah," Nell said. "I guess that's one of the possibilities for when you can't think of anything else to do. Or when—" She stopped, stuck a fork into the avocados.

"And think of how happy it would make Jerry Falwell," David said. "The possibility that you could give birth to a gun-toting Christian. He'd make you an honorary member of the I Love America Club."

"Any kid of mine pulled that on me I'd break its head," Nell said.

"Maybe you'll luck out and have a punker," David said. "I did—though I think she's getting a little tired of that routine. She said she's going to let her hair grow and buy some dresses."

"If you don't watch out, she'll end up wanting to go to Wellesley and major in art history," Lexi said.

"So you're moving up in the world," Roger Gaston said to Lexi. "Ivory towers and all that." David had wanted to invite Molly Compton and the only way to get her number was through Roger, so he had ended up inviting Roger too. Molly was around somewhere, with a new boyfriend. "But I bet you're going to miss the Center, being out there on the front lines all the time, making news, hustling politicians."

"It was mostly the other way around." She was working on a large handful of dry-roasted peanuts.

"I didn't think you were ready for retirement."

"It's not like I'm going to be teaching the philosophy of justice. I'm going to be supervising law students who have their own cases. I'll be in court more than I am now."

"When do you start?"

"Three weeks."

"Sounds like a nice little vacation."

She didn't think it would be. She had to sell Nell's car, do something with the furniture she was leaving behind, and do something about what was more than likely her own condition, if she decided to do something rather than nothing.

"What's happening at the Center?" Roger asked. "Has Reagan emasculated it yet?"

"He's working on it. They haven't had to lay anyone off yet, but that's mostly because so many people have left. It's pretty grim."

"I guess it's a good time to leave. I mean, before they fire you. Can I get you a refill?"

Lexi nodded. The room was beginning to fill up with people from the Center and a few from the paper and a few she didn't know. She saw Nell and Louise on the terrace. Louise was opening the present from Nell and there was a guy Lexi didn't know at her side. She hadn't gotten any program notes on him either. From across the large room, looking out to the dark terrace, about all she could see was that he didn't look like he was about to hit the road for Alaska on a motorcycle three days from now. He was maybe sixteen. Louise held up the unwrapped present to the light coming from the living room. It was a book. Lexi squinted. *Our Bodies, Ourselves.* So Louise wouldn't go around popping birth-control pills like they were Chiclets. It gave Lexi an idea for what she should give Nell when she took her to the airport later.

"Hey, Lexi," Edmundo Ramon tapped her on the shoulder. "Pretty nice place you've got here."

"Thanks, it's David's."

"I thought you lived here too."

She shook her head. "I'll probably move in at the end of the summer when his daughter goes back to New York. She changes her mind about moving back there every other week, depending on which guys are calling her up. When the right ones aren't calling, she figures her chances'll be better in New York." Lexi hadn't told her that she might spend the next fifteen years moving around, looking for better odds.

"Speaking of better chances, have you met—" Ed held on to the arm of the woman at his side. "Adela, Lexi." They said hello. "We just decided to get married," he said. "You're the first to know."

"More like the forty-first," Adela said. "Ramon, you're too much."

"I'm a happy man."

"Wait till we get married."

"When's the wedding?"

"She wants to wait. What do you want to wait for?"

"You might be out of a job next week. You think I want to marry a pauper?" She laughed and put her arm around his waist.

"Honey, you have to believe. Look at Lexi here. She got another job just like that." He snapped his fingers. "One day she's an indentured servant at the Center, the next day she's a professor."

"Hey, baby, wanna dance?" It was Nell, coming up to her

from behind, touching her waist. "This is our song." Lexi excused herself, took her hand and they went off to the side of the room.

"Since when is this our song?"

"I don't know. Isn't that what you have to say to girls so that they'll dance with you?" They started to dance.

Chubby Checker was singing, "C'mon baby, let's do the twist, take me by my little hand and go like this." They took each other by the hand and went like this. Not twisting but shaking their hips, moving their feet, making a wider and wider circle for themselves on the crowded living-room floor. They moved closer, held their entwined fingers up between their bodies. Lexi closed her eyes and tried to imagine the rest of their lives. It was like trying to imagine a country you've never seen. As much as you want to go there, you want to stay exactly where you are, dancing, familiar, at home. She gripped Nell's fingers tighter. "I can't believe you haven't told him yet," Nell said.

Lexi opened her eyes. "I told you, I'm going to when I get back from taking you to the airport." The guys singing backup sang, "Round and round and round and around," and Chubby Checker sang, "You should see my little sis, she really knows how to rock, she knows how to twist."

"I still don't understand why you waited so long," Nell said.

"Because I'm still not sure."

"About whether you are or what you're going to do?"

"Both." She flung her arm around Nell and said, "Dip me."

"What you?"

"Like in the movies. You be Fred Astaire." Lexi held on to Nell's shoulder, Nell held her waist and Lexi leaned back, kicking up her leg. But it was hard to dip and laugh at the same time. "I'm trying, don't let go." She didn't know who let go first, they were laughing so hard. They fell to the floor, a tangle of arms and legs, heaving, sputtering.

"What's your problem, Lexi?" Louise kicked her gently in the butt. "If you were wearing a dress, your underpants would be showing."

Lexi nuzzled up to Wiley in the kitchen. "Wanna dance?"

"No." He was emptying ashtrays, lining up empty bottles across the counter. "You know I never dance."

"Try it. Just once. It's easy." He watched as she danced in a little circle around the floor. "You just go like this." She clapped her hands and strutted toward him. She wasn't even listening to the music, she was just moving with him in mind, inches from his body. This would have been enough if they were in bed. It must have been three weeks ago that it happened, but how could you figure out which night, which morning? He moved toward her, more as if to kiss her than dance with her, but instead he spoke: "How will I know what to do?" He wrapped his arms around her, moved a few steps in place. She kicked off her shoes and stood on his feet. He might get used to the idea right away. He had gotten used to a lot of new ideas lately. They all had. "I'll lead," she said. This time she would lead. This time it would be her idea. Even if she decided to do nothing. "Kiss me."

"You guys are really quite gross. And there's no more ice cubes out there." Louise opened the freezer. They separated, held hands, leaned against the counter.

"Who's your new guy?" Lexi said.

Louise spun around, holding an ice-cube tray. "If you weren't making out, I'd bring him in."

"We're not anymore."

Louise turned on the faucet and ran the tray under the spray.

"Here, take this." David handed her a bowl.

Nell knocked on the open door.

"You!" Lexi said. She turned to David. "I told her to dip me and she dropped me on the floor."

"In all fairness, she asked me if I would dip her and I tried—" Nell laughed—"and then I dropped her."

Louise dumped the ice cubes into the bowl, grabbed a handful and left.

"I think this is my exit," Nell said and took a swig of beer.

"So soon?" David said.

"So soon and yet so far." She burped. "I've got a plane to catch, and I've got a few things left to pack. So I guess this is goodbye, Wiley." She finished her beer, stuck her hand out for him to take. "It's been grand."

He took her hand, leaned forward and kissed her on the cheek. "We'll miss you."

She nodded. "We'll miss you too."

"Write if you get work."

"I'll be back if I don't."

Lexi touched his arm. "I'll be back soon." He nodded. In the living room Louise was dancing with her new boyfriend. They looked to Lexi too much like kids to be doing it. As far as Louise had told her, she hadn't done it with anyone yet.

"Should we go?" Lexi took Nell's arm.

She shook her head. "C'mere." Nell led her across the living room, down the hallway and into David's bedroom. She closed the door behind them. "I need to be alone for a little while. I want to go back to my house and—" she stopped— "say goodbye. And I want to go to the beach for a few minutes."

"By yourself?"

Nell nodded.

"Are you all right?"

"I'm terrified."

"So am I."

"You don't look terrified at all. You look magnificent. Did I tell you that before? All of you looks a little bit rounder, kind of like you'd been inflated. But it's nice, it's sexy."

"It's only five days late."

"It might still come."

Lexi shook her head. "I feel different too." She folded her arms across her breasts. "They really hurt. I've been stuffing my face for days. What should I do?"

"Tell him."

"Then what?"

"I don't know what to tell you."

"I think I've almost decided." Nell nodded, coaxing her to continue. "I'll tell you on the way to the airport. I'll know by then."

"Pick me up in an hour and a half. Is that all right?"

Lexi nodded and flopped into the chair by the window. Nell turned to leave, and as she reached to open the bedroom door, she looked back at her. It was the look Lexi knew best, the look that said: one, I understand, and two, no matter what, we'll survive.

The door clicked shut behind Nell, and Lexi leaned back into the chair. They had been fugitives together, they had stolen horses together. They knew everything there was to know about each other, except what the country they were on their way to really looked like. That was a trip each would have to make on her own, or, rather, with a different partner. Another dance. Another set of steps. She got up and walked down the hall to the living room. David was in the corner, hands deep inside his pants pockets. He was nodding, talking to Ed Ramon. Easy, she thought as she approached them. She touched his arm and smiled. You just go like this. She reached inside his pocket for his hand and held it tightly. Signed, sealed, delivered.

An hour later, with the party breaking up, she drove through the maze of crowded, narrow Venice streets toward her house to pick up the present she was going to give Nell. It was eleven-thirty and the street people were just beginning to rock. Bottles and joints and pipes were going around. Radios blasted. People in clusters divided by age, race, intention. Out of one of the radios Rod Stewart shrieked: "If you want my body and you think I'm sexy, c'mon sugar let me know."

The parking space in front of her house was taken. She parked in the driveway of the abandoned house across the street.

As she shut the car door, she thought she saw someone at her front door. It was dark, it was hard to tell. She leaned against the car, peered over the roof. A man took a few steps away from her house and a sliver of his face shone in the faint light the street lamp gave off. He kept walking, in complete darkness now, down the street, away from her. He stopped at the second car in the row and opened the door, his face suddenly illuminated by the light inside the car. "Hey!" she shouted. "Boz, I'm here!"

He looked up. She ran across the street to him. They embraced. "What are you doing here?"

"On my way to Mexico. Comin' by to say hi."

"You got a new car?" She tapped the roof.

"Yeah. Two hundred bucks. All I had to do was rebuild the engine and put in a new clutch. It drives like a dream. AM-FM radio. The works."

"What happened to the Bug?"

"You got a few hours?"

"No, actually—" She started walking toward her house. Boz followed. "I'm on my way to the airport with Nell. I've got to pick her up in a few minutes. She's leaving." Lexi opened her front door.

"Where to?"

"New York."

"What's she doing, hustling some publisher again?"

"No, she fell in love. She's moving."

"The real thing, huh?"

"Yeah, I think so." Lexi went to the bedroom, opened the top drawer of her dresser and took out the present she was going to give Nell. She tore a page from the newspaper on her desk, wrapped the present in it and slipped it into her purse.

"You got any beer?" Boz asked as she returned to the living room.

"No, I haven't been here for days. You want to stay for the night?"

"No, I'm going to keep going. I figure I can get to Ensenada by five."

"Then what?"

He shrugged. "Sleep for a while. Keep going. I don't know. You still going out with that guy?"

"Yeah. You still going out with that woman?"

"No." He shook his head. "We called it off a few weeks ago. Things get neurotic so quick. One day you're all lovey-dovey and the next day you want to tear each other's eyes out. You know how it is."

"Yeah. Want to hear something weird?"

"Sure."

"I think I'm pregnant. Walk me to the car."

"What are you going to do?"

They walked across the street to her car. "Nothing." She got into her car, looked up at him. "Think I'm crazy?"

"A little, but what do I know?"

She started the car, looked back at him, smiled. "You know how it is."

"Yeah."

She knew that he did. "Stop by on your way back and I'll tell you if I've changed my mind. And I owe you a beer."

"I'll be back." He smiled.

"Call first."

"Don't count on it." He waved as he walked backward. "You know how it is." He blew her a kiss, turned and walked across the street.

She backed the car out of the driveway and then drove down the narrow back streets to Nell's house.

"I'm numb," Nell said. They were in the TWA waiting area. Passengers with seats in rows twenty-two to thirty-three were being asked to board. "You could stick a knitting needle in my arm and I wouldn't feel it."

"You think I'm doing the right thing?" Lexi needed to hear it one more time.

"Absolutely. Do you think I am?" Nell looked frightened and summery, wearing a straw hat with a wide brim, her arms laden with bags, carry-ons, a shopping bag filled with old shoes.

Lexi looked hard at her, felt her face constrict, eyes grow smaller, tighter. "Yeah."

"You're not sure."

"You know it's not that. It's just that—"

A voice came on the PA: "We are now boarding passengers holding seats in rows one to twenty-one."

"—I'll miss you."

Nell turned to look at the line that was forming and turned back. Lexi handed her the present wrapped in newspaper. Nell undid it and then wrapped it again quickly, her eyes wide. "You think I need a diaphragm that doesn't work?"

She stuck it into the bulging side pocket of her purse and, with great care, put down everything she was carrying, not looking at Lexi, so that their eyes had to meet for only a second as she stood up and reached with both arms for her. They held on tightly, as tightly as they ever had. People and luggage brushed against them. Women announced flights to Houston, Albuquerque, St. Louis. Connecting flights to London and Rome. Non-stop service to New York. This is how it would have been if they had made love. She would have felt Nell's breasts pressed against her own, and they would not have laughed. They would have just held on tightly like this, the way lovers do, the way you do when you can't let go because if you let go what you lose is a part of yourself. They cried. They held on tighter. They let go.

Nell loaded up her arms with her bags. Lexi plucked the boarding pass from the pocket of Nell's purse and wedged it into her fingers. They tried to laugh. Lexi straightened her summery straw hat, turned down the brim so that it covered one side of her face. She wanted Nell to look her best. Her foxy best. "Call me tomorrow. Don't forget." Tears streamed down Nell's cheeks. She couldn't speak. She nodded and turned and headed toward the entrance to the plane. Lexi walked the other way, through the crowds and waiting areas, past the shops, all the way through the serpentine terminal, and the words to a hundred songs played in her head. Songs about loving, leaving, coming back again, your best girl, your only guy, going to St. Louis but my next stop just might be L.A., going to a go-go, going to take you higher, going to the chapel of love, love the one you're with, don't let me down, come round at twelve with some Puerto Rican girls that's just dying to meetch you, you go your way and I'll go mine, now ain't that peculiar—

What was peculiar, stepping on the rubber mat, making the glass doors swing open into the warm, dry night, what was peculiar was that as she passed through the doors, she thought of how she had waited for Stephen Shipler to open the doors to restaurants and hotel rooms for her. Waited for the doors to open and the minuet of seduction to begin. Terrific, I mean really terrific, in bed. Sure I like my wife. Wouldn'ta thought someone who wears those kinda clothes—

What was peculiar, cutting a path through the lot, was that she had no idea where she had parked her car. It was there but not there, somewhere but not anywhere, like her sneakers that night on the beach. She stopped and listened to the roar of the planes. Wiley, best love. Kiss me. Dip me. Don't drop me. She whispered. There is something I have to tell you.